Readers love *The Necessary Deaths* by DAVID C. DAWSON

Award winner in the 2017 FAPA
for Adult Suspense and Thrillers

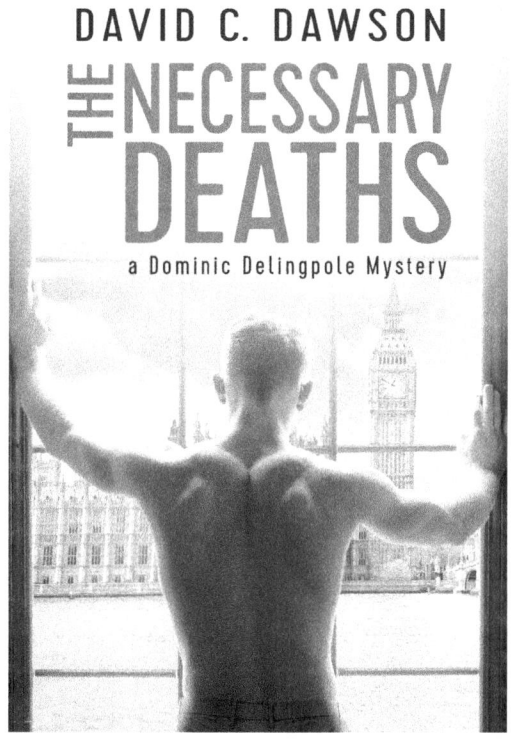

"A very successful blend of human interest and captivating, modern-day action adventure with political and international business conspiracies to keep me glued to the pages… I am already looking forward to more stories about Dominic and Jonathan!"
—Rainbow Book Reviews

"A fun and quick read, especially if you like figuring out a whodunit."
—Alpha Book Club

"Along the way you'll be thrilled and entertained and you'll most definitely laugh. There's some excellent dry humour in this book, and the main characters spark nicely against each other throughout. More, please, Mr. Dawson. More!"
—International Thriller Writers

"David C. Dawson did an amazing job on this book and I look forward to the next book in this series."
—Gay Book Reviews

By DAVID C. DAWSON

THE DELINGPOLE MYSTERIES
The Necessary Deaths
The Deadly Lies

Published by DSP PUBLICATIONS
www.dsppublications.com

DAVID C. DAWSON
THE DEADLY LIES

DSP PUBLICATIONS

Published by
DSP Publications

5032 Capital Circle SW, Suite 2, PMB# 279, Tallahassee, FL 32305-7886 USA
www.dsppublications.com

This is a work of fiction. Names, characters, places, and incidents either are the product of author imagination or are used fictitiously, and any resemblance to actual persons, living or dead, business establishments, events, or locales is entirely coincidental.

The Deadly Lies
© 2017 David C. Dawson.

Cover Art
© 2017 L.C. Chase.
http://www.lcchase.com
Cover content is for illustrative purposes only and any person depicted on the cover is a model.

All rights reserved. This book is licensed to the original purchaser only. Duplication or distribution via any means is illegal and a violation of international copyright law, subject to criminal prosecution and upon conviction, fines, and/or imprisonment. Any eBook format cannot be legally loaned or given to others. No part of this book may be reproduced or transmitted in any form or by any means, electronic or mechanical, including photocopying, recording, or by any information storage and retrieval system, without the written permission of the Publisher, except where permitted by law. To request permission and all other inquiries, contact DSP Publications, 5032 Capital Circle SW, Suite 2, PMB# 279, Tallahassee, FL 32305-7886, USA, or www.dsppublications.com.

ISBN: 978-1-63533-891-1
Digital ISBN: 978-1-63533-892-8
Library of Congress Control Number: 2017911710
Published December 2017
v. 1.0

Printed in the United States of America
∞
This paper meets the requirements of
ANSI/NISO Z39.48-1992 (Permanence of Paper).

To Nick, an inspiration and a source of support.

Acknowledgments

MANY THANKS to a great member of the cabin crew of a major airline, who must remain anonymous. He advised me how it might be possible to get access to the crew bunks on a transatlantic flight. Also to Paul Vates, a wonderful actor who helped me hone the dialogue in sections of this book. Finally to Andi Byassee, whose unfailing patience and sheer brilliance have added so much to this book.

DAVID C. DAWSON
THE DEADLY LIES

DSP PUBLICATIONS

Chapter 1

BERNHARDT FREUDE had just twenty minutes to live.

The tires of the crimson red sports car gripped tight to the twisting mountain road that snaked south of the Pyrenees, down to the east coast of Spain. As a lawyer specializing in European copyright law, Bernhardt Freude was a cautious man. He had bought the car earlier that year precisely because *Auto Bild* magazine had voted it the safest sports car of the year two years running. Before setting off on his cross-European journey, he had booked it in for inspection and maintenance at the workshop close to his apartment in Berlin.

Bernhardt had been on the road for just over two days. Last night he had stayed in a pleasant little *chambre d'hôte* on the French-Swiss border. He seldom drove when he was back home in Berlin. It was simpler and quicker to take the U-Bahn or the tram. But if he had to travel farther, he preferred the liberty and independence that a journey by car offered. He hated flying. His long athlete's legs were unsuited to the cramped cabin of a budget airline plane. And he found the other passengers noisy, crass, and shallow. In his youth, he often took long train journeys across Europe. They were exciting and romantic. Now at the wheel of his beloved new car, he could keep his own company, away from the noise, smell, and possible infections of the general public.

It was over an hour since he had passed the summit of the climb through the Pyrenees. Just after Girona, he decided to turn off the E15 *autopista* onto a smaller road that headed to the coast. It twisted and turned through the hilly, arid landscape, and there were few passing points. Bernhardt was a careful driver, and as such, he kept his speed at no faster than fifty kilometers an hour, much to the apparent annoyance of the driver in the large black limousine close behind him.

Bernhardt was very conscious of the car on his tail. It had been following ever since the last service area, where he had noticed it parked next to him. As soon as the road straightened out for a short stretch, he pulled over onto the dusty verge and stopped to let the driver pass. As the black limousine roared ahead, Bernhardt switched off the engine and got out. He crossed the road to enjoy the spectacular view he had just left behind: the peaks of the Pyrenees, rising up in snow-capped grandeur.

On that late-May day, a breeze from the mountains competed with the afternoon sun, which warmed his face. Bernhardt stretched his aching limbs and longed to be twenty years younger. To relive his carefree life as a prize-winning law student from Berlin's Humboldt University, driving his battered Volkswagen beetle on his first cross-Europe adventure. Confident, triumphant, and gloriously without responsibility.

Sighing, Bernhardt leaned back against a rock, drinking in the beauty of his surroundings. He was headed for Spain's Costa Dorada, the Golden Coast. Miles of sandy beaches bordering the azure blue of the Mediterranean Sea.

He took out his mobile phone and dialed Dominic's number. After several rings it switched to voicemail. Bernhardt hung up and stood for a moment, pondering what to do. He redialed.

"Hello Dominic. It's your boy from Berlin here. Not long now. I am no more than two hours away from Sitges, and you. Let's meet at the bar by the church. You know the one. To remind us of that wonderful time. I have everything with me. See you soon. Tchüss, Schatzi."

He turned and crossed the road back to his car. Slipping his phone into the pocket of his tan chinos, Bernhardt got in and fastened his seat belt. Then he began his final drive, headed for Sitges, the gay-friendly sanctuary he loved most.

"WHO WAS that, lover?" Jonathan lay languidly stretched out, facedown on the sun lounger. He aimed to expose every inch of his toned body to the rays of Spanish sunshine.

Dominic put down his phone. He paused to look out across the terracotta rooftops below their balcony to the Mediterranean beyond. Why go back to damp England, when they could live among this warmth and vividness forever? He and Jonathan were into their second week in this idyllic spot south of Barcelona. Dominic could get used to it.

"Oh, just a client trying to contact me," he said. He kissed Jonathan on his neck. "You'll be burnt to a cinder if you don't get some more sunblock on you. Here, let me rub it into your back."

Dominic picked up the plastic bottle of sunscreen and straddled his husband's prostrate body. Reaching across Jonathan's broad shoulders, he began to rub the cream in. Jonathan moaned appreciatively beneath him.

"Husband, you have very sensuous fingers, do you know that? And a wonderfully firm riding position." Jonathan reached his arms back and massaged Dominic's upper thighs. Now it was Dominic's turn to moan appreciatively. Jonathan's large, strong hands grasped his husband's thighs firmly, and his thumbs delved deep into Dominic's groin.

"Mm, is that a gun in your Speedos," asked Jonathan, "or are you just pleased to be newly married?"

Dominic dropped the bottle of sunblock to the ground and lay flat on Jonathan's back. "I don't think I'm going to be able to move from here for a short while," he said. "Not with any decency at least."

Jonathan transferred his massaging hands to the inside of Dominic's swim shorts. "You're such a shy, retiring country lawyer, my love. And that's why I want you above all others."

Dominic nibbled gently on Jonathan's ear. "Mr. McFadden. You're a very bad influence on me. Just for that, I'm going to have to leave you in a few hours."

Jonathan turned his head and clumsily kissed Dominic on the side of his lips. "Why? Where are you off to?"

"I'm going to hunt down something very special for you from the town," replied Dominic. "And I want to wander around a bit. You've seen Sitges many times, but remember it's only the second time for me. I still find it difficult to believe how beautiful it is. I want to drink it all in."

"You mean you thought I'd simply bring you to some gay ghetto for our wedding?" asked Jonathan. "You know that Sitges is far more than just a gay-friendly resort. The Spanish know what they're doing, and they're very relaxed about it. There are hetero families, gay families, singles—everyone is here. And yet we can hold hands. We can be arm in arm. I can kiss you in the street and no one bats an eyelid. This is what the world should be like. Remember, Spain was one of the first countries in the world to introduce equal marriage. Long before the UK or the US. It was fitting for us to come here."

Jonathan's hands resumed massaging Dominic's groin. "So what's this something very special you're going to get me?"

"I can't tell you that," replied Dominic. "It's a surprise. I saw it the other day. All I'll say is that it was in the window of that antiques place. You know? By the museum, just beyond the church. I've decided it's exactly what you need."

"Well that's remarkably generous of you. Especially as I have everything I need right here." Jonathan squeezed gently, and Dominic moaned in ecstasy. It would be a sweet couple of hours before his rendezvous with Bernhardt.

PUCCINI'S *La Bohème* was playing on the car's CD player. It was the aria "Your Tiny Hand is Frozen," which Rodolfo sang to Mimi. Bernhardt turned up the volume, and the rich sound of Pavarotti's classic 1972 recording filled the car. The aria was always intensely moving for him, bringing back memories of happier times.

Bernhardt remembered the first time he met Dominic, on the steps of the Berlin Opera House, nearly seventeen years ago. The poor young man had looked so lost as he searched for the returns ticket window. So lost and so cute. Bernhardt knew he had no choice but to treat this beautiful young English boy to the best seat in the house that night. During the interval they talked about opera, art deco furniture, and law. It turned out their passions were very similar. At the finale, tears were streaming down Dominic's face. Bernhardt was moved by the raw emotion this shy young Englishman showed. He put a comforting hand on Dominic's knee, reached across, and kissed him tenderly on the lips. "Stay with me tonight. Be a part of the new excitement that is a unified Germany. Our united Berlin."

Dominic had stayed in Bernhardt's bohemian apartment in the Schöneberg district of Berlin for several weeks. Bernhardt found the young man to be naïve and inexperienced sexually, almost racked with guilt. Moments of foreplay were abruptly halted when Dominic pulled away, as though in fear of liberating himself.

Blinded by his infatuation with Dominic's beauty, Bernhardt allowed their days together to fill with passionate discussions about the law and its role in a Europe now rid of communism. He tried to convince himself it was erotic intellectual foreplay that would resolve into a lustful sexual exploration of each other's bodies. Sometimes it did. Too often he had to leave the apartment to find sexual relief in the bars around Schöneberg.

Then one night, Bernhardt returned home late to find his apartment empty. Dominic had packed his rucksack and gone. It was a disappointment, but not unexpected. Anyway, Bernhardt had no shortage of beautiful men to play with in that increasingly fashionable sector of Berlin.

His lucrative law practice paid for a comfortable lifestyle. With the end of communism in Eastern Europe, software companies were taking advantage of exceptionally talented East European programmers willing to work for low wages. Bernhardt's fluency in multiple languages and his broad knowledge of the new European legal systems quickly built him a reputation as the number one expert on European contract law, especially software law.

As Pavarotti's voice soared in the closing moments of Puccini's aria, Bernhardt realized the twists and turns in the road were beginning to tighten as it descended into Spain. Distracted by the music and his thoughts, he had failed to notice his speed was increasing. He put his foot on the brake, but the car continued to accelerate. He stamped hard on the pedal. All the indicators on the dashboard went blank. It was as though the car had switched to autopilot. He could sense he was getting faster but had no idea what speed he was going. The long sweeping curve in the road ahead tightened around the cliff face. Perspiration on his palms greased the leather steering wheel, and Bernhardt gripped tight as he tried to force the car to follow the course of the road. Now terrified, he could see a large diesel-oil truck ahead of him. He was closing on it fast. Frantically he stamped on the brake pedal. Still his car accelerated.

After nervously taking his right hand off the steering wheel, Bernhardt pulled hard on the parking brake. The rear wheels locked momentarily. He smelled burning rubber as the tires, skidding along the road's surface, erupted in clouds of black smoke. The back end of the car lurched violently from side to side, and Bernhardt let go of the parking brake to seize control of the steering wheel with both hands.

He was little more than thirty feet away from the truck when its stoplights came on. Bernhardt reached for the parking brake again and pulled hard as the front end of the sports car hooked under the rear of the truck. The rear wheels locked, and the car spun on the road surface. The steering wheel was wrenched from Bernhardt's grasp. The truck braked hard, and the sports car catapulted across the road into the crash barrier. It flipped over the top and rolled several times before it came to rest on a wide, sloping shelf of rock a few feet from the cliff edge.

Bernhardt was hanging by his seat belt in the upturned car. The engine had cut out, and he could hear the truck accelerating away beyond the bend in the road. There was an eerie silence, broken only by the sound of twisted metal creaking on rock.

Bernhardt knew he had little time to escape, but there was something he had to deal with first. Rapidly, he reached into the pocket of his chinos and pulled out his mobile phone. He tapped in a code, then selected a number and clicked Send. Shoving the phone back in his pocket, he reached to undo his seat belt. The car slid several feet toward the cliff edge. Frantically, Bernhardt pushed hard on the belt buckle. Suspended in the upturned car, his weight pulling on the strap, Bernhardt could not release the mechanism. It felt like every bone in his body had been broken, and blood was trickling into his eyes. With an enormous effort, he pushed his left hand against the roof of the car to lessen his weight on the seat belt. The catch clicked open, and he collapsed painfully onto the upturned roof. The car rocked with an ominous creak. Bernhardt was still scrabbling for the door handle when the car tipped at the edge of the cliff, then tumbled to the rocks below.

Chapter 2

PETE YAWNED, stretched his aching limbs, and looked at the time on his mobile. It was just before five. In a few more minutes, he would have to get up. He curled into a ball and pulled the blanket over his head. *Two more minutes*, he promised himself.

"Hey, Pete. You got that job interview today, haven't you?" The man's voice came from the bed next to his. "Better shift your ass if you're gonna make it on time."

Pete groaned from beneath the blanket and stretched out his aching limbs. "Give me a break, Chuck! I gotta rest. My gut's playing up again, and I got no sleep last night."

"Just lookin' out for you, buddy. Don't want you screwin' up this one like you did the last."

Pete pulled the blanket down slowly and peered across at the bright, eager eyes of his early morning alarm call.

"Thanks for reminding me, Chuck. You know, you're a real pal sometimes."

"Will you guys shut the fuck up? Some of us are tryin' to get some shut-eye here."

Pete looked around him. His bed was at the far end of the dormitory. There were about ten more on his side of the room, between him and the door, with around the same number opposite. The voice had come from one of the beds on the other side.

"Sorry, Mo," Pete said in a loud whisper. "But it's nearly five. They'll be kickin' us out in half an hour anyway."

"All the more reason to shut the fuck up now. Jerk."

Pete sat up and pushed the blanket back. There was no point in holding out for a few more minutes of sleep. Now he was wide-awake. He reckoned he could get down to Planet Fitness for a wash and shave before heading to Walmart for the nine o'clock interview. Planet Fitness was one of his few indulgences. For ten bucks a month, the twenty-four-hour-a-day gym offered a warm shower and a place to shave and freshen up. His pal Mo had put him on to it when they had met at the shelter on a cold January night. Today he was going to give himself an extra treat and get the bus. Then he would turn up without his shoes looking scuffed and not be all sweaty after his cleanup at Planet Fitness.

As he walked down the hall to check out his bag from secure storage, he met Captain Roberts. As ever, she looked smart in her Salvation Army uniform. Pete stopped, stood to attention, and saluted.

"Stand easy, Sergeant," said the captain. "Pete, it's good to see you bright and early. Ready to do the Lord's work today, are we?"

Pete lowered his salute and shuffled his legs into a stand-easy position. "I've got a job interview, Captain. I'll be back in action before you know it. Don't want to be a drain on the shelter's good services for more than a minute longer than I need to be."

The captain smiled and patted Pete on the arm. "You're a good man, Pete. But it's been a while, hasn't it?"

Pete's shoulders drooped.

"Don't worry," she continued. "There are many opportunities for work in Seattle. Who's this interview with?"

"It's Walmart, ma'am."

"Good, good," said the captain with a broad, friendly smile. "Look, I've got a little time to spare. Why don't we go find an office upstairs and do a practice run for your interview? I can help you be real confident for later. By the time you're finished answering their questions, they'll be begging to hire you."

Pete followed Captain Roberts down the corridor and up three flights of stairs. There was no carpet on the first and second sets of stairs, just bare boards. The captain's flat shoes clattered noisily in front of him. Pete noticed that her calves were very shapely. Such a pity they were enveloped in heavy, dark tights.

The final flight of stairs was carpeted. Pete had never been up here before. He had been told it was not a place for the shelter's clients. As they neared the top, he paused and held on to the handrail to catch his breath. The captain turned and gave him a sympathetic smile.

"Aren't your legs as cooperative as they used to be? I know what it's like, Pete. I'm beginning to feel my fifty years now."

Pete looked up slowly and swallowed a gulp of air. "Fifty, eh? Well I've got thirteen years on you, young lady. And those include three of active service in 'Nam. They take their toll on you, those years."

The captain's face flushed briefly. Pete had not meant to embarrass her, but her attempt to say something nice had irritated him. He took a deep breath and resumed his trudge up the stairs. Captain Roberts entered a small dark office, where early morning sunlight filtered through its single grimy window. She pressed the light switch, and a solitary neon tube flickered into life. Captain Roberts sat behind a dark wooden desk and clasped her hands in front of her, resting them on its well-used surface. Pete hesitated in the doorway.

"Come in, Pete, and make yourself comfortable. I'm not going to role-play this with you or anything. I just want to make sure you're prepared for later. We want you to shine, don't we?" When she smiled, her dark brown eyes lit up her face, and her lips parted to reveal a row of almost even teeth. Pete entered the room, sat down on the hard metal chair opposite the captain, and waited for the interrogation to start.

"Now, Pete, have you got a copy of the résumé you filled in for the folks at Walmart?"

Pete shook his head.

"It's always a good idea to do that if you can. Do you remember what you put on it?"

Pete nodded. He could remember word for word. He felt he had written a thousand résumés in the last three years.

Captain Roberts's smile once again lit up her face. "Let's start with your employment record. What was your last job?"

Pete swallowed hard. Then he began. "Thirty-five years. I was with WRI for thirty-five years. I started on night patrols and worked my way up to be head of facility security. I had thirty people reporting to me when they pushed me out. That's when the crap started."

"Pete, it's not a good idea to use bad language when—"

"So I thought," Pete continued, ignoring the captain, "you know what? I'm not far off retirement. I'll take it early. I've served my country. They owe me. They owe me big-time. That's when the world turned real shitty—"

"Pete," warned the captain.

"Pardon my language, ma'am, but there's no other word for it. First, WRI said I had no pension entitlement. So I thought I'd fight them, and meanwhile I'd get my government pension. Add it to my Vet's pension. But the pension office says, 'There's no record of your pension entitlement. You get nothin'.' Assholes!"

"Pete! You must moderate your language—"

"So I go around to every goddamn government office I can. Then one day, the mortgage company comes knocking. Smart young man in a shiny suit says there's no record of my mortgage payments. But I show him. I show him the statements I'd kept all the years. But he says they're no good. The computer's not got 'em. And that means, so he says, they don't exist. Next thing, I lose the house. And the car. And you know what?"

Pete took a deep breath. Captain Roberts leaned forward to lay her hand gently on Pete's trembling arm.

"I hit sixty, and I've got nothing." Pete looked down at the captain's hand resting on his arm. "Diddly-squat."

His shoulders sagged. The captain squeezed his arm. "We've been through this before, haven't we?" she said. "You've got to move on, Pete."

Captain Roberts pushed her chair back and stood up. "Now, Sergeant. We both know you can do better than that. We're not going to let them see that you're beat, are we?"

Pete shook his head vigorously. He blinked hard and looked down at the desktop. He didn't want the captain to see his tears.

WHEN DOMINIC left for his mysterious shopping trip, Jonathan stood at the balcony rail of their sixth-floor holiday apartment, watching people wandering to and fro in the wide street below. The apartment was in a perfect central location. Directly on Passeig de la Ribera, the main promenade of Sitges, alongside the wide, clean beaches.

Jonathan waited nearly twenty minutes before checking his messages on Scruff. He felt a little guilty; he was technically breaking his promise to Dominic. Maybe they were on their honeymoon, but he convinced himself he was only being courteous to his correspondents. He was certainly not making plans for any hookups. Even Jonathan conceded that would be unfair to Dominic. He reminded himself of his husband's exact words as they waited in the departure lounge at London's Luton Airport for their flight: "Don't let me catch you looking at other men on Scruff. We're on our honeymoon." And Jonathan had promised faithfully he would not.

But Jonathan needed sex. A lot. He loved Dominic deeply. Dominic was caring, thoughtful, endlessly self-deprecating, and full of humility. All the things Jonathan felt he was not. He loved the fact that Dominic maintained these qualities in his professional life and could still remain successful. He was a compassionate lawyer. Now there was an oxymoron if ever there was one, he thought. Jonathan would die to save his husband and lover. But it took several years before he felt confident Dominic understood his need for an open relationship, his need for sex with other men, even the occasional woman.

It was not something Dominic needed. Certainly he was attracted to other men and flattered by their attentions. But his lust and sexual needs were fully satisfied by Jonathan's endless inventiveness. Jonathan knew his partner had experimented with occasional hookups in the three years before they married, but he felt Dominic was practicing bravado when describing them to him, that he was doing it out of a sense of duty to help Jonathan justify his own needs.

Perhaps he was overthinking the whole thing. Not something he would ever have done in a previous relationship. Dominic was different from the other men he had known. It took only three years for Jonathan to decide he wanted to spend the rest of his life with Dominic. So long as their relationship could be open. After all, love was about much more than simply sex.

The photo of a good-looking young man with a shaved head and soulful brown eyes lit up the screen of his phone. Jonathan tapped the incoming message icon alongside it.

Hey, horny. Bored with married life already? If not, why the fuck are you reading this?

Jonathan sighed. Steve knew him too well. He scrolled down as the message continued.

Seriously. If you are reading this, can you ask Dominic to do something for me? I might want some legal advice.

Jonathan and Dominic had first met Steve in a bar in Brighton at the end of last year. During the events that followed their meeting, Dominic was nearly killed in a car filling with exhaust fumes. Thanks to Steve's technology skills, Dominic survived. That moment of crisis made Jonathan realize he could not live without his partner. He had asked Dominic to marry him—something he knew Dominic wanted more than anything in the world—and of course, Dominic had accepted. It was all thanks to Steve. He was much more than a sexy guy. But he was that as well.

Jonathan wondered what free legal advice Steve needed. He knew the young man's principal work was in surveillance. Perhaps he was in trouble. Again. Jonathan looked back at the photo. Steve's brown eyes were very appealing. And his smooth-skinned chest was very defined. Perhaps he might be on hand for a Skype video call.

Chapter 3

ALFONSO DE la Torre pulled the earpiece of the two-way radio out of his ear as the crackly voice rose to an almost deafening pitch.

"What do you mean, you lost him?"

He put the earpiece back into his ear once he was sure the volume had subsided. "It's the mountains. Or something went wrong with the transmitter. Suddenly there was no signal. I kept on riding for several kilometers. But I'm sorry, Captain Ricardo. The car has simply disappeared."

Alfonso de la Torre sat astride his police motorbike, waiting for his captain's response. He idly wiped the dust of the road from his tall leather boots. Alfonso took pride in his appearance. He devoted a lot of attention to his uniform. His tight avocado-green breeches were a perfect fit, and the sleeves of his tunic shirt were just the right degree of snug around his biceps.

"I'll call the aerial team," replied Captain Ricardo. "We must find that man. And the documents he's taken." His voice betrayed a hint of panic as he berated de la Torre. "Europol is giving the Guardia Civil a real hard time on this. They won't say why they want the suspect, Herr Freude. But it's putting everything else on hold across Europe, so it's got to be some serious shit. They tracked him across Germany, through Switzerland and France. You can't just lose him now. Go back up the road and look again. Perhaps he had an accident and he's gone over a cliff or something. I'll put you in touch with the aerial team once they get the chopper up. Meanwhile we'll put a trace on Freude's mobile phone."

The radio went dead. Alfonso de la Torre took off his helmet and took out a packet of Ducados cigarettes from his top pocket. Lighting one, he leaned back and drank in the scenery and the heat of the afternoon sun. If the man had gone over the cliff, then there was no hurry.

THE VIDEO connection was intermittent, but Jonathan could clearly see Steve's shaven head, the collar of his pale blue polo shirt, and his red braces.

In the background was what looked like a high-class hotel bar. The people were smartly dressed, in contrast to Steve.

"Looks like you're somewhere very swanky," said Jonathan. "I'm surprised they let a lowlife like you in. You're not dressed as a skinhead again, are you?"

To confirm Jonathan's suspicions, Steve raised a 14 hole Grinders boot to the camera, revealing in addition a pair of skintight bleacher jeans.

"Fuck off, mate," Steve replied. "It's only an airport lounge, not the bloody Ritz. Mind you"—Steve's defined cheekbones and razor-smooth head leaned toward the camera lens—"it's the fucking executive lounge. I'm off to San Fran. First class." He leaned back, a cocky smile clearly visible.

"I'm impressed," Jonathan said. "But do you have to wear all your skinhead gear? They'll think you're some white supremacist and throw you off the plane."

Steve flicked his middle finger at the camera, and a broad grin spread across his face. "C'mon, Jonathan, you find it just as sexy as thousands of other gay men. When the British skinheads were kicking the shit out of gays in the 1970s and '80s—"

"I know, I know," interrupted Jonathan. "You don't have to give me the old lecture about adopting your enemies' uniform to defuse their attacks. And I know you're no racist. I just think there's a time and place."

Steve's face loomed in toward the camera. "Does getting married mean you have to become an uptight middle-class wanker?" he asked. "I can tell you, this executive lounge is the time, and it's definitely the place. I've been cruised twice already." He leaned back and raised a can of lager to the camera. "Cheers, you old fart."

Jonathan laughed. "So who's the innocent client you fleeced to pay for that?" He went on before Steve could answer. "No. Don't tell me. The client's only paying for economy, so you've pulled the gay network stunt. Yet again." Jonathan picked up his glass of cava and raised it to the screen. "Here's to Steve, always ready to service the ground crew."

Steve shook his head. "Nah, that's for pussies, mate. Much simpler than that. It took me just a few moments at the computer. These ancient airline-ticketing systems are full of holes. The companies are so fucking tight. They pay peanuts to their software guys. And you know what you get when you pay peanuts." Steve raised his can of lager again and waved it around his head. "Upgraded to first class, mate. On an Airbus 380. It's like taking candy from a fucking baby. I'm not servicing the ground crew this time. In a few hours, it'll be the cabin crew servicing me." He leaned into the screen again, a broad grin across his face. "It'll be more than fucking cruising altitude, mate."

Jonathan laughed and then choked as a mouthful of cava went down the wrong way. Once again, he held his glass up to the computer screen. "I salute you, young sir. You're always one to do things in style. Your own particular style, of course. Now why are you going to San Francisco? Apart from the obvious."

"It's work, mate. Well, it's a hackfest, actually."

"Hackfest? Is that a festival of hackers? You're not going to start sharing your hacking secrets, are you? You'll be flying back economy if you do."

"It's not that kind of hacking, you prick. Anyway I don't do hacking, me. I specialize in what they call 'unconventional entry.'"

Again Jonathan sputtered on a mouthful of cava as he laughed. "And you more than anyone know a thing or two about unconventional entries."

"Fuck off, Jonathan," replied Steve. "For an opera singer, you've got a fucking puerile mind. A hackfest is where clever people like me create some cool stuff for the unfortunates who are too thick to understand technology. Mostly arty twats like you. They'll pair me up with some designer or artist or, God help me, an opera singer. And we end up with some cool tech that no one's done before. We save the world from itself through tech."

"What do you mean, 'save the world through tech'?" asked Jonathan. "It's tech that got us into this mess. A billion cars guzzling the world's resources. The next must-have device eating up precious rare earths. It's people like me who'll save the world, through the power of music. And my fabulous garden designs, of course."

This time it was Steve's turn to roar with laughter. "I never saw you as someone with his finger on the pulse of the global crisis. Perhaps you should come to the next hackfest. They can pair you up with someone clever like me."

Jonathan leaned into the screen. "Well, Dominic and I will be in San Francisco in a few days' time. We're finishing off our honeymoon down the coast from there, at Big Sur. We've been invited to a wedding. Rather fitting, don't you think?"

"Dominic doesn't strike me as the jet-setting type," said Steve.

"Oh, he's changed," said Jonathan with a broad smile. "Sadly, my dear, it's a lightning visit. Five days only. So we won't have time for your little hackfest thingy, I'm afraid. Intriguing as it sounds. And positively philanthropic. Not like you at all. Don't tell me you're doing it for love?"

Once again Steve flicked his middle finger at the screen. "I don't know what Dominic sees in a cynical cunt like you. Oh, that reminds me. Can you ask him to do something for me?"

Jonathan thought back to the original message on Scruff that had prompted him to Skype Steve.

"Are you in trouble? He doesn't do criminal law, you know."

"Nah, mate. It's clever stuff I've invented that might need protecting. I'm branching out from security these days. The new horizon is control. Remote control. I can control anything, me. Phones, computers, houses. Cars. Hang on a minute. I'll show you." Steve began typing on the keypad of the laptop in front of him. A few seconds later, Jonathan's laptop started screening a raunchy porn film. He reached across to turn it off, but the keypad no longer responded. The video faded, and the words "Gotcha, tosser!" scrolled up the screen.

"Now who's being puerile?" Jonathan was disconcerted at how quickly Steve had taken control from hundreds of miles away. "Anyway, isn't that a bit old hat? Even I know you can use your mobile these days to turn your heating down when you're away from home—"

"Yeah, yeah," interrupted Steve. "And Google's got driverless cars. Any bastard knows that. But what I can do takes it to a whole new level. And that's where I need Dominic's help."

OFFICER DE la Torre surveyed the wreckage below him. The car had landed on its wheels, and the impact had shattered every piece of glass in the vehicle. Alfonso could see two airbags had deployed on impact. They were spattered with the blood of the only occupant, a middle-aged man wearing a once-white T-shirt and tan chinos.

Alfonso slowly dismounted his bike and pulled it onto its stand. He removed his crash helmet and placed it on the seat. Then he looked for a path down to the rocky plateau where the car had landed. He grasped at narrow ledges with his leather gloves. His boots found dubiously secure toeholds. Slowly, he eased himself down the thirty feet or so to the wreckage. In his teens, Alfonso had climbed regularly in the Pyrenees and in Spain's Sierra Nevada mountains. This short descent was a minor challenge for him. What he steeled himself for, with apprehension, was the corpse.

The body was still propped up in the driver's seat, pinned in position by the airbag. Alfonso carefully opened the door. He waited for splinters of glass to finish falling before he leaned in. Then he went through the routine he had been taught. First, check the body for vital signs. There were none. Then, trying to disturb the corpse as little as possible, he searched the clothes. All he could find was a mobile phone. With difficulty he extracted it from the driver's pocket.

Alfonso walked to the front of the car, leaned against it, and breathed deeply. He would never get used to this part of policing.

He looked down at the mobile phone. It lacked identifying marks and was locked with a PIN code. Alfonso walked around to the passenger door. Again, he opened it carefully, to avoid being injured by fragments of glass. The contents of the interior had been thrown around violently in the accident. He searched for the driver's documentation. In the glove box he found an expensive brown leather wallet. There was also a package, tightly encased in Bubble Wrap.

Alfonso took the two items around to the front of the car to examine them. The wallet contained a substantial amount of cash. He counted nearly two thousand euros in notes of varying denominations. There was a German driver's license in the name of Bernhardt Freude, aged forty-six. He also found two credit cards and a membership card for a car breakdown service.

He put the items back in the wallet and turned his attention to the bubble-wrapped package. Carefully, he unwrapped it. In his hands lay an exquisitely crafted bronze male nude.

Alfonso was sure he had seen something similar to it in the past. Gabriel, his husband of nearly eleven years, was a keen collector of art deco. Their apartment in the fashionable Sarrià district of Barcelona contained trophies from their frequent visits to antiques shops around Europe. Such beautiful objects were not affordable on Alfonso's modest police salary. But Gabriel was a senior executive for Spain's Banco España Internacional, where his father was the bank's chairman. It was not a job Gabriel particularly enjoyed, but it paid for a very comfortable lifestyle.

Recently, Gabriel had become an enthusiast for European expressionist architecture. In April, they had taken a seven-day holiday and flown to

Berlin, where they hired a large touring motorbike. It was an exhilarating way to see some of Germany's finest examples of art deco buildings.

They returned to Barcelona with a suitcase full of auction brochures, which Gabriel spent hours salivating over. They already planned a return visit in a few months.

Alfonso looked again at the figurine in his hands. He turned it over and over, admiring the simple beauty of its form. An idea crossed his mind.

Chapter 4

Steve was bored. The first-class lounge at Heathrow's Terminal Four was dull. Stuffed with tight-assed businesswomen and overweight men wearing badly fitting clothes. Steve's own Fred Perry top, bleacher jeans, braces, and Grinders boots were in sharp contrast. He amused himself for a while by catching the eye of his fellow waiting passengers. But he soon tired of their disapproving reactions. Steve felt like giving the lot of them the middle finger. Only the free food and drink stopped him. Periodically, he checked both Grindr and Scruff, but the talent was elsewhere in the airport. In desperation, he did what he always did in these situations—plugged in his headphones and called his mother.

Her face appeared on his laptop screen. "What's the matter, are you bored?" She knew him too well.

"Hi, Mom. Nice to see you too," said Steve. "Just thought I'd say hi before I got on the plane. We won't be talking for a while, I reckon."

"We only spoke this morning, Stevie. Now don't forget my Cinnamon Toast Crunch, will you? It's impossible to get here."

Steve was glad he was wearing his headphones. He hated anyone hearing him called Stevie. It made him feel five years old again.

"I told you where to buy them online, Mom. If I stuff them in my bag, they'll only get squashed. I'll get you something nice from Ghirardelli Square."

Candida Brown wrinkled her nose. "Oh, Stevie, you know how I hate American chocolate. It always tastes so stale. They make it far better here."

Steve felt his patriotic roots were under attack. "Dad always bought you chocolate when we lived in Renton. And you always ate it. Don't tell me that's the real reason you got divorced?"

Candida laughed. "Maybe part of it. He just got boring. You know that. He and I turned out to be very different. You and I, we're much more alike. We're restless. Can't just keep doing the same old thing. We have a need to do lots of different stuff. Crazy stuff. He didn't."

It was true. Steve's mother was unpredictable and wild. She was twenty years older than him and still had the capacity to shock. He loved her for it. When Steve was eleven, his parents separated. Candida and Steve left the three-room family apartment in a sleepy suburb of Seattle and moved to England. They lived with his mother's parents in Brighton, on the south coast. That was where they still lived, in a rambling, ramshackle townhouse. Steve had the basement, his grandparents lived on the ground floor, and his mother had the upper floors.

"While you're out there, you should go see him."

Why had he not seen that coming? When Steve made a trip to the States, it revived uncomfortable memories of his childhood. He thought back to his last visit, four years earlier, when he was invited to the headquarters of a major software company in Redmond. The company had wooed him over two days of negotiation, but he resisted the riches the company promised, preferring to remain a free agent. He remembered how his mother had tried to encourage him to see his father then. At the last minute, Steve called his dad from the Seattle airport while waiting for his flight back to England. There was no answer. His father was out somewhere. He had been relieved.

"Well, Stevie, why not? He isn't a bad man—"

"Just not a very good dad." Steve remembered the times his father had not been there. Absent for Steve's debut in the first-grade nativity play. Not there when Steve sang his first solo in the Renton Theater workshop production of *Oliver!* His dad made it very clear he disapproved of his son's passion for musicals. Even when his father was at home, he was not really there. He would disappear into his den in the basement for hours at a time, reading his books on the military. Steve remembered how he was obsessed with wars and the US Army.

"Okay, I'll see him this time. Where's he living now?"

His mother's face glowed with happiness on the screen. "Thanks, Stevie. It means a lot to me. He and I might have gone our separate ways, but he's your dad, and I don't want you to lose touch with him. The last thing I heard, the company was moving him down to Sacramento. But he may still be in Washington State—"

"Okay, Mom," relented Steve, "I've got a few days at the end of the hackfest. I was going to hang around in San Fran and cruise a few clubs. But the last time I was there, they weren't anything like they used to be. I won't be missing much. I'll pay him a visit. Just for you, Mom."

Steve glanced up at the TV monitor showing the flight departures and cursed. His flight was delayed.

DOMINIC LIFTED his head to the remaining rays of the sun. He shifted his bare legs out of the shadows, stretched, and basked in the warmth like a pampered cat. At his feet was a small carrier bag, the result of a successful visit to Antiquitats, next to the church, twenty minutes before. He was sure Jonathan would love the miniature bust of Handel, his most-beloved composer. Dominic had chosen his table outside the Restaurant Fragata so he could sit in the sunlight and have a good view of everyone who walked by.

There was always something interesting or attractive to see in Sitges. In most Mediterranean towns, the evening promenade began around 6:30 p.m. But in Sitges it lasted all day, with a burst of activity starting in the late afternoon. Couples, straight or gay, walked hand in hand, relaxing with their partners, pleased to be able to display their contentedness to all who watched. The openness and freedom of Sitges was perfect for Dominic and Jonathan. Here they could be themselves. Dominic was still getting used to walking hand in hand with his husband without seeing judgmental stares from passersby. In England, by contrast, even with equal marriage legal, few same-sex couples felt confident enough to hold hands in public, even in the heart of London. Here in Sitges, if people stared, it was only to admire Jonathan's well-crafted physique.

A pale-faced young man wearing a short-sleeved olive-green army shirt, camouflage shorts, and a baseball cap pulled low over his face sat on one of several benches less than a hundred feet away. Dominic was convinced the man was staring at him. He appeared to be in his late twenties and had a cigarette constantly in his hand. Dominic flattered himself that the young man was fascinated by his good looks. But in truth, he felt as though he was being examined, and it made him uncomfortable.

Dominic picked up his glass of cava. He took a sip and then looked down at the puzzling text he had received from Bernhardt. It had arrived a few hours ago, but he had not noticed it until he prepared to leave the apartment. Jonathan had proved a very passionate distraction after Bernhardt's first text.

This second message was bizarre. It contained twenty numbers—38 35 25.603 121 48 11.249—and the phrase *Turn to the feet of Adam*. This was followed by eight more numbers—03 15 26 21—and finally a date: *June 1*.

Once again, Dominic called Bernhardt's phone. It went straight to voicemail, as it had done on the half-dozen occasions he had tried to call since he sat down. It was nearly seven o'clock. He had expected Bernhardt to have arrived by now. More than that, Bernhardt would have sent him several texts, checking whether Dominic was at their meeting place. Bernhardt was always punctual and a stickler for detail.

Dominic looked up. The young man was staring at him again. Dominic decided now was the time to find out more about his observer. He finished his glass of cava, turned, and signaled to the waiter he wanted to pay. When he turned back, the young man had gone.

A few moments later, the waiter arrived with his bill.

"I was asked to give you this, señor."

From the metal platter the waiter left behind, Dominic picked up a note. It was tightly rolled and sealed with a cigarette paper. Carefully unsealing it, Dominic opened the note and read the brief message: *Balmins platges, 23:00. I am a friend of Bernhardt.*

JEFF WOODFIELD looked approvingly at the image on the screen. It showed a headshot of one of the developers booked into the fifth Embarcadero Hackfest. The biennial gathering of the world's finest hackers was due to start this coming weekend, here in San Francisco. Ever since he had launched the hackfests fourteen years ago, Jeff had spent his days finding the brightest and the best for the events. Attendance was strictly at Jeff's personal invitation. He trawled hacking conversations on the internet to find new programming talent. If they were cute as well, then so much the better.

The image on his laptop screen showed a man in his late twenties with a shaved head, wearing a blue Fred Perry top. Jeff flicked to the headlines of his research notes about the delegate.

Steve Brown. 29 years old. Brighton, England. Control systems hacker. New attendee. Demonstrates ability with power station and traffic controls. Specialty: vehicle control. Potential recruit for Charter Ninety-Nine.

Jeff flicked to the bottom of the page, where he had written miscellaneous notes. There was a single entry: *Originally from Washington State. British gay skinhead, unattached.*

After scrolling back to the top of the screen, Jeff studied the face again. The guy was thirteen years his junior. Just what he liked. Experienced but still fresh. Jeff had never met a real gay British skinhead before. He was fascinated how they had taken a right-wing political subculture and turned it into a gay sexual fetish. He knew many liberal gay men were turned on by the gear and the attitude but had no affiliation to the politics.

The heavy iron gates of the elevator clanged open behind him. Jeff turned to see his partner, Nick, step out onto the top floor of their apartment. Back in the early '90s, when it was just an abandoned warehouse, Jeff had lived in the building for free for two years as part of an occupying commune. It was in a perfect location. A block away from Coit Tower, close to the waterfront, with a view of the Bay Bridge. Seven years later, he made ten million dollars from the sale of his music sharing website at the height of the dot-com boom in the summer of '99. Enjoying the liberation of wealth, Jeff discovered the three-story warehouse was scheduled for demolition. He quickly bought it and turned the lower level into offices. The top two levels of the building became his home. It was an industrial architect's wet dream.

The sound of his partner's tan rigger boots echoed on the bare wooden floor as he walked toward the steel desk where Jeff was seated.

"Checking out the talent again, I see," teased Nick. "Which one have you gone for this time?"

Reflecting the image of Steve on the screen, Nick also had a shaved head. But the resemblance stopped there. Nick wore a loose-fitting, sleeveless white gym shirt that revealed his well-developed biceps and gave a glimpse of the muscles on his shaved chest. His faded blue jeans, which hugged tight around his buttocks and thighs, were tucked into his boots. He sported two days' stubble that hinted at the natural blond of his hair.

Jeff picked up the laptop and handed it to Nick for a closer look. "We've had an alert about this one. Nothing specific. But we're going to have to test his integrity. Do you want to go catch him? Helluva catch."

Nick took the laptop from his partner and admired the image of Steve on the screen. "Three years younger than me. What's the matter, am I getting too old for you?" Jeff kicked out at his partner playfully as Nick continued. "Sure, I'll go catch him if you're gonna let me. It's been a while since I've played away. Or did you want to be part of it? A threesome to welcome the horny Brit?"

The edges of Jeff's mouth turned upward slightly. It was the closest he ever came to a smile. "Much as I'd like to fuck the pair of you, I don't want him to sense he's getting any kind of special attention. I reckon he's a smart one, and we're going to have to be cool. No. Just play the innocent tech-support guy and get as close as you want. We need intimate trackers on him to find out what he's doing." Jeff grabbed his partner's crotch with rough affection. "And I know you're an expert at inserting them."

Chapter 5

WITH HIS flight delayed and nearly two hours to kill, Steve decided to call his father. There was no answer from the landline number he had, nor from the two mobile numbers. He went online to check the white pages. It took a while because his father's last name was the same as his: Brown. After ten minutes scrolling fruitlessly through a long list of people called P. Brown, he ordered another Peroni and decided to take a shortcut. He would hack into his father's online records.

It was usually a simple task for Steve to penetrate the security walls protecting the databases of millions of personal records across the world. With his dad living in the US, his first port of call was the Social Security records database. It took him just under eight minutes, with the help of a couple of contacts who were online, to work his way through the software barriers. A new personal best.

Steve scrolled through the long list of Social Security records for people called Peter Brown. None of the history records connected with his father's address or place of work or school or any of the numerous details about his father's life Steve had gathered over the years. He hacked into the pan-US phone records system for the area of Renton, Washington. But that also yielded nothing. Steve took another mouthful of his Peroni beer and stared in puzzlement at the laptop screen.

He sat back and thought for a moment. His father might have changed his name, but this was highly unlikely given how fiercely resistant he was to change. Even if Peter Brown was known by a different name, Steve would be able to find an electronic paper trail showing the history of his personal records. He took another swig of his beer and spent ten minutes hacking into the Washington State database of births, marriages, and deaths. Each state in the US maintained its own records for its citizens. The majority of states had transferred their records to computer databases with password-protected access. A few remained in paper form only. Washington was one of the more advanced and had a reputation for being comprehensive and accurate.

Steve looked for his parents' marriage record. He knew their wedding had been on Saturday, July 11, 1987, in Renton's registry office. It should have taken Steve no more than a moment to find it. But his parents' wedding was not listed as one of the four marriages celebrated in Renton that day. He struggled to remember his father's date of birth. He knew it was January 2, and his father was either sixty-four or sixty-five. As Steve searched, he already anticipated the result. Sure enough, there were no records for the birth of Peter Tomacz Zubryzcki Brown in Washington State. His father had simply vanished from the electronic records.

"Excuse me, Mr. Brown. They're calling your flight." Steve looked up to see the well-groomed young man who had welcomed him to the executive lounge earlier. Not his type, Steve decided. Perhaps there would be better talent onboard to while away the eleven-hour flight. Steve reluctantly closed the lid of his laptop. The mystery of his father's online records would have to wait until he could get onto the internet again.

ALFONSO DROVE his police motorbike onto the grounds of the gated apartment complex in Sarrià. He parked it in the reserved space, alongside his own touring bike. He removed his crash helmet and dismounted. From one of the panniers, he took out the bubble-wrapped package he had recovered from the wrecked vehicle earlier. He tucked it inside his helmet and went into the first of the apartment buildings.

His husband was cooking when Alfonso entered the hallway of their top-floor apartment.

"Gabriel, I'm back," he called as he placed his helmet on the console table in the tiled hallway. He removed the package from the helmet and walked the length of the hallway to the sunlit kitchen. The smell of pastry cooking in the oven hit his nostrils. He stood in the doorway of the kitchen and admired the tall, muscular frame of his husband. Gabriel was baking *empanadas*—pastry stuffed with meat, a dish he loved. On the stove sizzled a pan of *albondigas*, Spanish meatballs. To the side, Alfonso could see a large *tortilla*, freshly made.

Alfonso crossed the floor of the kitchen to stand behind Gabriel, who was stirring the pan of albondigas. Alfonso placed the bubble-wrapped package on the counter and wrapped his arms around Gabriel's taut waist.

As he kissed him several times on the neck, his husband leaned his head back appreciatively.

"Patrons are advised that they must *always* interfere with the cook when he's preparing tapas. It improves the taste of his meatballs." Gabriel put down the large spoon and turned slowly in Alfonso's arms. He wrapped his own arms around Alfonso's waist, squeezed tightly, and kissed him on the lips.

"You're very late, aren't you?" said Gabriel teasingly. "I've been slaving over this stove for hours. Have you been seeing another man?"

Alfonso ran his fingers through Gabriel's waves of black hair.

"A dead man, yes. Car crash on the N11 near Vidreres. It wasn't very pleasant."

Gabriel wrinkled his nose in disapproval. "I'm so glad I simply sit at a desk all day in the bank. I know I couldn't bear to see the things you do. Although—" He slid the palms of his hands over Alfonso's figure-hugging breeches. "—it's a shame I can't walk around in tight trousers and tall boots all day. I would enjoy that."

Alfonso laughed and leaned forward as though to kiss his husband. Instead, he picked up the large spoon Gabriel had been using to stir the albondigas and tasted the remnants of spicy tomato sauce still clinging to it.

"As ever, that tastes so good." He licked his lips approvingly. Gabriel leaned toward him, and for several moments their mouths embraced.

Alfonso looked into Gabriel's deep brown eyes and then pulled back slightly to gaze at the smooth arc of his lips.

"I will never tire of tasting, sensing, or looking at those beautiful lips of yours, Gabriel. You know, I still have that photograph of them I took on my phone the day we met in Sitges."

"I thought you a strange stalker then," replied Gabriel with a coquettish tilt of his head. "Thank God your uniform won me over."

Alfonso pushed his husband away with mock disapproval.

"And I thought you loved me for who I am, not for what I wear! Just for that, I won't give you the little gift I've brought."

"Ah, I saw my hunter-gatherer had been busy," said Gabriel. "What have you captured this time? And don't tell me where you got it. I know it's usually best for me not to ask."

He turned and reached for the bubble-wrapped package Alfonso had placed on the counter. He weighed it in his hands and turned it over several times.

"It's very heavy for its size," he said. "But then, good things can come in small packages. Or even large ones," he added as Alfonso pressed his crotch against him.

Alfonso laid his hands on Gabriel's shoulders and began to kiss around the base of his husband's neck. Gabriel rolled his shoulders appreciatively as he unwrapped the package. After a few moments, he discarded the last of the Bubble Wrap, and the bronze male figurine lay in his hands.

"Oh, Alfonso, he's beautiful." Gabriel raised the figure and turned it slowly in the fading sunlight. "German, I think, probably early 1930s. More than likely a representation of Adam in the Garden of Eden. He has no fig leaf, so it's before he was tempted by that wicked woman." Gabriel turned back to look at Alfonso with a rapturous smile on his face, his hands continuing to caress the figurine.

"I saw him, and immediately my thoughts turned to you," said Alfonso. "I found him when I was at that—"

"No, don't tell me," interrupted Gabriel. "It's best you don't. I'm presuming you didn't buy it in the flea market on Plaza Glories. I love it, and I will treasure it forever. From now on, when I look at my bronzed Adonis Adam, I will remember this moment. With the albondigas sizzling in the pan and you sizzling in my arms." He kissed Alfonso on the lips.

"Now," Gabriel continued, standing the figurine carefully on the worktop beside him. "Much as I love you in those wonderful breeches, you're hot and sweaty after the ordeal I'm sure you must have had today. Go and have a shower, and I'll finish getting supper ready."

Alfonso gave his husband one final, lingering kiss before he left him at the stove and walked into the bedroom. He sat on the side of the bed, removed his tall black motorcycle boots, and examined them carefully. He took great pride in their appearance, and today they had taken a battering. He set the boots aside to clean later.

Standing, he stripped off his clothes and looked at his reflection in the full-length mirror. It stood to the side of the glass doors opening onto their balcony. As he turned side on, he automatically held in his stomach. Gabriel's fine cooking was having a definite and lasting impact on his waistline, coupled with the hours of sitting on his motorbike in police speed traps. He made a resolution to resume his exercise routine. After all, the gym was on the ground floor of their building. He really had no excuse.

He was about to head for the bathroom when he noticed a letter addressed to them both lying on the nightstand. He picked it up and began reading as he returned to the kitchen.

"I see we've heard from the fertilization agency today," he said excitedly, still taking in the contents of the letter.

Gabriel looked up from his cooking at Alfonso's naked form. "My, my. If you stand around looking like that, I might just be in a position to make a deposit right now."

Alfonso put down the letter and rushed over to embrace Gabriel.

"Careful, careful," said Gabriel. "You don't want hot albondigas sauce all down you when you are quite so… magnificently exposed." Gabriel turned and looked admiringly at Alfonso's body. "Yes. It's wonderful news, isn't it? I was going to keep it as a surprise until we were having supper. They've said yes." He tilted his head to look lovingly at Alfonso. "We're going to be a family."

Alfonso cupped his hands around Gabriel's face. "So, will he have your beautiful eyes and wonderful hair, or my sticky-out ears and bowlegs?"

Gabriel pushed his husband gently away and turned back to the stove. "Who says he'll be a he? It might be a girl. Maybe, by some miracle of genetics, he or she will be a combination of the two of us. I understand that's even a possibility now. But whether it's a boy or a girl, we're going to have a child."

Alfonso picked up the letter once more and started to reread it.

"Have you emailed them? When does everything start? Shall I book my paternity leave now?"

Gabriel smiled. "Yes, I did email them. They're ready to go through the full assessment with us both. You'll need to take some time off, at least five days. More if we want to do a little sightseeing."

Alfonso punched his arms into the air and began dancing to an imaginary club soundtrack. "We're going to California! And when we come back, we'll be dads!"

Gabriel leaned back against the worktop and relished the spectacle.

"Sorry to spoil the celebration," said Gabriel, "exquisitely sexy to watch as it is. But we won't come back dads. I believe the gestation period is still nine months for a baby. But yes, given that we can't legally surrogate here, California is going to save us." Gabriel took a gulp from his wine. "And it will be extraordinarily expensive."

Alfonso dropped his arms, stepped toward his husband, and placed his hands on Gabriel's waist.

"It's all right, isn't it? You can pay for this? Because if in any way it's not possible, then you only have to say—"

Gabriel placed a finger on Alfonso's lips to stem the flow of his anxiety.

"Such beautiful lips," he whispered and leaned forward to rest his forehead on Alfonso's. "How lucky I am to be kissed by them every morning. Money is not a problem. I shouldn't have said anything. Really, it's not a problem. I just wish that Spain could change its stupid laws. But, as we both move into our midthirties, respectability is fast overtaking us. We're going to be fathers and loving parents. And if it means going to California to ensure we are completely legal, then that's what we'll do. Anyway," he continued, with a mischievous twinkle in his eyes. "Whilst we're out there, we can celebrate our years of unrespectability by behaving disreputably. You can hire a big Harley-Davidson and take us for a trip along the Pacific Coast Highway. I'll enjoy riding pillion, holding tight to your waist."

Chapter 6

"You're strangely quiet tonight, my love," said Jonathan to Dominic. "Is everything all right?" He tore a hunk from his bread roll and mopped up the remains of the mussels in tomato and garlic. "This is delicious, as always. How were the sardines? You've not finished them."

"Oh, I think I may have had a bit too much sun today." Dominic picked up his fork and tried one more mouthful of the sardines before pushing his plate away. "You know what I'm like if I forget my hat."

They were sitting on the terrace of the Vivero Beach Club restaurant. It was built into a rocky outcrop on the edge of the old town of Sitges and looked straight out to sea. About fifty feet below, the waves rhythmically lapped the shore of a small private beach. The restaurant was fast becoming their regular haunt. They both loved seafood, and after Jonathan had charmed the maître d' on their first night, they were offered a table with an exceptional view each time they returned.

"Oh, by the way"—Jonathan began to pick from the remains on Dominic's plate—"I've got a message from young Steve Brown for you."

"Oh yes?" said Dominic. "And when were you talking to him?"

Jonathan paused, a forkful of sardines halfway to his mouth. "Dominic, my darling. He called briefly this afternoon to ask you for legal advice. Apparently he's done something frightfully clever with whatever computer thingy he does. He was on his way from Heathrow to San Francisco for some programming party. Sounds ghastly." Jonathan took a mouthful from his fork and enjoyed its taste for a moment. "Given you were away being mysterious, all I could do was simply offer to take a message." He put down his fork and picked up another hunk of bread, using it to scoop up sardines and tomato sauce from Dominic's plate.

Dominic reached across and rested his hand on Jonathan's arm.

"Jonathan, you know I've always said I wanted us to be open about everything we do?"

Jonathan's hand froze in midair, and tomato and garlic juice began to trickle down his thumb.

"That's honestly it with Steve," said Jonathan. "There's really nothing else. Yes, I might have had the merest twinges for him before we were married. But that's completely in the past now."

Dominic rubbed his husband's arm. "Jonathan, just for once it's not about you. I have to tell you something."

Jonathan put the bread down on his plate and licked at the juice running down his hand. "Dominic, are you about to confess to *your* secret lover, who you've been keeping hidden? Is he gorgeous? Can I play too?" He put several tomato-stained fingers into his mouth and sucked them provocatively.

"It's nothing like that, Jonathan," said Dominic. "And that's exactly why I'm telling you! Good God, we're on our honeymoon." Dominic poured himself a glass of water and took a sip, giving his husband a disapproving look.

"Well, a threesome could have been fun. Not that I'm proposing it for a moment," Jonathan added hastily as Dominic's eyes widened. "So tell me, what is your deep, dark secret?"

"It's really nothing important, Jonathan." Dominic put his glass down on the table. "I simply have to go to meet someone later, and I must keep it confidential. It's to do with work." He reached out to massage his husband's arm. "It's a bit odd, I know. But I didn't want you thinking the worst when I suddenly slink off in half an hour."

Jonathan took Dominic's hand and squeezed it.

"I trust you to the ends of the earth, my lover. You know that, Dominic. That's why I wanted to marry you." Jonathan sat back in his chair and sighed contentedly. "I never thought I'd find someone like you. And it wasn't for want of trying. But I've met some real shits over the years. You are the man who lights up my life. You constantly prove to me there is beauty in the world. So tell me"—he leaned forward enthusiastically—"where are you meeting this mystery man?"

Dominic coughed and took another sip of water. "Actually, it's going to be on Balmins—"

"The nudist beach! At this time of night?" Jonathan grinned and leaned closer to Dominic until their lips were almost touching.

"You are becoming intriguing. Is this where the ride really starts? Now that we're married? I can't wait." He began to explore the periphery of Dominic's lips with his tongue. Dominic leaned in and reciprocated—until they were interrupted by the shadow of their waiter standing beside the table. The waiter coughed.

"Perdone, señores. Is everything all right with your food?"

Dominic pulled away from his partner, his face red with embarrassment. Jonathan turned to the waiter with a broad grin on his face.

"Everything is all right with *everything*," he said. "My husband—isn't it wonderful I can say that?—my husband is about to have a secret assignation."

"Jonathan!" Dominic's face was getting redder. "I told you in confidence. Please don't go blurting it out to—"

"I'm sorry, I'm sorry." Jonathan put his finger to Dominic's lips. "I will say nothing more." He turned to the waiter. "Please. Everything is fine. Thank you, young man. The chef, as ever, has excelled himself."

The waiter cleared their plates and left them. After an awkward pause, Jonathan reached for his glass of wine. "Dominic, I really didn't mean to…. I mean, I was only making a joke—"

"Jonathan, I'm sorry," Dominic interrupted. "It's me. I really want to tell you more, but it's work and it's complicated…." His voice trailed off into silence, and he leaned forward to rest his forehead against Jonathan's.

Jonathan stared for a moment into Dominic's clear blue eyes. It had been a long time since he had felt so lost for words. Finally, he sat back and spoke.

"I shouldn't need to know, Dominic. I shouldn't need to care. But I do. You must admit, for a business meeting, it's an odd time and an even odder place to hold it."

Dominic opened his mouth to speak, but Jonathan held up his hand.

"At the very least, let me come and wait by the roadway, to make sure you're safe. It will be pitch-black on Balmins beach. Dammit, Dominic, I've nearly lost you once. I can't let that happen again." Jonathan rubbed his eyes as they dampened with tears.

Dominic reached forward and gently cupped his hands around his husband's face. "Jonathan, when that Downpatrick woman tried to kill me, you were my brave knight, charging to my rescue. And here you are again, with your lance in your hand."

Jonathan giggled.

"Oh really, Jonathan," said Dominic. "And I thought you were getting so romantic."

KARL MICHAEL Meyer sat on a rocky promontory and looked back at the lights of Sitges. It was a very pretty town. The last time he had visited

Spain was over twelve years ago. It was just before he went to university and the last time he went on vacation with his parents. His father drove them from their home in Stuttgart, southern Germany, through Switzerland and France, then along the Spanish coast to Barcelona. He thought of it as his last months of innocence. That September, he began his studies at Berlin's Technische Universität and met Bernhardt Freude. And then his life turned upside down.

From this dark spot above the beach, lit only by the watery light of the waning moon, Karl Michael could see below him the now empty Balmins beach. Just over eighty yards behind him, a pathway linked the town of Sitges with Port Sitges, a smart modern development for the yacht-lovers who cruised the Mediterranean. He was far enough away from the path to avoid eavesdroppers and could easily see if anyone approached. He adjusted the earpiece connected to his phone and waited. After a few moments, he heard a distorted voice.

"This is Russia checking in."

A moment later, he heard another voice. "Britannia here," followed by "Hi, this is West Coast America checking in."

Then came "This is East Coast America checking in." And finally, "This is China checking in."

Karl Michael held the phone close to his mouth. "Good. This is Germany here. Before we go any further, please double-check your encryption and confirm. This is an irregular call and in breach of our agreed security protocols."

One by one, he heard the voices confirm they were encrypted.

"This is West Coast here. Could you tell me what the hell's going on?"

Karl Michael's voice was even and calm. "We have everything under control. The Originator left Berlin unexpectedly yesterday, but we tracked him to Spain. Unfortunately he is in possession of the DG chip. We will recover it—"

The voice from West Coast interrupted him. "Okay, so three questions. How the hell did he remove it without anyone noticing? Why the hell is it still out there? And finally, what's wrong with the guy? Has he flipped or something?"

The voice from the East Coast chimed in. "Hey, Jeff, you know that's four questions?"

Karl Michael frowned. "East Coast, respect the protocol. Never include names in our conversations, even when we're encrypted." He paused and a grunt of apology came through his earpiece.

"To answer your questions, West Coast. The first is very simple. He's the Originator, and therefore he, of course, has the access codes. The other questions are harder to answer. We tracked him up to the French border with Spain. We know that something went wrong because he sent an emergency locator code. But we know he also sent it to a third party."

"This is China here. Do you know who the third party is?"

"Yes. I've made contact, and I'll be meeting him shortly. I believe him to be benign, and so this may be a simple operation."

West Coast cut in again. "What makes you think he's benign? Anyone outside Charter Ninety-Nine has to be seen as a threat. If the Originator was making external alliances, he was compromising our security. And at a crucial moment in the rollout. Which brings me back to my third question: has he gone loopy?"

Karl Michael scowled again. "I will not have you question the mental state of the Originator in such a flippant way."

He paused and looked down onto Balmins beach. It was still empty. Then he continued, "Allow me to complete my answer to your second question. The third party is a British lawyer and was an acquaintance of the Originator from many years ago. Interestingly, I've established he has connections with another British individual. That person was identified some time ago as a possible candidate to join the Ninety-Nine. For the moment, he remains under observation. From flight schedules, I've discovered he's on his way to the hackfest in San Francisco as we speak. I'll send details to you, West Coast, so you can observe, and possibly intercept, if needed."

Karl Michael looked toward the beach again. He could see some figures scrambling down the rocks at the far end.

"I have to wrap this now, as I believe the third party's arriving for our meeting. Don't worry. I have reason to believe this will be straightforward—"

The voice of East Coast cut in. "Look. This is serious shit going down. If the DG chip goes AWOL, then Charter Ninety-Nine is fucked. And if it's in the wrong hands, then the world's data systems are going to be screwed for years. That will cause chaos like you've never seen. You say it's straightforward. Well, good luck with your sweet-talking, Germany. But we've got heavyweights in Barcelona. If you can't handle it, we will."

Chapter 7

STEVE STRETCHED out his legs as a glow of smug satisfaction spread through his body. If you had to fly at over five hundred miles an hour in a tin tube for eleven hours, he mused, then first class on an Airbus 380 was the way to do it. He contemplated taking out his laptop to continue research into the mysterious disappearance of his father's online records. Instead, he looked out the window and enjoyed the view as the plane banked slowly west and headed for its cruising altitude over the Atlantic.

A voice at his side shook him from his daydream. "Your beer, sir."

Steve looked up at the dark-haired flight attendant standing by his seat. The man was well over six feet tall, with a narrow waist and broad shoulders, his hair cropped very short. As he leaned in close to place the beer on the tray table of Steve's seat, their eyes met for a moment.

"Would you like to book a spa and shower for later in the flight, sir?"

Steve nodded. It would be the perfect preparation for the next three days, when he would be locked in a room with a bunch of computer programmers. If he could persuade this fine specimen to join him in the luxury of a first-class spa, flying at forty thousand feet, then he would have fulfilled the boast he'd made to Jonathan earlier.

GABRIEL LIFTED his head from the pillow and gently stroked the curls of black hair between Alfonso's well-formed pectoral muscles. Slowly, he let his hand slip farther down his husband's chest. Alfonso opened one eye while reaching down gently to stay any further progress of Gabriel's fingers.

"Gabriel, you're insatiable. We've just had two glorious hours here. I could happily stay in this bed with you forever. Every time we make love, I feel our love for each other is strengthened even more. But there's just one thing—"

"Yes, I know. Your stomach's rumbling." Gabriel rested his head on Alfonso's chest and stared up at him. "I think they can hear it up the coast in Figueres. It was wrong of me to desert my post at the kitchen stove, but you were just too irresistible. The way you reacted to the surrogacy letter from California made me so horny for you." Gabriel sat up and smoothed his hand across the valley of his husband's chest. "I feel we could almost think of this as our moment of conception."

Alfonso lay back and laughed. "I'm sorry to bounce you back down to earth, but doesn't that happen in a laboratory? In a test tube somewhere?"

Gabriel stopped moving his hand. "Honestly, Alfonso. You can be so prosaic. Allow me this moment of romanticism. Indulge me. Think of this as our second honeymoon. And tonight, after the fabulous supper that is even now incinerating next door, I want you to take me on the back of your motorbike on a ride to the bar in Sitges where we first met."

Alfonso sat up, pushed Gabriel over, and rolled on top of him. He kissed Gabriel a dozen times on his eyelids, his nose, his cheeks, and then explored his lips. Finally, he lifted his head and smiled.

"It's a good job I didn't have time to drink any of that wine I poured. Otherwise we'd be taking a taxi. Much less fun than feeling your crotch nuzzling my ass on the back of the bike at 140 kilometers an hour."

DISTRACTEDLY, DOMINIC checked his watch in the moonlight as he edged his way down the rocky path to Balmins beach. It was just after eleven. His foot slipped, and he flung out his arms to recover his balance. Jonathan grasped his waist firmly to steady him.

"This was really a very bad idea, wasn't it?" Dominic said in a half whisper.

"I don't know why you're whispering," replied Jonathan loudly. "It's your secretive friend who called this meeting. He's the one acting all clandestine. I want as many people as possible to know we're here. I don't want to end up as the subject of some bizarre story in a Spanish newspaper. 'Body of unknown, well-dressed Englishman found on Sitges nudist beach.' You know I'm wearing my best chinos, don't you?"

"Jonathan, I didn't ask you to come—"

"But you're grateful I did, now, aren't you? It may be a moonlit night, but there are an awful lot of dark crevices in those cliffs over there. Who knows what they're concealing?"

Dominic heard the sound of footsteps below them. He peered into the gloom and vaguely made out the shape of a man striding across the sand toward them. He seemed to be wearing nothing but a pair of sandals and carried a small rucksack.

"Hola!" called the man cheerily, waving an arm at them.

"Oh my God," whispered Jonathan to Dominic. "There are some people who are definitely not suitable on a nudist beach."

"Shh, Jonathan, don't be so rude," Dominic hissed. "He can probably hear you." Dominic clambered down the last few feet of jagged rocks onto the sand of Balmins beach. "Hello," he said as confidently as he could. "Did you leave a note for me at the Restaurant Fragata earlier?"

The man stopped a few feet away and looked Dominic up and down for a moment. Dominic had to admit Jonathan was right in saying the man would have been better off wearing clothes. A lot of clothes. He was very large, with multiple folds of skin making him look like a melting wax effigy. When the man finally spoke, it was with a lisping, high-pitched English accent.

"Not me, ducky. Must have been another man of your dreams. You two come down for a late-night skinny dip? I could join you, if you like." He put his hands on his hips and struck a pose with his chin jutting out. Dominic tried not to laugh.

"No, no. Don't let us hold you up" came Jonathan's voice at his side. "Otherwise you'll be late for your personal-trainer session."

The man tossed his head and reached into his rucksack for some clothes. "There's no need to be like that, ducky. There are a lot of men who would kill for the fuller figure." He started to pull a pair of large sweatpants over his flabby thighs. "If you're looking for your young German friend, you'll find him over there. You'll be well suited. He's just as rude as you."

With that, the man pushed past them and started to climb the stony path, swearing loudly as he did.

Jonathan whispered into Dominic's ear. "If I ever get to look like that, my dear, you have my full permission to suffocate me with the nearest plastic bag. Now, let's go and find your mysterious assignation."

THE LIGHTS in the first-class cabin of flight 391 to San Francisco were dimmed. The window blinds had been closed to create an artificial night, allowing passengers to sleep if they wanted to. Those who did had their expensive seats converted into beds. Wearing their Gucci eye-shades, they slept soundly. The flight attendants would wake them gently in several hours' time with early evening tea, shortly before their arrival at America's seventh largest airport.

Steve was bored and frustrated. His cute flight attendant had been thoroughly professional and declined Steve's invitation to join him in the first-class shower. Steve wanted to carry on searching for his father's online records, but his next move was to get onto the dark web, the shadowy world of the internet closed to search engine robots, or "bots." He preferred not to access the dark web through a public airline's onboard Wi-Fi.

He thought about breaking into the plane's control systems for amusement. He knew where to find the hidden cabin interface points and could probably get to them at some point in the flight. But he had packed two important cables in his hold luggage. To keep his mind occupied, he called up a bot on his laptop screen and sent it out to explore the passenger laptops and phones connected to the onboard Wi-Fi.

While he waited for the bot to work its way through the flimsy firewalls on his fellow travelers' computers, Steve sat back to ponder the mystery of his father's electronic records. He remembered he had forgotten to search a key database before he left London. The SSDI, or Social Security Death Index, was a publicly available service and needed no hacking to view. Perhaps his father had died and no one had notified Steve's mother. Or maybe his father had fallen victim to one of the ten thousand or so "accidental death registrations" that happened in the US each year. Even if his father was now electronically dead, there would still be some trace of him on the internet. But Steve had found nothing at all.

Steve's train of thought was interrupted by an alarm from his laptop. He typed in the password to unlock his screen and read the simple message "Gotcha!" displayed in flashing red letters. Steve watched as a trail of type began to arc across the screen.

Neat little bot, but sooo last year. I was going to erase your hard drive for being such a failure, but I'm curious to know who you are. See you by the aft galley in ten minutes. Otherwise the hard drive gets it. Top-to-Bottom.

Steve sat back and smiled. There was somebody with a brain onboard. Perhaps he was cute as well.

Chapter 8

STEVE WALKED down the aisle toward the aft galley of the twin-deck A380 airplane. He looked pityingly at the passengers crammed into the economy cabin, remembering his own aching, bedsore experience of sitting in their place for eleven hours. That was only a few years ago, before he learned how to manipulate the passenger manifest. Not only were the poor mugs confined like caged pets in a pet store, but there were far more of them here than in first class. Which meant less of the same rarified, partly recycled air to go round. No wonder they developed colds when they got home.

As Steve walked the last aisle to the back of the plane, a tall Mediterranean-looking man, probably in his midtwenties, stepped out from the galley. He wore slim-fit jeans, and his sleeveless white T-shirt revealed well-developed upper arms.

"So you're the guy with the steampunk bot?" The man's voice was deep, with an English accent that betrayed a southern European origin.

"If you're so hot with your code," replied Steve, "what're you doing languishing among the deadbeats of economy?"

"In with the prickless wankers of first class, are you?" the man asked. "No wonder your coding's crap. You've gone soft." He looked down at Steve's footwear. "Nice pair of Grinders, mate. Bet they had a field day with you at Heathrow security. I'm Sinon, by the way. Take the word *sin* and add *on* to the end of it. It's Greek."

Steve smirked. He glanced across at the restroom door opposite, then back at Sinon. "Sinon by name, sin on by nature?"

Sinon grinned and looked Steve up and down again.

"What? With a muscled skinhead like you? Sure." He looked around and then continued in a low voice, "Ever seen the crew quarters on one of these planes?"

Steve was impressed.

"Don't tell me you can get us in?" he asked.

Sinon thrust his hand into the pocket of his chinos and pulled out a small digital key. "Friends in high places," he said with a cocky smile. "It's a better place for a fuck than the restroom. And my mate Charlie, the purser, will even bring us some beers when we come up for air."

Steve grinned back. It was going to be a good flight after all.

DOMINIC AND Jonathan stood side by side on the sand, sharing the beauty of the moonlight dappling the surface of the sea. The air was warm and still; the hubbub of Sitges nightlife sounded muted and distant. Dominic slipped his fingers through Jonathan's, squeezed his hand tight, and kissed him on the cheek.

"Thank you, Jonathan."

"What for?" he asked. "I haven't done anything yet. I may yet need to protect you from the perils of the night. I anticipate we will imminently be attacked by international drug smugglers or carried off by white-slave traders to be sold in the markets of Morocco as the playthings of Arab oligarchs."

Dominic laughed, rested his head on Jonathan's shoulder, and watched the moon-silvered waves lap the shore.

"I think I want to say thank you for so many things. You make me very happy. And I feel guilty I wasn't honest with you about this evening, or the meeting earlier—"

"What meeting earlier?" Jonathan turned to look at Dominic. "So your visit to the antiques shop was just a cover story, was it?" His face appeared severe, but Dominic was certain it was mock anger. He knew Jonathan too well.

"No, not entirely. I did go to the antiques shop, and I did find the gift for you I was looking for. But the reason I didn't tell you about the meeting—"

"Dominic, stop." Jonathan kissed him gently on the lips. "We all have convenient lies to tell from time to time. I am confident—no, more than that—I *know* you love me enough not to want to hurt me. I know there's some good reason for your secrecy. I love you and trust you. You don't have to say any more." He looked into Dominic's eyes. "But if I find it's another man—"

"Hello! Good evening. Are you Dominic Delingpole?"

Jonathan and Dominic turned in the direction of the man's voice. He had a faint German accent. At first, all Dominic could see was the glow of a cigarette followed by the glint of very white teeth, forming what appeared to be a beatific smile.

"Who's there?" Dominic asked, peering into the gloom.

A man stepped toward them, aged in his late twenties or early thirties. He had untidy blond hair and wore a shapeless black fleece top. After transferring the cigarette to his left hand, he extended his right in welcome. Dominic recognized him as the young man who had been watching him outside the Restaurant Fragata earlier.

"My name's not important for the moment," the man replied. "I'm a friend of Bernhardt, and I know he was on his way to meet you. He's missing now, and I'm most concerned for his safety. I was hoping you might help me find him."

The man smiled again and waited for Dominic to shake hands with him. Dominic hesitated. In that moment, Jonathan stepped forward and grasped the man's hand firmly.

"Well my name's Jonathan, and I don't take kindly to being dragged away from a very pleasant late-night dinner with my husband to meet a man who won't even tell us his name."

Jonathan jerked the man's hand down, at the same time hooking a foot between his legs and pulling sharply backward. The man fell to the sand. Jonathan jumped astride him and placed a hand firmly on his throat. The man fought back and attempted to stub his cigarette on Jonathan's neck, but Jonathan intercepted it and thrust it into the sand inches from the man's face.

"Let's start again, shall we, sonny? My name's Jonathan. This is my husband, Dominic. And now, be so kind as to tell us your name."

The man tried to twist his head aside, but Jonathan simply squeezed his throat tighter. After a few moments, his struggling stopped, and he lay still, his eyes staring wide and angry at Jonathan.

"Now," continued Jonathan, "in a moment I'm going to relax my grip on your throat. If you do anything stupid, you'll be in a lot of pain. But first...." He turned to Dominic. "My love, could you just check his pockets for anything unpleasant? In this boy's case, that could mean virtually anything."

Dominic squatted down on his haunches and gingerly patted down the outside of the man's jeans.

Jonathan gave him a despairing look. "Darling, you'll never get a job with airport security. This little toe rag has just tried to use my neck as an ashtray for his disgusting habit. Do you think you could display him a little *less* respect?"

Dominic flushed with fury and embarrassment and decided he would talk to Jonathan later about insulting him in front of a complete stranger. He thrust his hand deep into a pocket of the man's jeans and pulled out a mobile phone. Then he reached into the opposite pocket and retrieved a battered packet of cigarettes, a lighter, a pen, and a small bunch of keys.

Jonathan relaxed his hold on the man briefly and, with an almost casual movement, flipped him over to lie facedown on the sand. As the man lifted his head in protest, Jonathan thrust it back into the sand.

"Just a moment, sonny. We'll check your back pockets now. If the sand's getting in your mouth, try not to breathe."

"Jonathan, really," said Dominic. "I'm worried you're starting to enjoy this. Do you have to be quite so rough?"

"Well," said Jonathan, "as in all good S&M encounters, if he'd told me his safeword at the start, I could have stopped by now. But clearly he wanted to go all the way. Come on, Dominic. The longer you dither, the more sand he's going to swallow."

Dominic fumbled his hand into the single back pocket of the man's jeans and pulled out a bank card. He turned it over in his hand and peered at it.

"His name's Karl Michael Meyer," he announced. "Nothing else in his pockets. I presume you don't want me to go any further, Jonathan? I do think you should let the young man turn over now."

"The trouble with you, Dominic," said Jonathan, flipping Karl Michael onto his side and watching him spit out a mouthful of sand, "is that you're just too nice."

Jonathan stood up and offered his hand to Dominic. "But then, that is one of your adorable features as well."

Dominic got to his feet. "Jonathan, a word. Don't ever criticize me in public again. It's grounds for divorce, however many times you rescue me from dangerous German boys armed with lighted cigarettes."

Jonathan laughed and kissed Dominic on the lips. "I'm going to give you lessons in hand-to-hand combat and airport frisking. It could come in very handy in the bedroom."

The sound of retching at their feet interrupted them as Karl Michael choked out the last of the sand he had ingested. He looked up with fury in his eyes.

"That is so touching. In love. Even married. And Mr. Delingpole was only getting fucked by Bernhardt the week before your wedding. Perhaps it's a new kind of British stag party? A bridegroom visits all his former lovers for a final fling. Oh yes, Mr. Jonathan McFadden. You're not the only one who yearns for a so-called open relationship."

"WHAT THE hell are you two doing down here?"

Steve pushed his head past Sinon's naked torso, to see a short, red-haired female flight attendant staring furiously at them.

Sinon levered himself up on Steve's chest and poked his head out from the tiny bunk bed situated eight feet above the floor. It was one of fourteen similar bunks in the compact crew quarters hidden below the plane's economy deck. "I can explain, really. Charlie said—"

"I don't for a minute believe Mr. O'Donnell gave you permission to come down here to—" The flight attendant struggled to find words. "—do that." Her voice, hardened by the edge of a strong Glaswegian accent, seemed to explode across the cramped cabin.

"Right, gentlemen," continued the flame-haired woman firmly. "You have exactly one minute to put your clothes on and get back upstairs. Otherwise we'll be getting the flex cuffs out to restrain you two reprobates for the rest of the flight."

Sinon jumped down from the bunk bed, stretched out his arms to the flight attendant, and grinned. "Flex cuffs? Yes, please. A bit of bondage is always welcome—" He peered at her name badge. "—Margaret. Didn't know you were such an accommodating airline."

Margaret looked Sinon up and down with disdain. "I thought that tall boys like you were supposed to be well-endowed. I was clearly misinformed."

Sinon dropped his arms and reached down to pick up his clothes from the floor. Steve jumped down beside him and began to dress. In the cramped space of the crew compartment, he towered over the diminutive woman.

"Well, love," said Steve, "you should know more than most that size doesn't matter. It's what you do with it that counts." He winked at Margaret, pulled up his briefs and bleacher jeans, and reached for his polo shirt.

"Margaret? Are you all right?" At the sound of a man's voice, Steve turned. Another member of the cabin crew had joined them. His name badge showed him to be Charles O'Donnell, Inflight Services Manager. O'Donnell looked to be in his early forties, with crew-cut salt-and-pepper hair and a deeply tanned face and forearms. He looked past Margaret, saw Steve and Sinon, and rolled his eyes.

"It's all right, Margaret," he said. There was a strong Northern Irish accent in his voice. "I'll take care of this."

Margaret looked from her boss to the giggling figures of Steve and Sinon. "If I had my way, I'd tan their backsides," she said and pushed past O'Donnell to climb the stairs back to the passenger deck.

O'Donnell folded his arms, leaned against a bulkhead, and closed his eyes. "Of all people to discover you, it had to be Margaret the Mouth. I'm really going to be in the shite now." He opened his eyes. "Couldn't you two wait a few more hours until you were back on the ground before you got your dicks out?"

Sinon finished buttoning his fly. He stepped forward and clumsily tried to hug O'Donnell. "Sorry, Charlie boy. But you did slip me the key. I didn't think we'd been spotted."

"With him dressed like that?" O'Donnell pushed Sinon away and refolded his arms, glowering at Steve. "Shaved head, tattoos, braces, Doc Marten boots—"

"Grinders, Charlie," interrupted Sinon. "Steve's got a really smart set of Grinders."

"Whatever," Charlie continued. "It might be an attractive look for some people—"

"People like you and me, Charlie," added Sinon, grinning. "You know it makes you horny."

"All right, all right." O'Donnell sighed. "Look, I've had several people ask me why we're allowing a Nazi thug to fly with us. He's been scaring the life out of my passengers. Couldn't he have toned it down? Just for a few hours?"

"Why should I?" asked Steve, stepping forward. "Why should I be forced to dress like everyone else? I'm Steve, by the way. And for your information, I'm not a Nazi thug. I've been a member of Unite Against Fascism since I was sixteen. Just because I like the look—as do you by the sounds of it—"

Charles O'Donnell's face flushed red.

"—doesn't mean I like the politics."

"That's a bit naïve, isn't it?" replied O'Donnell.

"No, Charlie boy," Sinon said. "What's naïve is judging people by appearances. Just because someone's wearing a smart suit and tie doesn't mean they're a good little boy." He turned to Steve. "You should have seen Charlie in his leathers during London Fetish Week. On Masters and Slaves night, he had them eating out of his—"

"Enough, you little shite," said O'Donnell, holding up his hand. "Get up those stairs, the pair of you." Steve and Sinon squeezed past him, kissing O'Donnell on the cheek as they went. "And keep a low profile, please," he continued.

When he heard the hatch slam shut at the top of the stairs, O'Donnell leaned back against the bulkhead and closed his eyes. "For my sake. I've got a boyfriend and two Yorkshire terriers to feed."

Chapter 9

GABRIEL AND Alfonso arrived in Sitges shortly after midnight. Gabriel encouraged Alfonso to take a brief detour along the waterfront and into the old town. Finally, they rode up the narrow streets that led to the heart of the town's gay nightlife. The 1200cc touring bike drew a small crowd of admirers, particularly as Gabriel and Alfonso had dressed to impress. Alfonso brought the motorbike to a halt, and Gabriel dismounted. He removed his helmet and casually unzipped his black leather Dainese jacket. He watched as Alfonso dismounted and pulled the bike back smartly onto its stand. Alfonso gathered together their helmets and gloves and locked them in the bike's top box. The two men stood for a moment, their arms wrapped around each other's waist.

"We haven't been here for over five years," said Gabriel.

"You haven't been here for over five years," corrected Alfonso. "Remember, I have to come catch the bad boys of Sitges sometimes."

"Oh, I quite forgot." Gabriel held his husband at arm's length and looked him up and down. "You must be quite a distraction when you roll into town in your close-fitting breeches and boots." He glanced to his left and smiled at a man who was staring in their direction. The man was wearing shorts far too tight for him. "Rather like now, in fact. Mind you, I don't fancy the competition's luck tonight. Where do people get their dress sense from these days? The magazines in the doctor's surgery?" He took Alfonso's hand. "Come on, my love. Let's see if they're as badly dressed inside. I think we could make ourselves the focus of attention."

"SATISFIED?"

Dominic looked at Karl Michael with contempt. "I should have left Jonathan to suffocate you in the sand. He's right. I'm too soft when it comes to poisonous liars like you."

Despite Dominic's pleas, Jonathan had stormed off when Karl Michael made his allegations of infidelity. Dominic had only seen Jonathan this angry once before, and he knew better than to chase after him. He would wait half an hour and then go look for him in the nightspots of Sitges. Anyway, he had some business to finish with Karl Michael.

"You know you can't deny it, Dominic Delingpole," replied Karl Michael, still wiping away sand from his face. "You were in Berlin from the twenty-eighth to the thirtieth April. While you were there, you stayed at Nollendorfstrasse on two occasions."

"I didn't stay there on two occasions. I visited Bernhardt once at his apartment. And where did you get this ridiculous idea he was fucking me?"

Karl Michael's eyes gleamed in the darkness. "Because he told me. And he told me you came back for more. I know it's reliable information. Bennie has always been open with me about his lovers."

The two men stood on the sand, glowering at each other. Dominic was the first to break the silence.

"How long have you and Bernhardt been together?" he asked quietly.

"It's our twelfth anniversary this October." Karl Michael sat down on the sand and stared out at the sea. "He was the most wonderful thing in my life. And now he's gone missing, and all I know is that the last message from his mobile was sent to your phone. Why?"

Dominic sighed and sat down next to Karl Michael. "I've got no idea. And I've also no idea why you told Jonathan such a dirty lie."

"It's not a lie!" Karl Michael turned to face Dominic. "It's what Bennie told me. He fucked you twice. Once in the bedroom, and when you came back for more, he fucked you on the settee in the sitting room. I don't believe he ever lied to me. Why are you denying it?"

"Because it's not true," Dominic tried to protest.

"No, you're wrong, Mr. Dominic Delingpole." Karl Michael rose slowly and stood looking down at Dominic. "I know a lot about you. I know you first met Bennie at the Berlin Opera House seventeen years ago. I know you saw *La Bohème* together, and after that, you spent fifteen nights with him in his studio in Fuggerstrasse. Then you simply left one night. But you've been back, haven't you, Mr. Delingpole? You've been back many times since. Just who is the liar here?"

THE HEAVY industrial elevator doors clanged shut as Nick stepped out into the cavernous warehouse space on the ground floor of their waterfront building.

He flipped a row of switches on the pillar in front of him and watched as the bright overhead lights flickered into life, filling the space with a warm-tinted luminance. This was what he and Jeff had christened the "Creative Cavern." Tomorrow, it would be occupied by more than fifty highly intelligent and creative people from a range of backgrounds and from across the world. Half of them would be computer coders. Nick and his partner, Jeff, would team them up with designers, artists, sociologists, writers, even actors. They would set them the simple task of thinking without boundaries, imagining the impossible and then trying to create it.

Jeff Woodfield had researched the science of designing creative spaces when he built this home for the Grain Street Hackfest in 2001. Although the space was vast and industrial, thick carpet on the floor and sound-absorbing material on the walls gave it an intimate acoustic. Plentiful soft seating areas with beanbags and battered, fading leather armchairs and sofas were scattered about. A web of electrical cables hung down from the ceiling, bringing power outlets to about a dozen large round tables equipped with huge flat-screen monitors. Six or eight chairs were arranged around each table. This was to be the fifth hackfest. Jeff organized them every couple of years. On the exclusive membership list Jeff and Nick had drawn up, there were now more than a hundred people from across the world.

Nick crossed the floor to an iron spiral staircase and climbed thirty steps to a silver steel motor home, tethered thirty feet in the air by a series of taut metal cables. It served as the control room for the three-day hackfest. From here, Steve could monitor the creative dramas playing out on the floor below. Over the years, he had built an increasingly sophisticated computerized tracking system that alerted him to coding developments that might be of interest at any moment.

Inside the motor home, he powered up a bank of monitors on the back wall, took his seat in a large leather swivel chair, and picked up a keyboard. As the screens flickered into life, he selected a video feed from one of the ninety cameras installed around the building. It showed him the sidewalk outside 101 Grain Street. Two men approached the ground floor entrance to the building. He recognized them as Fortran and Cobol, the chosen names for two organizers of a half-dozen or so eager volunteers who helped out during the hackfest. Before either of them could press the intercom button, Nick buzzed down.

"Hey, guys. Welcome!" He enjoyed the startled look on their fresh, young faces. "Come on in. I'm about to get things going here. I could sure do with your help."

Nick reached behind him and pressed the main door-release button on the wall of the control room. He watched on the monitor as the heavy wooden entrance door slowly swung open. Fortran and Cobol strode enthusiastically into the building and disappeared from view. Nick waited until the door closed securely before he stood up and walked out onto the small platform surrounding the suspended motor home.

"Right, you two," he called to Fortran and Cobol as they emerged into the Creative Cavern. "Get yourselves coffee and doughnuts. Then the first thing I need you to do is check the table monitors and finalize the seating plan with me. I've worked out the groupings. I want you guys to print out the table cards so we can get everyone seated in the right place. When's the rest of the team arriving?"

Fortran looked up. "They'll be here in a while. Tomorrow, the call time is 0800. Briefing at 0900. I can go through that later with you, Nick. We'll kick off with the tech check first."

He and Cobol walked over to one of the four kitchen areas, which were each equipped with commercial-sized chrome coffee machines. As they started brewing their kicks of caffeine, Nick reentered the motor home control room and took his seat in the leather swivel chair. He leaned back for a moment, deep in thought. Then he reached forward and started typing rapidly on the keyboard in front of him. It took him only a few moments to call up Steve Brown's travel plans. He pulled a small gooseneck microphone toward him and pushed the button.

"Fortran?" Nick heard his own voice, strangely muted by the heavy soundproofing of the Creative Cavern below. "Come up here a moment, would you? I've got a little exercise for you."

Nick pushed the microphone away and looked back at Steve's travel records on the screen.

"Now, young British skinhead," he muttered to himself. "Let's see how good you really are. Fortran's going to send you a minor zombie attack for your arrival. Welcome to the city of broken dreams."

DOMINIC STOOD up and dusted the sand from his clothes.

"Karl Michael, there's something that doesn't add up with your paranoia over Bernhardt," he said. "If you know as much about me as you claim, you'll know I'm a lawyer, just like Bernhardt. I'm not nearly as clever as him, but nevertheless, he values my opinion when it comes to matters affected by English jurisdiction." He looked down at Karl Michael. "Over the years, he's consulted me on several issues relating to rights—"

"I don't believe you. Since twelve years, Bennie and me have not just been lovers and partners in life, but business partners as well. We work on the same projects together. If he was consulting you on business, I would be involved. Yet why has he not included me in these meetings with you?"

Dominic hesitated. His professional obligation of confidentiality was to Bernhardt, but he had never heard Bernhardt refer to Karl Michael as his business partner. He wondered which of the two was telling the truth. But then, there were elements of his long relationship with Bernhardt that, for the moment, he preferred to keep from Karl Michael.

"I'm not in a position to say, Karl Michael. Bernhardt told me you wrote computer programs for him—that's all he ever said."

Karl Michael slammed his hand down on the sand. "No! We were always equal. I'm sure of it." He stared down at his hand, sweeping it back and forth in the sand beside him vigorously. Then he stopped and looked up at Dominic. "Except in the last few weeks. He was planning something, I know it." He scrambled to his feet and gazed intently at Dominic, their heads a few inches apart. "I need to know why he was coming to see you. You must tell me what was in that final message he sent."

Dominic took a step back from Karl Michael. He could see the man's shoulders were shaking, and his fists were clenching and unclenching at his side.

"Karl Michael, I need you to calm down before we go any further." He waited and watched the blond-haired German breathe deeply. "I've lost my husband tonight. I hope I can get him back, but I hold you responsible if I don't. You've lost your lover, and now, so you tell me, your business partner." He held up his hand as Karl Michael opened his mouth to speak.

"I will help you. I promise. But you must help me. I can't think straight when people throw petulant tantrums like the one you just did. I don't have my phone with me, but I'll happily give you Bernhardt's message. It made no sense to me. It said something about Adam and a series of numbers. Do you know anyone called Adam?"

Karl Michael frowned. "No, there's no one. But why was he coming all the way by car to see you?"

"Oh, that's easy. He said that neither of you could get to the wedding. But then a business trip came up in Spain, so he said he would meet us here to give us our wedding present."

Karl Michael turned away to look at the sea. "I knew nothing about your wedding. He never told me about it." He turned back to Dominic. "I am feeling he has betrayed me."

Dominic placed a hand on Karl Michael's shoulder. "Don't say that. Perhaps he was protecting you from something. I do know he loves you very much." He turned back to look at the twinkling lights of Sitges. A siren sounded in the distance. Dominic looked back at Karl Michael. "And I love my husband very much too. So the first thing I must do is find him. Will you help me?"

Karl Michael nodded. "And in return, you will help me find Bernhardt, yes?"

"Agreed. I'm going back into town. Why don't you come and collect the message now?"

"Not immediately," said Karl Michael. "I must attend to something first. I will come to your apartment in a few hours. Will you still be up?"

"I imagine so," sighed Dominic. "Even if Jonathan is there waiting for me, we've got a lot to talk about. But why can't you just give me your number, and I'll text it to your mobile?"

Karl Michael shook his head.

"I would rather the message did not go into the ether again. It may already have been intercepted. But that may not matter, because I imagine Bennie's text only makes sense in conjunction with you." Karl Michael turned to go, then stopped and looked back at Dominic.

"Be careful, Dominic Delingpole. With Bennie missing, I think there may be others who will be very eager to get this information. And they may need your assistance to decipher it. Be very careful." He turned and began to walk away.

"What others?" called out Dominic to the retreating figure.

But Karl Michael gave no answer.

Chapter 10

As he trudged along the beach, Karl Michael vigorously ran his fingers back and forth through his short hair, brushing out the last grains of sand. He was furious with Jonathan and suspicious of Dominic. Why had the man not carried his mobile phone with him? If he had, he could have handed Karl Michael the code from Bernhardt then and there.

Karl Michael was convinced Dominic was not telling him the truth about his relationship with Bernhardt. He was certain the two had been fucking in Bennie's apartment just a few weeks ago. Karl Michael stopped. He thought about turning around to catch up with Dominic, demand he take him to his apartment to retrieve the phone message.

But he needed to keep Dominic on his side, at least for the moment. If he had to wait for a few more hours, it would not be of any consequence.

Karl Michael resumed his slow progress toward the path that would take him off the beach. The moonlight had gone. He stumbled several times as he moved from soft sand to the smooth, slippery rocks that formed the steep track.

After several minutes, he neared the path's summit, and he could see the rough track of the road above him. He reached up to grab on to a rock to pull himself up the last few feet.

The thin pointed heel of a woman's shoe came down hard on a fleshy part of his hand. Karl Michael cried out in pain. He lost his footing on the smooth rock and started to slide backward. His chin scraped against stone, his fingernails grasping desperately for a handhold.

He slid nearly twenty feet before he came to a halt, his feet resting on the sandy beach. Karl Michael lifted his head and tentatively felt his chin. He winced as he touched the grazed flesh, feeling blood oozing from a wound.

"Well, you fucked that one up didn't you, Herr Meyer?" The woman's voice came from above him. It had a soft Irish lilt to it.

Karl Michael groaned and looked up into the darkness. "Janet Downpatrick. Why are you here? I told you, I'm handling it. If anybody sees me with you, it will jeopardize the whole mission."

The woman bent down and shone a flashlight on Karl Michael's face.

"Why didn't you go back with Delingpole and get that message when he offered?" she asked. "We've lost time. What was so important you couldn't go with him straightaway?"

Karl Michael held up his hand to shield his eyes from the beam.

"I must check in again with Charter Ninety-Nine. We have a schedule to work to. If I deviate from it, they'll get suspicious."

Karl Michael slowly began to climb back up the steep rocky path.

Downpatrick bent down and held out her hand to help him onto the cliff path. Reluctantly, Karl Michael took the offer of assistance and hauled himself up. Despite her slight frame, she was remarkably strong. Karl Michael let go of her hand and slowly massaged his shoulder.

"Leave me to manage this," he said without looking at her. "I didn't realize you were bugging my phone; otherwise I'd have left it behind."

"It's as well I did," Downpatrick replied. "Now I know I must take care of things. You run along and make your call to your little friends in the Ninety-Nine. I'll deal with Delingpole."

As the white Lexus drew up to the curb, Jeff leaned forward to the uniformed driver. "All right, Robbie," he said. "You can take off for an hour or so. I'll call you when I'm through. Don't go too far away."

Robbie turned around awkwardly in his seat. "Yeah, okay, but don't be all night. Why do you have to make me wear this fuckin' uniform? It itches like a wrestler's jockstrap."

Jeff stepped out of the car and closed the door. He leaned in Robbie's open window. "Appearances, you asshole. I'm the multimillionaire. A successful entrepreneur. Remember? I've got to look the part, haven't I? Now piss off. And don't show me up later if I manage to hook her and I'm reelin' her in."

Robbie turned and grinned. "I just love it when you talk dirty like that, Mr. Multimillionaire, 'sir.'" He leaned forward and kissed Jeff on the mouth. "Now don't you forget, I'm the one who coded that first piece-of-shit website you made your money on. At the same time as sucking your dick."

Jeff laughed. "I'll never forget. That's why, when I wanted the best-goddamn-looking chauffeur in San Francisco, I immediately thought of Robbie Wakeling. Ex-lover, champion coder, lead guitar player, male model—"

"Yeah, yeah, flattery will get you most places, Jeff," interrupted Robbie, still grinning.

It was all true. Robbie Wakeling had been modeling Vivienne Westwood bondage clothes when Jeff first met him backstage at the Marriott during San Francisco Fashion Week. He told Jeff it paid better than working as a hack programmer.

"All I can say is, thank God you got bored with modeling." Jeff smiled. "Otherwise I could never have built MusicScene and sold it to the greedy dot-com market boys, who had more money than sense." He pressed his forehead against Robbie's. "You're a smart boy in so many ways. Even in that ridiculous uniform."

Robbie turned his head slightly and playfully bit the end of Jeff's nose. "Fuck off, you asshole. Go do what you do best. Charm."

He put the Lexus into drive and eased the car back into traffic. Jeff strolled over to the entrance of the Montgomery Street Bar and Grill. It was coming up to seven o'clock in the evening, and the place was crowded. Jeff pushed his way to the bar through the jostle of suits and wineglasses.

"Hey, Jeff, good to see you," hailed the barman, reaching out to shake his hand. "Your usual bottle? Just two glasses tonight? I've got you a table over in the corner. Go take a seat. I'll bring it over to you."

Jeff smiled and nodded. Jeremiah was not just the barman, he was the owner of the Bar and Grill. A man who knew his customers like an encyclopedia. It was Jeff's preferred restaurant above all others in San Francisco. The design was a modern take on the classic French art nouveau brasserie. Exquisite, large contemporary chandeliers and mirrors on every wall of the vast interior. Not since the superb Stars of the 1990s had a restaurant been so successful in attracting San Francisco's socialites and celebrities. Located as it was in the heart of the city's financial district, it was a perfect place for Jeff to pitch his exclusive stable of loyal programmers.

He walked the length of the restaurant to a table tucked in an alcove against the wall, away from the noise and bustle. Jeff settled into his seat and looked around to make sure he was unobserved. He reached into the jacket pocket of his suit, pulled out a small wireless camera, and tucked it discreetly into the wall light. Once more, he reached into his pocket, pulled out a small wireless microphone, and hid it under the rim of the flower vase. Jeff took out his laptop, set it on the bench beside him, and opened the lid. Eyeing the screen, he adjusted the angle of the camera. Finally he connected a small earpiece and checked the microphone.

Satisfied, Jeff closed the laptop and turned to watch the professional courtships of the clientele. The majority were alpha-male financier types, their tailored shirts cut to enhance their gym-worked chests. The few women in the room had power-dressed in black. They were bare-armed, tanned, and wore minimal jewelry. Most of them wore high heels to elevate their stature. Almost everyone used the copious supply of mirrors frequently to check their appearance on this important social stage.

Within a few minutes, Jeremiah arrived at the table. "I presume your guest will ask for you at the bar?" he inquired as he placed a chilled bottle of Argyle Blanc de Blanc, two champagne glasses, a jug of water, and a bowl of olives on the table. "When are you expecting them?"

Jeff looked at his watch. "She's due any moment. Sure, just send her over, Jeremiah. We might get a bite to eat later. See how it goes."

Jeremiah opened the blanc de blanc and poured Jeff a glass. He placed the bottle in a cooler next to the table and returned to the bar to keep an eye on the steady trickle of customers coming through the doors of the Montgomery Street Bar and Grill.

Jeff swallowed a mouthful of the chilled wine and turned to scrutinize his reflection in the mirror behind him. He complimented himself that he could still pass very well for a successful dot-com millionaire. Jeff was careful to keep his growing collection of tattoos below his neckline and above his elbows. His tattooed, lean physique could be cloaked with expensive clothes when business called. The rest of the time he dressed in T-shirts and sweatpants. This evening, wearing a two-thousand-dollar suit tailored by London's Ozwald Boateng, he knew he was very appealing, to both men and women.

"Jeff, darling, it's wonderful to see you."

Jeff stood to greet his guest. She was nearly as tall as him in her high-heeled Manolo Blahniks and was wearing a narrow black dress, slit up to the waist on one side. Her hair was cropped short, and her makeup was subtle, highlighting naturally high cheekbones and deep-set brown eyes.

The Deadly Lies

"Tanya, you look ravishing," he said with sincerity. They kissed on both cheeks. Then Tanya kissed him a third time on the lips. Jeff pulled away gently and sat back in his seat.

"I took the liberty of ordering *the* California champagne I know you love. And before you protest," he continued as Tanya opened her mouth to speak, "I call it champagne whatever they might say. And whether you're on a diet or not, you're going to have a glass. You can always have a water chaser to follow."

Tanya laughed and kissed him gently on the lips once more. She sat and looked around at the other customers in the restaurant.

"It's busy for a Thursday night," she commented. "But it's been a good day in the markets, and"—she looked around at Jeff—"they don't take much encouragement to celebrate."

"What do you mean, 'they'?" he asked teasingly. "You're just as much a part of them."

Tanya looked sideways at him and set her head to one side coquettishly. "I may walk in the same corridors as some of them, Jeff, but we are worlds apart. I just run their IT for them. They're simply salesmen—"

"And women," Jeff continued to tease.

"Whatever. It's more than I can do. I couldn't sell a life raft to a drowning man. Or woman," she added and took a sip from her glass.

"You undersell yourself, Tanya," said Jeff. "You know you don't just 'run their IT for them.' You control pretty well all the financial systems in the US—"

"Nonsense," interrupted Tanya. "The banks do that very successfully for themselves. I just make sure they all link up. You're trying to flatter me, as ever, Jeff. Which means you're trying to sell me something. What is it?"

Jeff smiled and leaned in toward her. "Security, Tanya. I've been watching your perimeter breach ratios recently. They're increasing, aren't they?"

Tanya carefully placed her glass back on the table. "That's confidential, Jeff. And you shouldn't have access to them. I certainly won't discuss those figures with anyone outside WRI."

"Six months ago," Jeff persisted, "they were less than .001 percent. And they'd been that way for the past five years. This morning they were .01 percent. A tenfold increase in six months. Don't tell me it's not at the top of your agenda every day. And what have you done about it?" He cocked his head. "Whatever it is, the problem's not gone away."

Tanya stared at him for a moment, her eyes unblinking.

"So tell me," she said. "What are you proposing?"

Jeff picked up the water pitcher, poured two glasses, and handed one to Tanya.

"You can stop drinking the wine now, Tanya. I can see you're counting the calories."

She smiled and took the water glass. "Jeff, our security parameters remain well within our service delivery requirements."

"Please don't tell me you're sleeping at night. Although I must say you're disguising the bags under your eyes very well."

Tanya pouted in mock anger.

"But we know the reality, don't we?" Jeff continued. "One day, maybe one day soon, WRI is going to receive a concerted attack. Maybe from Russia, most likely China. Can you really be sure your systems are robust enough?"

Tanya took a sip of water, then placed her glass on the table.

"So," she said, "I'll ask you again, Jeff. What are you proposing?"

"Get me a way to meet your head of analysis and your head of operations," replied Jeff. "And give me your support. You know I supply programmers to five of the major banks in the world." He laid a hand on her bare forearm. "The system's failing, Tanya. The last time we met, you said WRI would give us a chance. Maybe this is the time?"

Tanya placed her hand on top of his for a moment. "The last time, it was one helluva party." She looked at him wistfully. "And it was a very good night." She stroked his hand for a moment. Then she reached into her leather satchel and took out a slim laptop.

"But I did say we'd consider you," she continued, "so let's see what we can do." She opened the computer and began to type. "Let me log in to the group calendar and fix a date."

Jeff felt a Manolo Blahnik shoe gently rub his calf. Without looking up, Tanya added, "You know, I'm not counting calories as much as you might think. Did you say dinner was on offer?"

ALFONSO AND Gabriel walked up to the bar of XXL and peered into the smoky gloom of the club. It was a quiet night, and there was very little to see. Three or four groups of men gathered along the length of the bar, which stretched to the dance floor at the back of the club. The dance floor was empty. Gabriel looked forlornly at Alfonso.

"We'll be taking an early night, I think. Let's have two Shirley Temples, then head back home." He leaned across the bar and placed the order with the bored-looking, tattooed barman.

The loud, pulsating beat of "One More Night" by Maroon 5 segued into the cover version of "Sexy and I Know It" by LMFAO. Alfonso grabbed Gabriel's waist.

"I don't believe it!" he shouted. "They're playing our song. Come on, leave the drinks. Let's show this place how to party."

The two men strutted to the dance floor and threw themselves into a celebratory exhibition of nostalgia for the night they had first met, twelve years previously. The barman pumped smoke into the small dance space and wound up the music volume. After a few minutes, several men at the bar, who had been admiring their display, put down their drinks and joined them. Gabriel smiled as he watched, and admired Alfonso's clumsy but charming approximation of dancing. Gabriel leaned close to his husband's ear and shouted, "Tell me again. Who is it who sings this?"

"It's LMFAO," shouted back Alfonso. Then, seeing the look of puzzlement on his husband's face, he added, "Laughing My Fuckin' Ass Off. American." He stopped dancing and turned Gabriel's head to look at a tall man with sun-bleached hair who was leaning on the bar, watching them.

"What do you think, Gabriel? Do you want to be really disreputable for just one more night? Very soon we must be well-behaved parents for years to come." Alfonso glanced again at the man, who was still looking their way. "I bet he's English. He looks very cute."

Gabriel nodded and laughed. Then he beckoned the man over.

Alfonso shouted into Gabriel's ear. "He's coming over. You're a bad man, Gabriel de la Torre. Did anyone ever tell you that?"

"Yes," shouted Gabriel with a smirk. "My father, shortly before he kicked me out of the house. I've never looked back."

Gabriel extended a hand to the tall man as he joined them on the dance floor.

"Are you from England?" Gabriel shouted in English into the man's ear. The man nodded, and Gabriel continued, "You're very cute. We saw you looking. Come and help me and my husband celebrate a night of nostalgia. I'm Gabriel, and my handsome man is Alfonso."

The Englishman leaned toward him. "Pleased to meet you. I'm Jonathan. I've just run away from my honeymoon."

Chapter 11

STEVE AND Sinon shuffled forward in the immigration line at San Francisco International Airport. It was nearly eight in the evening, and they were both tired and irritable. Their delayed flight from London had arrived at the same time as several others, and the immigration hall was packed. The two men had been waiting in line for over fifty minutes. Finally, they were close to the front. Sinon reached into his rucksack and retrieved his passport in readiness. To pass the time, they checked out each other's passport photographs and made critical comments.

"So what kind of a name is Sinon?" asked Steve. "Not one I've ever come across before."

"I told you before. It's Greek," responded Sinon. "My dad's Greek. He was from Athens. He named me after my grandfather. Never read your classics?"

"I watch *Spartacus* on TV for the horny guys. Are you ever in that?" Steve said with a grin.

"Not me. I'm from Manchester. My dad came over to the UK in the '80s. Anyway, my namesake was in Troy, not Sparta," replied Sinon. "You should read a bit of Virgil some time. Sinon was the guy the Greeks pretended to leave behind with the wooden horse. The Trojans took him into Troy with the horse, thinking he'd been abandoned by his mates. Little did they know it was packed full of Greek soldiers. Remember the Trojan horse?"

"Never read it," responded Steve. "But I've created a few software Trojan horses over the years." He winked at Sinon. "Maybe that's why they want me at the hackfest. Is this your first one as well?"

Sinon shook his head. "This'll be my second. It's a hell of a buzz. I'm surprised you've not been invited before."

Before Steve could answer, the crowd shifted a little, and Sinon nudged him. "Go on. Our two booths have finally come free." He studied the grim-faced immigration officers who beckoned them forward. "Don't fancy yours. Or mine. She looks like she could kick-start a jumbo jet just by glaring at it."

Steve grinned. "See you on the other side?"

"Sure," replied Sinon. "I've got your number anyway. If I don't see you at the baggage claim, I'll catch up with you in the city. I'm staying in a neat place in the Castro I've used for a few years." He bent down to pick up his bag and then winked at Steve. "Welcome to the hackfest. Maybe you'll get invited back."

Steve ambled up to the booth opposite and handed his passport to the thin-lipped, balding man behind the glass. The man looked far older than retirement age, and he seemed to resent every minute of his job. He placed Steve's passport in a scanner and stared at the screen next to it. Finally, with an impassive expression, he looked up at Steve.

"Purpose of visit?"

"I'm at a conference in the city for a couple of days," answered Steve. "Then I'm going to see my dad in Seattle for a couple more."

"Address where you're staying?"

Steve handed him the printout from a booking with GayBnB. "I'm staying with this guy on Mission. Hoping he's hot," he added with a wink.

The immigration officer looked back at the screen for a moment. Then he turned his head to Steve, and his thin lips formed into a crooked smile.

"Without a visa you're staying nowhere." The man's eyes narrowed. "Did you forget to complete your online ESTA visa waiver, skinhead boy?"

Steve rummaged in his bag and then slammed a sheet of paper down on the narrow countertop beneath the glass.

"No, I didn't forget my ESTA," he said furiously. "And here's the printout to prove it."

The man behind the glass sighed, picked up the paper, and compared it with what was showing on his screen. He looked back at Steve for a moment and then made a phone call, turning his head away while he did.

"Hey, Steve. See you on the other side, mate."

Steve turned to see Sinon with his passport in his hand, about to head off to baggage claim.

The immigration officer's phone conversation seemed to go on for several minutes. Finally, he turned back to Steve. "Wait here. Someone will come collect you for further processing."

"What the fuck is further processing?" demanded Steve.

"If you use that kind of language," said the immigration official, "you'll be held in jail before they put you on the next plane home." The man's voice was quietly threatening. "The computer has no record of your ESTA."

"But I registered it online two weeks ago," Steve insisted. "That printout is the proof."

"Easily faked," the thin-lipped man said. "I'll trust the computer, not your scrap of paper. Stand aside and wait for the investigating officer. Next!"

A<small>LFONSO GRABBED</small> hold of Jonathan's arm as he staggered toward the steep spiral staircase that led back down to the bar of XXL. From below came the muted thud of music from the dance floor. Around them, in the half-light, a steady shuffle of men entered and left the club's upper-floor darkroom.

"Jonathan, wait," Alfonso said. "You're in no condition to go anywhere at the moment."

Jonathan struggled to escape, but Alfonso twisted his arm behind his back and pushed him forward onto his knees. A few men stopped to watch—most simply moved away to another part of the floor.

"Alfonso," mumbled Jonathan, "I think I've been on my knees quite enough in the last half an hour. Just let me get outside to the fresh air. It's only a poppers rush. It will soon clear."

"What's wrong with Jonathan?" Gabriel emerged from the bar below, pushed past a small group of men, and walked up the iron spiral staircase to Alfonso and Jonathan. "I leave you alone for five minutes, Alfonso, and you get into trouble."

"It was nothing to do with me," replied Alfonso, still resisting Jonathan's struggles. "He nearly collapsed in the darkroom. Says he had a poppers rush. So I managed to get him out here. The problem is, I don't know if he's taken anything else. Help me get him onto that seat. Then I can shove his head between his knees."

Gabriel and Alfonso positioned themselves on either side of Jonathan with his arms over their shoulders. They lifted him onto a low iron bench, and Alfonso pushed Jonathan's head down firmly.

"I'll go get him some water," Alfonso said. "Stay here and make sure he doesn't try to stand up again. We don't want him to get light-headed."

Gabriel leaned across Jonathan's prostrate form and kissed Alfonso on the lips. "Well, my love. This evening hasn't turned out how I planned. I wasn't expecting to play nursemaid to an English stranger tonight."

Alfonso smiled, stood up, and disappeared down the stairs, leaving Gabriel sitting beside Jonathan's hunched figure.

"Tell me truthfully, Jonathan, have you taken anything else?" asked Gabriel.

Jonathan shook his head and mumbled indistinctly.

"What was that? What did you say?"

Jonathan lifted his head. "I've really fucked things up this time. I can't believe what Dominic's done, but then I shouldn't have run out on him like that."

Gabriel leaned toward him and put an arm across his shoulder. "Is Dominic your husband?" Jonathan nodded. "Did you have an argument?"

Jonathan sat up and pushed Gabriel's arm away. "You could say that, in a manner of speaking." He leaned back against the wall and groaned. "And now I've fucked it up more. Oh God, I really shouldn't have come in here." Jonathan stood up and launched himself at the top of the stairs.

"Jonathan, stop." Gabriel stood up, but he was too late. Jonathan's legs buckled beneath him, and he fell headlong down the iron staircase, landing at the feet of Alfonso, who was about to climb the stairs with a bottle of water. Alfonso bent down to examine Jonathan's motionless body. After a moment, he raised his head and shouted, "Emergency! Someone call an ambulance. He's out cold."

By the time the ambulance arrived, Jonathan had recovered consciousness, and Alfonso had moved him into the recovery position. A large crowd had gathered outside the club. Three police officers from the Policia Local struggled to push people back as the ambulance made its way up the narrow side street to Club XXL.

Alfonso walked outside to meet the paramedics. "He's English. He fell down the stairs and banged his head," he reported. One of the paramedics was unloading a folding gurney from the back of the ambulance. He wheeled it through the club entrance to the foot of the spiral staircase. Alfonso followed, helping to clear a way through the crowd of onlookers. "He was out for several minutes, but he hasn't lost consciousness since."

"Has he taken anything?" asked the paramedic. He crouched down to Jonathan's motionless body and felt his pulse.

Alfonso shrugged his shoulders. "He said it was a poppers rush. I've no idea if he took anything else. We'd been dancing together, and then he left the dance floor to go upstairs. Next thing I knew, he was falling down the stairs." It was an approximation of the truth, Alfonso justified to himself.

"Alfonso!" The second paramedic, who had been driving the ambulance, entered the club. "Are you still on duty? I thought you were on patrol way out by Girona these days?"

"Philippe, it's good to see you," replied Alfonso unenthusiastically. He knew straightaway that, by morning, Philippe would have reported this encounter to the emergency services throughout the east coast of Spain. "No, I'm here with my husband. It was a trip down memory lane. We were just leaving, but then we stopped to help this Englishman who fell down the stairs."

The first paramedic turned to look up. "Is this the Alfonso de la Torre you were telling me about, Philippe?" He turned to Alfonso. "I thought you said you were dancing with this man? And yet you were here with your husband?" He looked across to Philippe. "I don't understand these people. And you say they want to have a family together?"

Alfonso was furious, but now was not the time to say anything.

Philippe shrugged and turned to get the gurney ready to transfer Jonathan to the ambulance. Gabriel put a reassuring arm on Alfonso's shoulder.

"Don't worry about him," he whispered. "I'm sure we'll get far worse comments than that in the years to come. Let's be helpful here, instead of angry. Why don't I go with Jonathan in the ambulance, and you follow behind on the bike? I think we should at least help Jonathan find his husband before we leave him. It doesn't sound like he's having a very good time right now."

Alfonso nodded. He turned to speak to Philippe. "We rode down on the motorbike tonight, Philippe. Can Gabriel ride with Jonathan while I follow on the bike? Jonathan's going to need some help, as he doesn't speak Spanish. Are you taking him up the road to Saint Camil?"

Philippe looked around as he secured Jonathan to the gurney. "They've closed their emergency room to new admittances tonight. There was a major accident on the C-32 earlier. We're going to have to go to Barcelona. To l'Hospitalet."

"Okay, good for us. We won't have so far to get home afterward," replied Alfonso. "I'll be ready by the time you've got him on board."

He leaned over to speak in Jonathan's ear. "Don't worry, my English friend. You're in safe hands. They're taking you to the hospital to have your head checked. It's just a precaution. If you have blacked out, they need to observe you for twenty-four hours. Gabriel's coming with you, and I'll follow behind. Where can we contact your husband?"

Jonathan stared at Alfonso in bewilderment. "I can't remember. We're staying in Sitges. In an apartment overlooking the church. I don't know where it is. I just follow Dominic." Jonathan was beginning to look panicky. "I don't even know his mobile number. I just push the button on my phone." He grabbed Alfonso's arm. "You've got to find him. His name's Dominic Delingpole. We were at the Vivero Restaurant earlier this evening. Then we went to Balmins beach—"

"For a naked midnight swim? I didn't think you British were so adventurous." Alfonso smiled. "Don't worry, my friend. I'm a police officer. We'll soon find him."

"Police?" exclaimed Jonathan. "Oh God. Have I just spent half an hour in a darkroom with a Spanish police officer? On my honeymoon? Oh God. Please don't tell Dominic."

Chapter 12

THE BABY had been crying for over half an hour. Periodically, it would draw up its little legs to its stomach, as though in agonizing pain, and then kick out hard against its mother's chest.

Steve watched the poor mother try to console her child and felt a wave of sympathy for her. Back home in Brighton, his own mother was a part-time childminder—babysitter, as they called it in the States—and he was used to babies and young children being around the rambling Georgian house they shared with Steve's grandparents. He had often been roped in to help out with a tantruming two-year-old. The mother in front of him tried every technique to placate her baby, but without success.

He already had a headache when they landed. A consequence of failing to drink sufficient water during the dehydrating flight. The immigration holding room was airless and starkly lit. The baby's cries made his headache ten times worse. But he could not blame the child. Instead, he cursed the U.S. Citizenship and Immigration Services for its shoddy computer system. Steve checked his watch again. Nearly two hours had passed since the humorless official had shown him into the room, which Steve now shared with about twelve other unfortunates. The mother with the crying baby sat opposite him on one of the hard plastic chairs. She looked to be in her early thirties, and her head was covered with a hijab. A few seats away from her sat an Asian couple with three children. They had come in shortly after him. Alongside Steve was an elderly couple, possibly from India or Pakistan. Next to them was a smartly dressed family who spoke Russian to each other in hushed voices from time to time.

At the far end of the room sat two immigration officials, a man and a woman. Steve had been watching them ever since he was shown into the room. Much of the time, they seemed to do nothing more than chat to each other. Then the phone would ring, and a person or group of people would be called to the front and escorted through a side door.

After the first hour of waiting, Steve had walked up to the desk and asked how long he was going to be held in the room.

"As long as it takes, sir," replied the male immigration officer. "I suggest you go back to your seat and don't make a fuss. We've got a lot on tonight." He had said it in an emotionless, monotone voice. Steve guessed he had repeated the same answer to countless stranded passengers in the past.

Steve leaned forward to the mother and her baby. "How old?" he asked with a sympathetic smile.

The woman turned from her baby with a weary look on her face. "She is just twelve weeks. I am worried she has an infection. She is very hot and won't stop crying. I am very sorry." She looked at Steve and tilted her head as she apologized. "It must be very annoying for you."

"No worries, love," he said. "My mom's a childminder back in England. I'm used to it." He gestured to the two immigration officers at the end of the room. "If you think she's ill, why don't you ask them to help?"

The woman smiled at him. "You are very kind to be understanding. I am returning to my husband, who lives in the Valley. I lost my bag with my passport and papers and mobile phone in it when I got off the plane. I cannot think where it has gone. I can only believe it was stolen. The immigration people do not believe me. They think I am lying."

"Why don't you just get them to call your husband?" asked Steve.

The woman tilted her head again. "I know this sounds very silly, but I do not know his number. You see," she said with a smile, "it is stored in my phone."

"Well, that's easily sorted," said Steve. "What's your husband's name, address, and mobile phone company? It won't take me long to get that. I've got my laptop in here." He gestured to his rucksack.

The woman shook her head and pointed to a sign on the wall. "You cannot use electronic devices in here. You are not through US immigration yet. We will only get in more trouble."

Steve grinned. "Don't worry, love. That's not a problem for me."

"WILL YOU stay for the night?" As Tanya spoke, she slowly traced her fingers over the intricate detail of a tattoo across Jeff's chest. The Maori-inspired design flowed up to his broad shoulder and down his upper arm.

"I seem to remember," she continued as she lifted her head and gently kissed his nipple, "that after that party, I woke to find you alongside me in the bed." She laid her head on Jeff's smooth, shaved chest. "Stay again."

Jeff raised his head from the pillow for a moment and looked down at Tanya's athletic body, nestled against his. He smiled. A very successful night overall, he thought.

After a light supper at the Montgomery Street Bar and Grill, Jeff had called Robbie and offered Tanya a ride back to her apartment on Nob Hill. She had said yes immediately. When they arrived, she invited him in "for a nightcap." That was two hours ago. Tanya had wasted no time in getting Jeff to the bedroom.

She was a passionate, fiery, and, Jeff sadly admitted, much fitter lover than he was. It was now around midnight, and he felt exhausted. The prospect of not moving any farther for the night, of wrapping himself in the comfort of Tanya's bed, was very appealing.

Jeff looked across to the huge bedroom window in Tanya's top-floor apartment. It framed the spectacular sight of the Golden Gate Bridge, lit by the low-hanging moon. This view alone was worth over a million dollars. The apartment was in one of the most sought after locations in San Francisco. Tanya had done well. Once upon a time—fourteen years ago to be precise—she had been Jeff's intern. He had plucked her from a young cohort of programmers who had joined one of the first hackfests he had put together. Jeff recognized her potential immediately, both professionally and as an occasional playmate in the bedroom.

He looked down at her smooth ebony body again. The temptation to stay the night with her was strong. But he needed to contact Charter Ninety-Nine and send them the information he had retrieved from Tanya's laptop. With the Originator missing, there was now a greater urgency for the group to push on with its task. The financial access details he had retrieved would have a very short life cycle. He needed to get them to Russia and China quickly.

"You're miles away, Jeff. What are you thinking about?"

He kissed her tenderly on top of her head. "Fourteen years ago, that night you stayed over at Grain Street—"

"And we slept among the building rubble."

"I don't remember getting much sleep that night." Jeff laughed and slid his hand up her thigh. "Maybe the next day—"

"When you were supposed to be doing the final presentation," Tanya said. She looked up at him. "Why do you keep coming back to me? You've got Nick now. Doesn't he satisfy you?"

Jeff lay back on the pillow and spread his arms wide across the bed.

"Don't overanalyze everything, Tanya," he said with a sigh. "Just enjoy the moment. Nick doesn't begrudge me this. He encourages me to—"

"You've told me before, he's got his own fuck buddies," she interrupted. "Is that why you do it? To get your own back?"

Jeff sat up and allowed Tanya to slide away from him. He reached out his hand and stroked her cheek. "Sex isn't about revenge, Tanya. I don't use it as a weapon to harm Nick. We're in love. And even more, we're soul mates."

Tanya smiled and looked away.

Jeff eased himself off the bed and walked across to the window. He stood with his back to her, looking at the view across the bay. "Yeah, maybe it sounds corny," he said, "but it's true. I've known him for over five years now. I wouldn't want to harm him, and neither would he want to harm me. We trust each other completely."

He turned to look at Tanya. She wrapped her arms around a pillow and hugged it close. "You men are really something else," she said. "You dress all tough. You flash your tattoos and your muscular bodies. Underneath, you're soft as butter. What is it you see in that gym bunny?"

Jeff moved away from the window and gathered his clothes from the floor.

"Everything," he said, getting dressed. "He's more than a gym bunny. Far more. And for your information"—he turned to Tanya—"we've always been completely honest with each other. There are no lies between us. If ever there were, that would end our relationship immediately. He knows I'm with you tonight. And he'll get a full report when I get back." Jeff looked down and started to button his fly. "But remember, Tanya. I not only find my gym bunny man real hot—" He paused and looked up. "—but tall, sexy women are a real turn-on for me as well."

Tanya hugged the pillow closer. "And when are you next going to find me a turn-on, Jeff?"

STEVE SAT in the dirty washroom cubicle, rapidly tapping away on his laptop. He knew he could not be away from the immigration holding room for long, or they would come searching for him.

It had taken him less than a minute to find the mobile number for Ramesh Panchal of Queens Drive, Mountain View. When he called it, the phone was answered quickly. Steve could hear airport sounds in the background.

"Mr. Panchal?" said Steve.

"Yes?" said a voice at the other end.

"My name is Steve Brown. Is your wife Nisha Panchal?"

"Oh my God, has something happened to her?"

"No," Steve reassured him. "I'm with her here in immigration. She's lost her bag and mobile phone, so they're treating her as a suspicious immigrant. I guess you're waiting in Arrivals. If you get your ass over to immigration on that side right now, you can get your wife and baby released real quick."

"But we have lived here nearly fifteen years!" protested Ramesh Panchal. "Why do they still treat us in this way? Here in the Valley, I am president of the second biggest security software company—"

"Yeah, yeah, prejudice sucks doesn't it?" replied Steve. "Put it down to bureaucratic blindness, mate. They reckon that if they lock up every person who differs even slightly from their societal norm, they're bound to catch a bad guy eventually."

Steve leaned back against the wall and tried to read some of the graffiti on the scruffy cubicle door in front of him. He wished he had a pen to add to it.

"The fact is," he continued, "the bad guys know this, so the smart ones simply blend in. Now go get your wife out. Your daughter's got a temperature by the looks of it."

"You are a very kind man," said Mr. Panchal. "I don't know why you have taken your time to do this, but I am most grateful. Can I do anything for you?"

"If I'm still here in a day, I'll give you a call. But I reckon I know how to fix things."

Steve ended the call and turned back to his laptop.

It took him longer than he expected to hack into the Homeland Security database containing the electronic travel authorization records, or ESTAs. Once there, it was just a few moments before he found his own damaged record. It looked to Steve like an inexpert hack. Either that or the person had been interrupted before they could tidy up all the loose ends after deleting the record. The field chains in the database entry had only been partially severed. A few remained intact. Steve spent several minutes tracing the pattern of other entries in the database. Then he painstakingly applied the necessary fixes to his own database entry. Rechecking his work, he felt confident that his US visa waiver record, essential for a visitor from the UK, would now appear to the immigration officials.

"Mr. Brown? Are you in there? You must return to the immigration holding room immediately." The voice was followed by someone banging on the cubicle door.

"All right, all right, I'm just finishing up, mate," replied Steve. He rapidly closed his laptop and stuffed it back into his rucksack. "You guys have seriously spooked me this evening. It's no wonder I've got the shits now."

He was about to push the flush button when he felt his mobile vibrate in his pocket. Pulling it out, he read the message on the screen:

Not bad. Took you a while, though. I've got a car waiting outside once you've got your bags. Nick

"You bastard," Steve muttered to himself, shoving the phone back into his pocket. "But I'll get you yet."

Chapter 13

DOMINIC PAUSED at the top of the long, wide flight of steps that wound past the church of Sant Bartomeu & Santa Tecla on the northern end of Sitges. He looked out over the seafront boulevard of Passeig de la Ribera. It was nearly one in the morning, and the nighttime promenade was in full flow. Couples meandered along, chatting and laughing or simply enjoying each other's company. Some stopped at one of the many ice-cream stands along the seafront. Dominic caught sight of a few serious clubbers and watched with amusement as they wove their way with speed and intent through the crowds.

On his first visit to Sitges, these young men had fascinated Dominic. Perfectly preened, wearing expressions of haughty exclusivity, they started to appear between eleven o'clock and midnight. Jonathan had christened it the bitching hour. They were on a mission to fuck, moving between more than twenty or so gay nightspots in Sitges, hoping to end up in someone else's bed or, if they were unsuccessful, sullenly slinking back to their own at dawn. Once, when Dominic awoke before six in the morning, he stood on the balcony and watched a few stragglers doing the walk of shame.

He looked up at the floodlit church, sighed, and started down the steps. He was not a passionate clubber, but tonight he would reluctantly join the ardent young men. Not to party, but to look for his missing husband. He thought about the confrontation on Balmins beach half an hour earlier and wondered how he might have handled things better.

He wanted to tell Jonathan the truth, but there was information that he could not reveal, and that made him feel uncomfortable. Before they encountered Karl Michael at Balmins, it seemed like Jonathan had understood. As they held hands on the beach and watched the waves, Jonathan had talked about the importance of respecting the occasional "convenient lies." Dominic sighed again and wondered if straight couples had the same complications in their relationships.

In his head, he drew up a route map of possible venues where Jonathan might seek sanctuary. The first was just a hundred yards from the church. Bar 7, in Carrer Nou, was one of the longest surviving bars in Sitges and a regular drinking place for both Jonathan and Dominic. The bartenders at Bar 7 were always welcoming, friendly, and cheeky. Some of them were English, which made it a popular haunt for British visitors.

When Dominic opened the double doors to Bar 7, he paused. The place was heaving. A raucous rendition of Madonna's "Like a Prayer" assaulted his ears. Dominic took a deep breath and pushed his way through the crowd. When he finally reached the bar, Adriano, the burly and bespectacled barman, beamed at him. Adriano leaned across the counter, held Dominic's head in both hands, and kissed him full on the lips.

"Mi delicioso Dominic!" he proclaimed to the whole bar. "Eres un inglés muy guapo!"

Dominic gently pulled his head away from Adriano's bearlike hands. He avoided looking around, certain the eyes of every man in the bar were, at that moment, staring at him. His face flushed.

"Adriano, I'm sorry. I can't stop. I'm looking for Jonathan. Has he been in tonight?"

Adriano stepped back and raised his hands in the air. "You may search me if you like," he said, winking to the men standing on either side of Dominic. "I have not seen your charming husband this evening." He lowered his hands and folded his arms across his growing paunch.

"But, *chaval*, it is your honeymoon, is it not?" Adriano narrowed his eyes as he looked at Dominic. "Something is wrong? You two are the perfect couple. Everybody here say it is true. Come"—he reached for a glass—"I will make you one of my special gin cocktails. It is my gift to you." He reached forward and kissed Dominic again. "You must tell me all about it."

Dominic smiled wanly. He knew he had no choice but to accept Adriano's generosity.

NICK STOOD waiting patiently, carrying the small whiteboard on which he had written the words "Steve Brown" with a thick black marker pen. The arrivals hall at San Francisco Airport was crowded. Nick had positioned himself in front of a set of automated doors, which swung open periodically to release another handful of relieved-looking passengers from the customs hall behind them. After a wait of nearly twenty minutes, the doors burst open, and he recognized the tall, lean figure of Steve Brown striding forward, pushing a trolley with two large rucksacks balanced on it.

"Don't say a fucking word, mate," said Steve as he thrust the trolley at Nick, "or I'll fucking nut yer. Just take my bags and get me out of this shithole."

Nick grinned, took hold of the trolley, and led the way through the crowds in the arrival area out into the damp May evening. They crossed the street in silence to the entrance of the multistory parking deck. Nick pressed the button to call the elevator and turned to Steve.

"Hey look, Steve. You did good, really. I'm running the hackfest. No hard feelings, eh? One of my new recruits did the hack. How did you rate it?"

Steve said nothing.

The elevator doors in front of them opened, and they stepped in. Nick pressed the button for the fifth floor.

As soon as the doors slid shut, Steve grabbed Nick by the throat and pinned him against the wall of the elevator. Then he shoved his knee into Nick's crotch.

"I don't care if your name's Tim Berners-fucking-Lee," Steve breathed, his face inches away from Nick's. "It was a shit hack, and you should rip the little fucker's balls off who did it."

With a twist of his arm, he shoved Nick's head down, until his face rested on Steve's Grinder boots. As Nick flailed his arms behind him, Steve grabbed one of them and twisted it hard.

"Want me to treat you rough, do you?" hissed Steve. Nick moaned softly in assent, and Steve twisted his arm tighter. "Well, you can start right now by learning obedience. That's if you want to enjoy some more punishment from me on this trip. You've pissed me off big-time, shithead."

Steve gave Nick's arm a hard flick, and his body twisted over on the floor of the elevator. Before Nick could move, Steve brought his boot down firmly on the side of Nick's head.

"That's better," said the English skinhead. "Compliance. That's what I like. We can do some more of this later."

He paused for a few seconds.

The elevator shuddered to a stop at the fifth floor, and the doors opened.

"Time to go," said Steve. He lifted his boot off Nick's head. "I'm fucking knackered. Good to see you're into the obedience side of skin culture." He reached down to help the American up but then paused. "You're not a fucking Nazi, are you? You're definitely only into the gear and stuff?"

Nick stood up and brushed himself down. "Yeah, of course I am." There was a crooked grin on his face. "I'm a member of Anti-Fascist Action here in the Bay Area. We've got enough fucking fascists in this country without me adding to them."

Steve grabbed the handle of the trolley and pushed it out of the elevator. He turned to look at Nick. "You're all right," said Steve. "For a fucking Yank. Now. Where's yer car?"

Steve followed him and took hold of the trolley.

"You got a place booked?" he asked. "I can take you there now if you want. Or you can come back to the loft, and we can get some action. We've kitted out a pretty cool playroom."

AROUND ONE thirty, Dominic kissed Adriano the barman goodbye, apologized once again for being gloomy, and thanked him profusely for the powerful gin cocktail. He emerged into the narrow side street of Carrer Nou and swayed for a moment as he breathed the fresh air. Then he strode off through an alleyway to arrive at the entrance of the club he liked least in Sitges, the cruisey Zona X. Jonathan had persuaded him to go into the place on their first visit to the town, and Dominic had sworn he would never return. It was designed solely for men to find anonymous sex. There was some subdued club music but no dance floor. Beyond the bar lurked dark corners and the essentials for sleazy man-on-man sexual encounters—a couple of slings, three cubicles fitted with glory holes, and a set of prison bars. Dominic paused on the threshold to read the sign on the wall: Naked Nite! He shivered as the vision of a room full of testosterone-fueled men, staring straight ahead, thrusting their erect cocks toward him, filled his head. A wave of anger washed over him, and he decided if Jonathan was inside, their marriage would end right there.

He was about to turn back into the street when the inner door swung open and a man in his early forties stumbled out. The man swayed slightly as he stopped and leaned forward to peer at Dominic. His breath smelled strongly of stale beer.

"Wouldn't go in there tonight if I were you," he slurred in a strong Birmingham accent. "Fucking twinks at every turn." He leaned back heavily against the wall with a thud. "I'm the oldest one by about fifteen years, I reckon." He heaved himself forward with a grunt, resting a paw-like hand on Dominic's shoulder. "Don't suppose you'd be interested…?"

Dominic pushed the man back against the wall and summoned up his best Spanish. "Lo siento, amigo, no le entiendo. Si usted está borracho, quizá debería irse a casa." (I'm sorry mate, I don't understand. Perhaps you're pissed and should go home.")

The man closed his eyes and belched loudly. "Just my luck. A fucking dago."

Dominic thought about kicking the man's legs from under him and then decided against it. At least the ignorant racist had confirmed there was no need for him to join the nightmare of Naked Nite.

From Zona X, Dominic moved on to the heart of Sitges' gay nightlife. Two hundred yards down the street was Carrer de Bonaire and Queenz. Dominic thought the club's regular cabaret a great night out in Sitges. The show had long since ended, and Dominic knew the bar would be packed with well-groomed men who considered themselves the elite of the town's gay population. Men who spent a fortune on their gym memberships, their cologne, and their dance lessons. Dominic doubted his husband would be here. Jonathan needed wittier conversation than any the self-regarding peacocks of Queenz could ever muster.

Dominic turned around to look down the length of the street that was the heart of gay Sitges. Carrer de Joan Tarrida was named after the owner of the region's largest shoe factory, now long defunct. Dominic wondered what the owner would think of the high-heeled sling-backs and boots worn by the drag acts who played at the famous Parrots Pub, which now dominated Carrer de Joan Tarrida.

Before he got to the Parrots Pub, Dominic had two bars to check out along the way. He knew they were popular with Jonathan, because Jonathan had eagerly dragged him into both of them when they first came to Sitges for a holiday two years ago.

The first was El Horno (the Oven). The tiny bar was always full, its numbers frequently swelled by a loyal bear community. Because it was so small, the clientele of El Horno spilled out onto the street, jamming the narrow alleyway outside, waving plastic pint glasses of lager in their hands as they spoke in animated conversation. Dominic slowly fought his way through the raucous crowd of large, hairy men. Some wore token items of leather such as a harness or leather waistcoat. Finally, he reached the bar's tiny backroom space without any sighting of Jonathan. Dispirited, he returned to the street.

Directly opposite El Horno was XXL. Dominic disliked this bar almost as much as he disliked Zona X. A crowd of ten or fifteen men stood outside the entrance, talking quickly in Spanish. Dominic tried but could not understand what they were saying. Their excited, rapid speech was almost drowned out by the heavy beat of the music seeping through the heavy steel doors of the club. Dominic dreaded the task ahead of him. If he failed to find Jonathan, either at the bar or on the dance floor, he would have to climb the spiral staircase to the upper floor. At the top lay the club's sweaty, airless darkroom, full of men with eager, grasping hands and thrusting, tumescent cocks. Maybe there he would find Jonathan immersed in the bacchanal. Dominic took a deep breath and cursed his husband. There was only one way to find out.

Chapter 14

"SHIT, IT'S a Tesla 101X!" Steve allowed his hand to glide over the curves of the matte black wing of one of the fastest electric cars in the world. "You didn't pay for that with the proceeds of a couple of hackfests. What do you really do? Hack into bank accounts?"

Nick's face formed a lopsided smile as the driver and passenger doors slid open with a faintly discernible hum. "Like it?" he asked as he threw Steve's bags on the back seat. "It's not quite the latest model, but we're going to get that in a few months."

"We?" queried Steve as he stepped into the black interior of the car. It was softly illuminated by the glow of hundreds of hidden LED lights. As he sat down, the lights shifted slowly through indigo to lilac and then a deep red.

"Blimey, it's like a fuckin' disco in here," Steve commented as Nick pushed the driver's seat back into place and sat alongside him. "What music you gonna play me on the drive? Donna Summer?"

By way of an answer, Nick touched a pad on a side console, and a mellow woman's voice, singing a cover of the Carpenter's song "Close to You," filled the inside of the car.

"You're kiddin' me!" said Steve. "You're into Rumer? I love her music." He waved his hand from side to side in midair, conducting the easy lyricism of the song.

"No one believes me when I say I like this stuff. They all think I should be into British punk, or some ersatz American copy. But not me." His hand paused in midbeat, and he turned to look at Nick. He reached over, laid the palm of his hand on the back of Nick's head, and pulled him close. Their foreheads touched, and their eyes locked for a few seconds.

It was Nick who moved first. He brought his hand up to pull Steve's head closer while he hungrily explored the inside of Steve's mouth with his tongue. Steve reciprocated, stimulating the back of Nick's mouth with his own tongue. He leaned in farther to Nick and lifted himself off the seat to get closer.

Nick's hands slipped down from Steve's neck to the front of his jeans. Expertly, the American's fingers undid Steve's button fly and worked their way inside his briefs. Steve could feel them exploring around the base of his rapidly hardening cock. All the while, Nick's tongue caressed and explored deep inside his mouth. Steve wrapped both hands around Nick's head and pushed it back and then down, redirecting the warm, moist, relentless stimulation to pleasure his penis. He leaned back against the passenger window as he felt Nick's tongue explore every erogenous point on his cock.

Suddenly, he felt a stab of pain around his perineum. He pulled away and sat back in the seat, massaging the base of his penis.

"What the fuck are you doing?" he asked. "I'm not into cutting or shit like that." Angrily, he carried on rubbing as the initial sharp pain subsided.

"Sorry, Steve," said Nick, "I need to cut my nails again, I guess." The lopsided smile reformed on his face. "Anyway, I thought you might be into a bit more pain than that."

"Yeah, well I'm not. I don't do piercing."

Nick reached for his seat belt, secured it, and rapidly reversed the Tesla out of the parking space. He paused to look across at Steve.

"It's probably not a good idea for us to get up to much in this car anyway," he said. "Jeff would be livid if I got cum on the upholstery. Wait until we get to the loft. If he's back from his business meeting, we can have a threesome if you like."

"I think I'll call this a night," Steve replied, fumbling with the buttons of his fly. "Just take me to my B and B, it's supposed to be round the corner from your place. The guy from GayBnB said he'd be up late, and I should get me some sleep."

"Suit yourself," said Nick. He put the car into drive, and they shot toward the exit of the parking lot, screeching to a halt just before the barrier. While Nick lowered his window and dealt with the exit ticket, Steve shoved his hand inside his briefs to explore the injury he felt between his legs. Gingerly, he used the tips of his fingers to trace the contours of the skin. The pain was rapidly disappearing, but he could definitely feel a tender spot around the edge of his scrotum.

Steve looked up to see Nick watching him with amusement.

"Want me to take over?" Nick asked with the same lopsided smile. "You can still come back to the loft if you want."

"Just drive, mate, will you?" replied Steve, withdrawing his hand and fastening the last few buttons. Nick shrugged and turned up the music, and the Tesla shot out of the parking lot toward route 101 and the city.

IT WAS well after one in the morning when the white Lexus pulled up outside 101 Grain Street. A single streetlamp lit the discreet entrance to the building. Clouds had gathered overhead, and a chill wind blew in from the bay. Jeff shivered as he stepped out of the car.

Robbie lowered his window and leaned out. "I'll do that delivery for you to Jeremiah's place first thing in the morning. But if you need a pimped-up driver this weekend, Jeff, just remember I'm performin' at the gig down in Santa Clara."

Jeff laughed. "Yeah, no problem, Robbie. You can dump the uniform now. Anyway, I'm not moving from here this weekend. It's the hackfest, and I'm going to be busy myself."

Robbie tipped his head to one side. "Lookin' for new programmers, or lookin' for new meat?" he asked, a grin revealing his expensive, perfect set of white teeth.

Jeff laughed. "Whatever comes my way, Robbie. I'm getting a bit old to expect too much anymore."

Robbie waved his finger at Jeff in mock admonishment. "Shame on you for talking that way. I know you too well. You like your menfolk lean and young and your womenfolk a bit more mature. And from what I've seen," he continued, "there's a constant stream of both just lining up for you." He dropped his hand and laid it flat on the door panel of the Lexus. "I imagine you got what you wanted tonight, didn't you?" He grinned again.

"Yeah, Robbie." Jeff smiled. "You could say that."

Jeff closed the car door, waved his arm in salute as the Lexus eased away from him, and crossed to the building entrance. Once inside, he took the industrial-style elevator to the top floor. As he opened the heavy iron gate, he could see a large cinema screen flicker in the loft space ahead of him.

"Hey, Nick," he called out. "You still up?"

Nick's head appeared above one of the long black leather couches ranged in front of the screen. He had stripped off his shirt, and his lean, muscled torso glowed in the reflected light from the cinema screen. Jeff noticed he was rewatching an episode of *Queer as Folk*.

"How many times are you going to watch that series?" Jeff asked mockingly, carefully placing a leather satchel down on a steel-topped table, hand-built for Jeff by a designer in Carmel. "It's gotten so old now. Other queer TV is available, you know." He pulled off his jacket and began to unbutton his shirt. "I've got to get out of these damn clothes. I feel like one of the mannequins in Nordstrom's window."

Nick rested his hands on the back of the couch and straightened his arms, flexing his neck and the muscles across his back.

"This is classic television, Jeff. No one's come close to achieving what Russell T. Davies did on British TV in the '90s." Nick started to do push-ups on the back of the couch. "This first show blew the minds of those uptight Limeys. Anal sex, rimming, and masturbation, all in one episode? And Stuart's so hot, even with all that hair."

Jeff had heard this from Nick many times before. He took his cue to prompt for the next section of the critique. "And the American version?"

Nick stopped in mid muscle-flex and looked witheringly at Jeff.

"Tame but worthy. Why does American drama always have to be about 'issues'? Why do they have to lecture us? Just give us a good onscreen fuck. That's what we want to see. Talking of which—" Nick leapt over the back of the couch and swaggered toward Jeff. "—wanna know where your new British protégé is right now?"

Nick reached into his back pocket and took out his mobile phone. He pulled up a map on the screen showing downtown San Francisco. A red dot pulsed over a street a few blocks away.

"So you got a tracker on him?" asked Jeff with admiration. "Did you manage to fuck him as well?"

Nick grinned. "Not sure he was in the mood after the injector did its magic. Fucking difficult doing it virtually blind, in a car, with a guy who's pretty damn hot."

Jeff's fingers paused on the last few buttons of his shirt. "Where the hell did you put the tracker?" he asked.

"Right between his two pleasure parks," Nick replied triumphantly. "I was hoping to carry on with the oral and distract him, but I guess he's a bit oversensitive just around there."

Nick shoved the phone back in his pocket and helped Jeff remove his shirt. He caressed Jeff's smooth chest for a few moments, gently massaging his nipples between finger and thumb. Jeff groaned appreciatively. Nick squeezed a little harder, then paused.

"So tell me, why did I need to go to all that trouble with the injector? Why couldn't we just track him with his mobile, like you'd normally do?"

Jeff sighed and gently took Nick's hands in his.

"We know he's a bright guy. So if he goes off anywhere special, he could be wise to us and simply leave his phone behind. Or just turn the thing off." Jeff placed his hands on Nick's shoulders and pushed him to his knees. "Okay?"

Nick looked up with a grin for a moment, then started to unbuckle Jeff's belt.

"Has this one been busy tonight?" he asked, patting the bulge on the front of Jeff's pants. "Did the lady get the attention she was looking for?"

Jeff held Nick's head firmly in both hands. "She's not complaining. Tanya Gould is going to be useful to us for a while yet. Tonight she yielded some very useful information from World Resources Inc."

Nick looked up at Jeff. "Voluntarily?"

"Let's say she offered no resistance. Although I'll admit she knew not what she did." Jeff caressed Nick's head and began to massage the lobes of his ears. "I need your help to check I got everything before we send it on to Charter Ninety-Nine."

Nick unzipped Jeff's fly, pulled down his pants, and wrapped his hands around Jeff's firm thighs. He looked up with the puppy-dog face that was always an instant trigger to give Jeff a hard-on. But tonight, Jeff continued to hold Nick's head away from him.

"Fuck, Nick, I think this is going to have to wait. It's morning, or close to it, in the rest of the world. We should get the new information to them as soon as we can. And there's another reason."

Nick swore and stood up. He helped Jeff pull his pants back on.

Jeff walked over to the table and held up the slim leather satchel he had placed there a few moments earlier.

"I slipped Tanya's laptop out of her room as I left. Robbie's going to take it back to the Montgomery Street Bar and Grill first thing in the morning. That way, she'll just think she carelessly left it there."

"Carelessly?" repeated Nick. "Imagine the news reports if that got out. 'Director of Operations for world banking security company WRI leaves laptop in restaurant.' She'd be toast."

Jeff took the laptop out of the satchel and placed it on the table. "Well, just like the major banks that WRI serves, it seems their security is pretty shit." He opened the laptop and started it up. "While we were in the restaurant, I watched her log in to her account without even double-touch security. No fingerprint, no iris scan. Nothing. I've seen tougher security on porn sites."

Nick walked over to Jeff and wrapped his arms around his waist. "This is going to be gold dust for the Ninety-Nine," he said. "That means everything's ready."

Jeff turned to face Nick. "No, it's not. There's still more to be done. And if we don't retrieve the Dormant Gateway chip that's gone missing, we can't risk planting the histories. All we can do with this information from Tanya is rob a few banks." He watched the smile form on Nick's face. "And no, that's not enough. The Ninety-Nine have been planning this for five years. We're not going ahead until the DG chip is recovered."

"So what's the British skinhead got to do with it?" Nick hoisted himself up on the tabletop and sat cross-legged in front of the laptop. "Have you got the log-in, by the way?"

Jeff picked up his jacket and retrieved a memory card from the pocket. He walked over to a console near the cinema screen and inserted the card. A few moments later, a video of Tanya in the restaurant filled the screen.

"Here. You can watch what she typed. Shouldn't be difficult." He went to stand square in front of Nick. He placed his hands either side of him on the steel surface of the table.

"As for young Steve Brown. He's our best chance for recovering the DG chip. And we've been told to do whatever it takes to get the information out of him. Could be fun."

Chapter 15

DOMINIC LEANED against the wall outside XXL and inhaled mouthfuls of the warm evening air. He felt angry and humiliated. He had been rebuffed and rejected in almost equal measure during the twenty minutes he had spent fruitlessly peering at men's faces in the shadowy maze of narrow corridors forming the cruising area on the upper floor of XXL. He did not feel the same thrill for encounters in darkrooms that he knew Jonathan still experienced. To Dominic, the artificial setup seemed comically serious and pseudo macho. It depressed him to see scores of men stand in the dimly lit corridors, waiting for anonymous physical fulfillment. It reminded him how he used to feel at school when the boys were lined up on the football field as the seniors picked their players. He was usually one of the last to be chosen.

Dejectedly, Dominic turned his back on the noisy hubbub of Sitges gay nightlife. He headed for their honeymoon apartment a few hundred yards away, located in a quiet street of modern holiday apartments. As he approached the entrance to the six-story block, he fumbled for the passkey in his pocket. He opened the heavy entrance door and stepped into the dimly lit lobby, walked over to the elevator, and pressed the call button. The doors opened immediately, and Dominic stepped into the small steel cabin. He selected the sixth floor, the doors closed, and the elevator climbed slowly to the top of the building.

The entrance to their holiday apartment was opposite the elevator and slightly to the left. When the elevator doors opened, Dominic could see immediately the front door to their apartment was ajar.

"Jonathan?" he called as he stepped out the elevator. There was no response.

Dominic paused. He knew the door had been shut when they left earlier that evening. He knew because he had locked it himself. Dominic looked around. The emergency staircase was to the right of the elevator. Handy, if he needed to make a rapid exit. There was a bright red fire extinguisher hanging on the wall opposite. It was the only potential weapon he could see.

Dominic stood on the hinged side of the front door, extended his arm, and slowly pushed it open.

"Karl Michael? Is that you?"

Still no response. The door opened straight into the large living room of the apartment. The main lights were on. Opposite him, Dominic could see the glass doors to their balcony. One of them was also open. He remembered distinctly he had closed and locked them before they left, despite Jonathan's mocking comments about cat burglars at six floors up.

Gingerly, Dominic stepped into the living room. He checked there was no one behind the door. At first glance, everything seemed to be in its place. Books and papers were on the round glass-topped dining table, where he and Jonathan had left them. Dominic looked across at the small kitchen area. Empty glasses and a partly finished bowl of olives were still on the countertop. There was no other apparent sign of a burglary, only the open front and balcony doors.

He turned to the bedroom on his left. The door was slightly ajar, and he could see the bedside lights were on. Dominic paused and listened intently, but he could hear no sound. He contemplated taking one of the knives from the kitchen to protect himself before he ventured into the bedroom. But he had never used one in combat before. If there was an assailant hiding in the bedroom, he reasoned, he risked handing him, or her, the perfect weapon to kill him with.

Summoning his courage, he strode forward and slammed the bedroom door fully open. No one leapt out at him. Dominic felt confident that any would-be burglar had gone. But someone had been here. Clothes had been tipped out of drawers, pulled from hangers in the wardrobes, and deposited in a pile by the window. The bedding had been ripped from the bed and the mattress upended on the floor. Through one of the open wardrobe doors, he could see the steel door of the room safe had been forced.

Dominic picked his way through the debris to get to the safe. As he passed the chest of drawers, he stopped. When they left the apartment for dinner, both their mobile phones had been sitting on top of the chest, plugged into their chargers. Now they were no longer there.

Dominic sat down heavily on the bare bed frame. "Shit," he said out loud. "So how the hell do I call the police at two in the morning when I haven't got a phone?"

"I TELL you I'm fine, really. All this fuss. I'm very grateful for everything you've done, but I'd really like to go home now."

Jonathan's protests were met with an amiable, uncomprehending smile from the orderly who pushed his wheelchair along a neon-lit corridor, heading for ward B21 in l'Hospitalet. When Jonathan had arrived at the ER reception fifty minutes earlier, Gabriel had been very helpful, explaining to the admissions doctor what had happened. Jonathan was impressed at the speed with which the hospital had dealt with him and how quickly they had found a bed to admit him to a ward for one night's stay, "for observation," as Gabriel had explained.

The orderly spun Jonathan's wheelchair through 180 degrees, ready to reverse him through the heavy swing doors of ward B21. It was then Jonathan saw Alfonso running up the corridor toward them, dressed in full bike leathers.

"An angel in leather!" Jonathan pronounced, throwing his arms wide in supplication. "I do hope you're wearing a harness and jock under that wonderful outfit."

The doors to the ward swung closed on them as the orderly pulled the wheelchair inside. He swiveled it around and pushed the chair alongside one of the beds. As Jonathan stood up and prepared to climb in, the doors of the ward opened again, and Alfonso strode in.

"Good evening, my injured Englishman!" said Alfonso in a loud whisper. "Now, don't you cause these nice people any trouble, or I will bring the full force of the law upon you."

"Oh, I do hope so," said Jonathan, his leg lifted in readiness to get into the bed. "I have nothing to protect me except this hospital gown, which, as you can see, has full rear ventilation and offers total access." Jonathan gave the flimsy gown a flick, like a coquettish debutante at a dance, before settling himself into the bed.

Alfonso grinned and stood at the end of the bed. He watched as a male nurse came over and checked Jonathan's charts. The nurse turned and started talking to Alfonso in Spanish. After a few moments, they both laughed, and Jonathan sat up in bed.

"What are you two saying?" asked Jonathan. "I know you're talking about me, and I insist on nothing but flattery."

"Apparently you're not going to be able to keep this evening's events quiet," said Alfonso. "Luis here is an avid follower of *Noticias de Rosa* online. One of their journalists was at XXL this evening. You're already headline news on their website."

Jonathan threw himself back on the pillow and groaned.

"This is terrible. I just hope it stays in the Spanish version only. I couldn't bear it if Dominic gets to hear about it."

He sat up suddenly.

"Alfonso. Please, do whatever you can to find my husband. His name is—"

"Dominic Delingpole. You've told me ten times at least. Don't worry. I'm sure it won't be difficult. And anyway, he'll be looking for you, I'm sure."

Jonathan threw himself back onto the pillow once more. "Not after the way I've behaved tonight. If he's got any sense, he'll catch the first flight home in the morning and file for divorce immediately." He put his fist up to his forehead and squeezed his eyes tight shut.

"My friend," said Alfonso, "have you heard of the Spanish phrase *la reina del drama*?"

Jonathan opened his eyes and shook his head.

"You should, my friend," continued Alfonso. "It describes you perfectly."

DOMINIC'S SHORT walk to the Passeig de la Ribera proved immediately successful in his search for the police. A patrol car from the Policia Local was still parked on the seafront, its two occupants watching with evident boredom as the dwindling trickle of late-night revelers dispersed.

The woman police officer walked back to the apartment with Dominic. She was at least six inches shorter than him, with a round face and a large mouth that frequently broke into a smile as they talked. He discovered her name was Officer Juanita Serrano, and she had learned her excellent English while working as an au pair in Oxford. Dominic was pleased to be able to talk about his home city at length as they walked.

At the entrance to the apartment, Officer Serrano paused and turned to Dominic.

"I'm afraid it's very easy to break into these holiday apartments. The keys change hands so often, anyone can make a copy. We know the owner. He tells us he changes the keys at the start of each season. But you know"—she shrugged—"I am not sure he does. It's probably too much effort for him."

She walked into the living room and looked around. "They're very tidy burglars," she said. "They don't make a mess."

"You should see the bedroom," said Dominic glumly. "You'll have a different view then."

They walked together to the bedroom, and Officer Serrano stood in the doorway, surveying the scene of devastation. Dominic had left it exactly as he found it twenty minutes before.

"So you say they forced open the safe but chose to ignore your passports, tickets, and your English money?" asked Officer Serrano.

"That's right," replied Dominic. "I haven't checked everything yet. But as far as I can see, they only took our two mobile phones and my laptop."

Officer Serrano started to make notes. After a few minutes of scribbling, she stopped and turned to Dominic.

"And where is your husband tonight?"

The whole time they had been walking, Dominic had avoided talking about Jonathan with Officer Serrano.

"I'm afraid I don't know, Officer," replied Dominic with embarrassment. "We had an argument earlier, and I haven't seen him for over two hours. I went looking for him, and when I couldn't find him, I came back, hoping to find him here. Instead"—he looked around—"I found this."

Dominic sat down on the bed frame with a sigh. "I'm afraid it's been a terrible evening altogether."

Officer Serrano remained standing and looked down at Dominic sympathetically.

"Señor Delingpole, I'm sure he'll come back here soon." She smiled broadly. "You are on your honeymoon, after all. But I'll take a note of his details. Just in case his name comes up on any reports overnight." She paused and then said, "Forgive me asking, and I know you're on your honeymoon, but have you looked for him in any of the clubs in Sitges?"

Dominic smiled wanly. "Officer Serrano, believe me. I've searched all of them tonight."

ALFONSO THREW his motorbike keys on the marble-topped console table in the hallway and placed his helmet and gauntlets beside them. He turned as Gabriel closed the front door of their apartment and smiled at him.

"So, *mi chico*," said Alfonso, "was that the second honeymoon you said you were so looking forward to tonight?"

Gabriel laughed. He placed his own helmet and gloves on the console table and wrapped his arms around Alfonso's waist.

"No, but I saw a new side of you tonight."

Alfonso looked quizzically at him. "I do hope it was my good side."

"Oh yes, a very good side." He kissed Alfonso tenderly on the lips. "I saw you as a professional tonight, working calmly in a moment of crisis. You are clearly very good at your job, Alfonso. But you also remind me just what a caring man you are. You are even more the man I love than when I first married you."

Alfonso rested his arms on Gabriel's shoulders and slowly drew his husband to him in embrace.

"I feel sorry for Jonathan," said Alfonso. "And also for his man, Dominic. Just think. They're on their honeymoon, and they have such a terrible argument." He leaned back against the wall of the hallway and pulled Gabriel to him. "Do you think their marriage will last?"

Gabriel rested his head on Alfonso's leather jacket and nuzzled his partner's neck.

"Well, Officer de la Torre, I should remind you, eleven years ago, we nearly didn't make our own honeymoon because someone…." He looked up at Alfonso with a glint in his eyes. "Someone decided that going on a fruitless manhunt in the Pyrenees was more important than catching our flight to Florida."

Alfonso held his hands in the air in mock surrender. "Gabriel, in my defense, it was only four months after I'd been fully commissioned into the motorcycle force. It would have looked bad if I didn't go."

Gabriel unzipped Alfonso's jacket, slipped it off his shoulders, and let it fall to the tiled floor. "Do you think the force would have put so much pressure on you to join the manhunt if you'd just got married to a woman?" He tugged at the base of Alfonso's white T-shirt and pulled it up.

Obediently, Alfonso raised his arms in the air as Gabriel removed the shirt and let it drop to the ground. Alfonso unzipped Gabriel's bike jacket and then paused.

"Yes," said Alfonso. "I think they would. Don't try to read homophobia where there is none, Gabriel. I remember at the time, Jose Gonzalez was asked to come in from compassionate leave. His wife had just died two days before. And he did come in. There is a strong sense of duty in the force. Which reminds me."

Alfonso kissed Gabriel once on the mouth, then eased him to one side and strode down the hallway to the kitchen.

Gabriel watched admiringly. "Those leather breeches fit you so well, Officer de la Torre." He followed Alfonso into the kitchen. "I think you should keep them on for a little while longer. What are you doing?"

Alfonso picked up the phone.

"I'm just going to see if control has any record of a Dominic Delingpole this evening," he said, rapidly dialing a number. "Maybe he's filed a missing person report about our friend Jonathan." He looked back at Gabriel standing in the doorway.

"After that, perhaps you'd like to put a collar on me," he said with a wink. "It may be late, but it is our second honeymoon tonight."

Chapter 16

DOMINIC LAY naked on top of the thin bedsheet and stared at the ceiling fan above his head. Its blades created cooling currents in the sultry air of the bedroom. Although exhausted after clearing up the mess of the burglary, Dominic found it impossible to sleep. His mind was full of conflicting thoughts. His honeymoon holiday with Jonathan, which until a few hours earlier had been so blissful and uneventful, was now a nightmare. Jonathan was clearly furious with him. And after what Karl Michael had revealed, Dominic admitted, Jonathan probably had good reason to be angry.

A laptop and both their mobile phones had been stolen. That meant Jonathan had no way of contacting Dominic, assuming Jonathan could remember his phone number in the first place, which Dominic doubted. The impulsive Karl Michael had dredged up awkward memories of events from the past. Dominic had hoped one day he could explain everything to Jonathan, but the time had not yet come. He knew it would be a difficult conversation. He probably was procrastinating, but he wanted to pick the right moment.

Then there was the mysterious text from Bernhardt. Dominic so wished he could recall what it had said exactly. He remembered the phrase "feet of Adam" and some numbers. But he had not attempted to memorize the numbers or the exact words. He felt certain the robbery was connected with Karl Michael. The man had seemed so desperate to retrieve the message from Dominic's phone. Perhaps he was responsible for the break-in.

But why? Despite their furious argument, Dominic thought he had done his best to reconcile with Karl Michael and part on reasonable terms. So if not him, then who?

Dominic sat up abruptly. The intercom was buzzing. He leaned across to look at the digital clock on the bedside table. It was just after 4:00 a.m. He rolled off the bed and picked up a pair of Jonathan's sweatpants from the back of a chair. He pulled them on and made his way quickly to answer the door. The buzzer rang again, more insistent and persistent this time.

Dominic picked up the white plastic receiver from the cradle on the wall.

"Hello, who's there?" he asked.

"This is Officer Alfonso de la Torre from the Guardia Civil. Is that Señor Delingpole?"

DOMINIC FOUND himself very distracted by Alfonso's handsome features and leather-clad body. The officer stood in the middle of the living room, explaining what had happened to Jonathan. Normally, Dominic was more attracted to fair-haired, blue-eyed men—like Jonathan, in fact. But Alfonso's short-cropped black hair, long dark eyelashes, and deep brown eyes were extremely appealing. And that figure. The police officer could do with losing a few pounds around the waist, admittedly, but the leather breeches enhanced the curve of his buttocks in a very fetching way.

"Señor Delingpole?"

Dominic realized with a jolt that the officer had asked him a question, and he had no idea what it was.

"I'm so sorry, Officer," he said with an embarrassed cough. "I was miles away. What did you say?"

"I asked if you would be able to get to the hospital later this morning?" repeated Alfonso. "They don't normally allow visitors until much later in the day. But I have a day off, so I could meet you there and help get you in to see your husband earlier."

"That's very kind, Officer," replied Dominic. "But you really don't need to go to all that trouble."

"Oh, it's really no trouble, Señor Delingpole. Your husband is a most entertaining man. Although I understand that during the evening, you and he—"

Alfonso stopped, unsure what to say next.

"Yes," said Dominic, breaking the awkward pause. "We had a bit of a quarrel. Jonathan found out something about me under rather unfortunate circumstances. I'm embarrassed about it, and I feel that I've hurt him badly. I just hope he'll forgive me."

"Oh, don't worry, Señor Delingpole. He'll forgive you," said Alfonso with a smile. "He was desperate to find you when I left him, and he was very—*arrepentido*. Contrite. We need to get you two back together again as quickly as possible. Then you can continue your honeymoon here in peace."

"Sadly, we only have another day," replied Dominic. "Then we have to fly to San Francisco. We're going to the wedding of one of Jonathan's former lovers." Dominic smiled at Alfonso. "He's had several of those in the past, as you can imagine."

Alfonso laughed. "Oh yes, señor. I can certainly imagine."

PALE SHAFTS of early morning Mediterranean light filtered through the high windows of ward B21 at l'Hospitalet. It was almost 7:00 a.m. The handsome nurse called Luis had promised Jonathan a doctor would be in the ward by 7:30 a.m. at the latest. Luis explained the doctor was the only person with authority to discharge him. Jonathan was confident he could persuade the doctor he was fit and healthy, despite having had virtually no sleep. The man in the bed next to him had snored like a foghorn on the cliffs at Dover. Despite Jonathan's prodding and poking, the man seemed beyond unconscious, and his snoring had been relentless.

Jonathan lay in the semidarkness, listening to the rasping noise of the sleeping man, wondering how he might ever find Dominic again. He resolved to leave the hospital as soon as possible, even if the doctor told him he had to stay longer. He missed Dominic terribly and felt full of remorse for the events of the evening.

Impatience finally got the better of Jonathan. He decided to get dressed and be ready for the doctor when he arrived. As Jonathan pulled on a pair of trousers, he heard the doors clatter open behind him. He turned to see Dominic and Alfonso enter the ward.

"Oh my God, Dominic!" he cried, stepping forward. The loose leg of the trousers caught under his foot, and he fell headlong onto the hard floor.

"Jonathan! Not again," shouted Dominic and Alfonso, almost as one. They rushed forward and helped Jonathan to his feet.

"I should kill you, really I should," said Dominic as Jonathan steadied himself, his trousers sliding down below his knees.

Jonathan said nothing, but he wrapped his arms around Dominic in a bearlike embrace and hugged him tight. He felt as though an enormous weight had been lifted from him, and his shoulders heaved in a deep, contented sob.

"Oh, my love, I'm so sorry," Jonathan said eventually, loosening his grip on Dominic but still clinging to his husband's shoulders. "I don't know if you can ever forgive me for running off like that. After all I'd said about nearly losing you before and never wanting to lose you again. I'm a fool, and I don't deserve—"

"Jonathan, please," interrupted Dominic gently. "Shut up. I've spent half the night worried to death, wondering where you are. Then I find out you actually did go to XXL. On our honeymoon. I'm not sure what to think at the moment. But at least you're safe."

Jonathan looked at Dominic for a moment through watery eyes, then wrapped his arms around his husband and hugged him again.

After a few moments, they heard Alfonso clear his throat behind them. "Um, if you two are going to be all right now, I'll leave you to it," he said.

Jonathan and Dominic separated hastily. Jonathan looked down at the front of his white Armani briefs. They were struggling to contain his obvious enthusiasm for being reunited with Dominic. Jonathan grinned, then bent down, hoisted up his trousers, and buttoned his fly.

"Dominic my dear," he said enthusiastically, as he fastened his belt. "Alfonso is the hero of the hour. He, and his beautiful husband, Gabriel, who was so helpful last night." Jonathan looked at Alfonso and winked. "My dear Alfonso. And your Angel Gabriel."

Alfonso laughed.

"Husband?" asked Dominic with embarrassment. "Oh my. I hadn't realized—"

"Oh, Dominic," said Jonathan teasingly. "As far as the Spanish police force is concerned, Alfonso is their motorbike queen of the road." He turned to Alfonso. "Now, we must do something to repay both of you for your sweet kindness. Why don't we take you out for a meal tonight? We can call you when we get back to the apartment—"

"Jonathan," interrupted Dominic. "Shut up, please. There's something I need to tell you. We don't have any mobile phones at the moment. Or a laptop for that matter. Last night we were burgled."

Jonathan paused as he buttoned his shirt.

"Burgled? Our apartment?" He sat down on the bed and sighed. "Oh, Dominic. Not another one of your adventures. I thought we'd had more than enough last year, when that ghastly Downpatrick woman and her henchman tried to kill you. We could do without this just now."

Alfonso stepped forward. "Gabriel and I can help you replace your mobile phones, if you like," he said. "It will be much easier for us, as we speak Spanish. Then you'll be equipped for your trip to America."

"That would be so helpful, Alfonso," said Dominic. "Are you sure?"

"Of course." Alfonso smiled, reaching into his jacket and pulling out a card. "Here. This is our address. It's no more than ten minutes away. Get a taxi. I'll ride on ahead, and we'll meet you there. Gabriel will make you one of his famous *desayunos* while I call the phone company."

Jonathan jumped off the bed and threw his arms around Alfonso and Dominic. "What did I tell you, Dominic? There's no end to this man's generosity. Together, we are the three caballeros. Invincible!"

The two men laughed as Jonathan tried to lead them in a clumsy approximation of a kick line dance. There was a clatter as the doors to the ward burst open. A woman wearing a white doctor's coat strode in. Her chestnut-brown hair was secured in a tight knot on the top of her head, and there was a severe expression on her face.

"¿Qué está pasando aqui?" she demanded.

Luis, who had been watching and laughing from the nurses' station, hastily stepped forward. "Señores, this is Doctor Jurado. I asked her to come here especially early to assess Jonathan."

"Good morning, gentlemen," said Doctor Jurado, the hint of a smile forming on her face. "Which one was the acrobat in the sex club last night?"

"Acrobat in a sex club?" repeated Dominic, turning to Jonathan. "Just what did happen at XXL?"

IT WAS shortly before eight o'clock when Dominic and Jonathan's taxi collected them from the hospital. Doctor Jurado quickly declared Jonathan fit to be discharged but advised him to return immediately if he felt dizzy or nauseous. As soon as the taxi set off, Jonathan began to apologize again. Dominic stopped him before he could get into full flow.

"Jonathan, can we forget about last night for a while? It's true we've got a lot to talk about. We're going to have to do it soon. But not just yet. I'm really worried about the break-in. I think someone's targeted us. And they might come back."

"But surely they're not going to bother us again?" replied Jonathan. "Not now they've got your phone with the message from your German lover on it?"

"Bernhardt is not my lover," said Dominic, irritated at the phrase. "Last night, Karl Michael said the message would only make sense 'in conjunction with me.' That's why I'm worried they might come back."

Dominic turned to face his husband.

"There's something that Karl Michael said, and it scares me." Dominic rested his hand on Jonathan's arm.

"What was that?" asked Jonathan.

"He said that others would need my help in deciphering the message," replied Dominic. "I'm worried about what Karl Michael and Bernhardt are involved in. And I wish Bernhardt had never sent me the text."

Dominic leaned back in the seat and looked out the window. The car was passing some of Barcelona's finest buildings. The taxi stopped for a moment by the stunning Gaudi architecture of Casa Milà. Normally Dominic would be transfixed by it. This morning he was too annoyed and distracted.

"So what did the message say?" persisted Jonathan.

"That's the trouble. I can't remember. It was just a series of numbers." Dominic turned away from the window to look back at Jonathan as a thought crossed his mind.

"Oh, but now I remember. Karl Michael was supposed to come and see me last night. When we left the beach, I invited him to come back to the apartment and get the message off my phone. But he said he wouldn't come straightaway. He had something important to do first. He was supposed to come over later, but he never did."

Dominic took Jonathan's arm. "I completely forgot, what with Alfonso turning up in the middle of the night with the news about you."

"Perhaps he'd already been," said Jonathan grimly. "Perhaps young Karl Michael got impatient, went straight to the apartment while you were searching for me, stole both the phones, not knowing which was yours, and took the laptop for good measure."

Dominic turned to look out the window again. Their taxi had entered an elegant suburb of Barcelona. The apartment buildings on either side were modern and sophisticated. Trees lined the boulevard. As they waited at a stoplight, Dominic saw a charming pavement café with several well-dressed people sitting outside, taking coffee in the early morning sunshine.

"But it makes no sense," said Dominic, envying the carefree scene. "Before we left the beach, we made an agreement to help each other. We shook hands on it. Karl Michael said he would help me find you, and I agreed to help him find Bernhardt."

Dominic turned to his husband and rested his hand on Jonathan's chest. "No, Jonathan. I think something's happened. And it worries me a lot."

Jonathan leaned across and kissed Dominic on the lips.

"Don't you worry, my almost perfect English husband," he said. "Your white knight has now returned, and he will protect you." Jonathan leaned across again to kiss Dominic once more but was flung forward violently as the taxi came to an abrupt halt.

"Hemos llegado," announced the taxi driver. And then in a lower voice added, "Putos maricones!"

"Are we here already?" asked Dominic absently, looking out the window at the imposing gates of a modern apartment complex.

"That's what our foul-mouthed little taxi driver just said," replied Jonathan angrily.

"Now what's the matter?" asked Dominic as he reached for his wallet.

"Just when I thought we were making progress," continued Jonathan, unbuckling his seat belt and slamming the car door open. "That little worm just called us dirty faggots. I thought we'd got past all that." He turned to Dominic. "Don't give him a tip, my love. In fact, let's simply show him what he's missing out on."

Jonathan pushed Dominic back against the seat in a passionate embrace.

Chapter 17

DOMINIC WAS overwhelmed by the scale and elegance of Alfonso and Gabriel's apartment. On their arrival, Alfonso greeted them enthusiastically at the door. He led the way down a wide entrance hall, its walls lined with extravagant twentieth century artwork. The entrance hall emerged into a vast, high-ceilinged reception room. There was a mezzanine floor suspended at the far end. A wall to the left was partly given over to tall glass doors. These opened onto a long balcony overlooking the city. Everywhere, Dominic could see fabulous pieces of art, paintings, sculptures, and glassware. He looked down to admire the fine art deco rugs scattered across the white and black tiled floor.

"¡Hola, amigo!" called a voice from the mezzanine floor in front of them. "You must be the famous Dominic I've heard so much about."

Dominic looked up and saw a tall, broad-shouldered man in his early thirties. He was wearing a white shirt, open at the neck, with sand colored chinos belted around a narrow waist. His wavy black hair was well-groomed, and his smile displayed gleaming white teeth. His bare feet padded on the wooden spiral staircase as he descended rapidly to greet Dominic.

"I'm so pleased to meet you. I am Alfonso's husband, Gabriel." He grasped Dominic's shoulders and kissed him on either cheek.

"Can I get you some coffee?" said Gabriel after their embrace. "Breakfast?"

Dominic shook his head. "Coffee would be lovely, but we really don't want to put you to so much trouble—"

"I'm famished!" interrupted Jonathan, stepping forward. "Breakfast would be perfect, my dear Angel Gabriel. Especially after a night in hospital." He embraced Gabriel and kissed him passionately on both cheeks. "I'm Jonathan, Dominic's husband," he added proudly.

Gabriel laughed. "How could I possibly forget so quickly, Jonathan? I'll go start fixing some coffee. Please make yourselves comfortable." He went into the kitchen, and a few moments later they heard the sounds of an espresso machine hissing into action.

Dominic crossed the floor to a large glass-fronted display cabinet on the far wall. On its middle shelf sat an angular black-and-chrome cocktail shaker, surrounded by eight cocktail glasses. To the side were a glass olive bowl, silver cocktail stirrer, and chrome ice bucket.

"You have a marvelous collection of art deco," he called to Gabriel with admiration. "My little collection at home pales into insignificance by comparison."

Gabriel reemerged from the kitchen, carrying a circular black-and-chrome tray. On it were two small cups of espresso and a sugar bowl. Dominic noticed Gabriel was now wearing an apron emblazoned with the words Rennie Mackintosh Museum, Glasgow in large letters.

"I'm so pleased to know you are a fellow fan," Gabriel said, setting the tray down on a glass-topped coffee table. "I've been collecting since I was fifteen. My father is chairman of the Banco España Nacional and gave me an allowance," he added by way of explanation for his expensive hobby. "But he doesn't share my passion for art deco. He calls it vulgar." Gabriel wrinkled his nose in distaste at the comment.

"Your father doesn't approve of a lot of things you like," said Alfonso, walking across to Gabriel and putting an arm around his waist. "Including me." He looked at Gabriel and arched an eyebrow. "I don't know why you continue to work with him in that tediously boring place."

Gabriel laughed and gestured at the apartment. "Because it pays for this, my husband." He turned back to Dominic.

"Alfonso just brought me a most exquisite bronze statue. Come and see. I have it on the mezzanine. I am deciding where to display it."

Dominic followed Gabriel as he strode up the spiral staircase two at a time. At the top was a sunlit library, the walls lined with books. Light streamed in from three large skylights filtered by electrically operated blinds.

Gabriel reached into one of the shelves, picked up the bronze statue, and presented it to Dominic.

"Here. Isn't he beautiful? My perfect Adam."

JEFF LAY back on the large black leather couch, a beer in his hand. Next to him sat Nick, hunched over Tanya's laptop, checking and rechecking multiple log-in sequences for the banking service networks of WRI. The vast loft space was lit by the warm glow of LED lights, discreetly embedded in the six wrought-iron columns that supported the roof structure. A vinyl copy of *Electric Dreams* by the guitarist John McLaughlin played softly in the background.

Jeff took a swig of his beer and turned to Nick. "The call's about to start. All good?"

Nick nodded. "The log-in sequences are all there, as far as I can tell. I don't want to do any more work on them. We need to hand this over to China now. They'll be able to create a permanent, secure pathway that will remain undetectable. They can keep it dormant until the Ninety-Nine's ready for the assault." He looked up at Jeff. "Let's get on with it. I'm fucking done in, and we've got the hackfest starting tomorrow."

Jeff initiated the call on his iPad. He turned off John McLaughlin and switched the conference call to the main speakers in the loft. Within a few minutes, they heard the rest of Charter Ninety-Nine, confirming they were online.

"Why hasn't Germany checked in?" asked East Coast.

"We'll hold on a few moments more," replied Jeff. "I don't want him missing this. Besides, we need an update on the DG chip. I want to know if he's got any news. The British guy's landed here in San Francisco, and we're tracking him."

At that moment, there was a click on the conference call, and a distorted voice began speaking.

"This is West Coast," interrupted Jeff. "Could you repeat, please? The sound's pretty shit."

There was a pause, then "Hello, West Coast. This is Germany checking in." The sound was still badly distorted, but the voice was just about audible.

"Okay, we're all here," said Jeff. "I'll be brief. There's been a breakthrough today. We've now got a way into the global bank networks. China, you've got some work to do, but we're confident you'll build us a tunnel, ready for the assault. This new development, coupled with Britannia's success on personal records, means we should be ready to launch the assault, maybe sooner than we planned."

"Hey, just a minute," said East Coast. "Aren't we forgetting something? This whole thing could get blown out the water if we don't get the DG chip back. And what's happened to the Originator? Do we even know he's still on our side?"

There was a crackle on the call as a voice interrupted. "Germany here. We're close to securing the DG chip. We've obtained information sent by the Originator that should lead us to it very soon. West Coast? We may need your help on this."

Jeff took another swig of his beer and set the bottle down on the floor. "Sure. What do you need?"

"The Originator made contact with a British man called Delingpole," continued the voice on the speaker. "He's currently in Spain. But we've now learned he's flying to San Francisco tomorrow. We believe he may have the DG chip. If we fail to intercept him before he flies, you must take over when he lands there."

Jeff looked across at Nick. "Is he linked with this other British guy, Steve Brown? If so, we're already on to him."

"It's possible," replied Germany. "We'll find out what we can in the next twelve hours. But I have a question for the group. What if the DG chip is already destroyed? We may have to go ahead with the assault without it installed. Be prepared for that. We know the Originator never copied it. Deliberately. It's unique."

Jeff sighed. "Germany, you know as well as we do that it's taken five years to build the DG chip. Once in place, it has the power to help us change the course of world events. It's essential if our global rewriting of personal records is to succeed. You warned us before—if we launch the assault without the DG chip, we're certain the assault will fizzle out in a few days, if not hours." He looked across to Nick again, who nodded in agreement.

"Which means," cut in the voice of East Coast, "you gotta get that DG chip back. And if you have to, use extreme force."

DOMINIC HELD the finely formed statue of Adam and turned it slowly. He caressed its smooth surface while his mind desperately tried to recall the exact detail of the message he had received from Bernhardt the day before.

Turn to the feet of Adam

And there was a set of numbers and a date. If only he still had his phone. If only he could remember those numbers. His fingers explored around the base of the statue, gently rubbing across the sculpted feet of the figure. Then he held it up to the light and peered at the figure closely.

"He's beautiful, isn't he?" said Gabriel. He watched proudly as Dominic scrutinized his latest acquisition. "I think he's from Germany, probably early 1930s."

Dominic had now turned the statue completely upside down. The base of it was about five inches square and half an inch thick, with a narrow step on each edge. Dominic gently slid his thumbnail around the step.

"What have you got there, my love?" Jonathan strode up the spiral staircase, two at a time, to join Dominic and Gabriel on the mezzanine floor. Alfonso followed a few paces behind him.

"Oh my," continued Jonathan as he saw the look on Dominic's face. "I can see you're in love again." He turned to Alfonso with a knowing look. "My husband has found another art deco romantic in darling Gabriel."

"No, Jonathan, it's more than that." Dominic turned to his husband, his eyes wide with excitement. "Jonathan, this is a statue of Adam. Gabriel has just acquired it."

He held it out, and Jonathan took it in his hands. He weighed it for a moment and then turned it over a couple of times.

"Very pretty," he said. "No fig leaf? Very daring." He turned to Alfonso. "Far too risqué to be British." Alfonso laughed and nodded in agreement.

"But Jonathan," said Dominic excitedly. "Bernhardt's text. It said, 'Turn to the feet of Adam.' What if this was the Adam he was referring to?"

Jonathan laughed and handed the figure back to his husband.

"I'm sorry, my love. I think you're clutching at straws. Why would Bernhardt send you a text about a statue that belongs to Gabriel?"

"Bernhardt?" asked Alfonso sharply. He turned to Dominic. "Who is Bernhardt?"

Dominic looked embarrassed for a moment. "Bernhardt Freude. He's just a friend of mine from Germany. We knew each other long ago. He was driving down to meet us here as he couldn't make it to the wedding. Yesterday I received a strange text from him. And since then I've heard nothing."

Alfonso reached out and gently took the statue from Dominic. Then he looked up at Gabriel. "Gabriel, can I have a word with you in private for a moment?" He turned to Dominic and Jonathan. "Please excuse us, gentlemen. I mean no disrespect, but there is something that Gabriel and I must discuss alone."

The two men descended the staircase. Dominic and Jonathan leaned over the handrail of the mezzanine floor and watched as Gabriel and Alfonso walked out onto the balcony.

Jonathan looked across to Dominic and raised his arm. "Something wrong with my deodorant today?" he asked and turned his head to sniff his armpit. When Dominic rolled his eyes, he lowered his arm and draped it over Dominic's shoulder.

"Anyway, my love," he continued as he pulled Dominic toward him and slipped his hands around his waist. "Could you see anything on the bottom of that statue? I could certainly see something on the front. He was very well-endowed. Just like my own beautiful—"

"Jonathan, not here," interrupted Dominic. He placed his own hands over Jonathan's and intertwined their fingers.

"You know, I was almost ready to pack my bag and go home last night." Dominic leaned his forehead on Jonathan's. "I was very angry with you. But I was also worried you might have been kidnapped." He lifted his head to look closely into Jonathan's eyes. "Then I find you were in that god-awful nightclub. I can't put up with this much longer, Jonathan. This could be the shortest marriage ever."

Jonathan opened his mouth to speak but closed it again as he heard feet ascending the spiral staircase. Instead, he pulled Dominic close and kissed him tenderly on the lips.

"Adam appears to have inspired love in my art deco Garden of Eden," Gabriel said with a laugh as he reached the top of the stairs.

Dominic looked around awkwardly, Jonathan's arms still wrapped around his waist. Jonathan began to nibble at his ear.

Alfonso put his arm on Gabriel's shoulder as he joined his husband at the top of the stairs.

"Adorable! The lovebirds on their honeymoon." He turned to Gabriel. "Do you think we should leave them alone again for a bit longer?"

"No," said Gabriel, holding out the statue of Adam. "We need to explain where this beautiful bronze man came from." He turned to Alfonso. "Tell them what you just told me."

Chapter 18

STEVE LAY on the bed in his guesthouse bedroom, exhausted but wide-awake. It was 3:00 a.m. in San Francisco but 11:00 a.m. in London. And Steve was on London time. Nick had dropped him off at the guesthouse just over an hour ago. It was a traditional-looking timber-clad building close to Coit Tower. Steve had booked it through GayBnB. He chose it because it was a short walk from the location for the hackfest. As he had walked up the short flight of wooden steps to the front door, he had wondered what kind of welcome he might receive for being so late.

After several minutes of ringing the bell, the door was opened by a genial bear of a man, who introduced himself as Anders. He dismissed Nick's apologies for being delayed, welcomed him in, and closed the door. As he led the way down a gloomy corridor, he explained he liked to play his guitar late into the night and smoke a joint or two. Anders was originally from Finland. He was an easygoing man about fifty years old. He had long thick hair that was almost white and tied in a ponytail, and a white beard.

Anders invited Steve into a comfortably shabby sitting room, lined with books and furnished with large scruffy settees covered by multicolored throws. He offered Steve a joint and a cup of mint tea, and they talked intermittently while Anders improvised a tune on his guitar. After an hour, Steve thanked him for his hospitality and headed for his bedroom, leaving Anders still strumming the guitar.

The bedroom was large and furnished with dark wood furniture. Steve threw his clothes on the floor and climbed into the king-size bed set against the wall opposite a large sash window. He turned out the bedside light and attempted to get some sleep.

As he lay in the darkness, desperate to sleep, he realized the joint he had smoked had failed to relax him as he had hoped. Besides, the puzzle of his father's missing computer records irritated him, and he could not dismiss it from his mind. Worse, he was feeling increasingly sore underneath his cock after the encounter with Nick in the front seat of the Tesla.

Annoyed, Steve sat up, turned the bedside light back on, threw back the covers, and examined his crotch. Contorting himself in front of the lamp, he could see a red mark below his cock. When he slid his fingers over the mark, he could feel it was raised and sore, like a large insect bite.

"Jesus, what was that fucker doing?" muttered Steve to himself. He pressed a little harder on the raised area and felt a sharp pain.

"Shit, you bastard," he continued, and he threw himself back on the pillow, gingerly massaging the pain away with his fingertips. "I'm not even going to be able to wank myself to sleep tonight."

After several minutes, the pain subsided. Steve sat up, reached for his laptop, and connected it to the Wi-Fi, using the code Anders had given him earlier.

As he prepared to resume the search for his father's online records, a message flashed up on the screen.

There you are at last. We need to talk. Urgently. Dominic needs your help.

Steve set the laptop to one side, climbed off the bed, and reached for his backpack. After a few moments, he found headphones, plugged them into the laptop, and made himself comfortable on the bed.

"Good morning, young man!" Jonathan's voice rattled the tiny earphones, and Steve hurried to turn down the volume. "How splendid to see you," Jonathan continued. "And with no clothes on! An extra treat for us." On his laptop screen, Steve could see the faces of four men smiling back at him. Hurriedly, he switched off his computer's camera.

"What's the matter?" asked Jonathan in his ears. "You're not shy all of a sudden, are you? And I'd promised our dear Spanish friends you'd give us a floor show as well."

Steve could hear giggles in the background. "Fuck off, Jonathan. Do you know what time it is here?"

"I do, my dear," replied Jonathan. "Which is why I did you the courtesy of not telephoning. But I rather hoped you might be geeking on the interweb. And of course I was right."

Steve had no chance to reply as Jonathan continued in full flight.

"So, young Steve, Dominic has got us into a big adventure again. When all we wanted was a quiet honeymoon in the sun. I'll start from the beginning—"

"Jonathan, will you shut up, please," Dominic's voice cut in. His face appeared on the screen. He looked somber, and Steve could see a tension in the body language between him and Jonathan.

"Steve," said Dominic. "My mobile's been stolen, and it's got a very important text message on it. Are you able to retrieve it somehow?"

Steve thought for a moment. "How big is this big adventure, Dominic? If it's like the last one, we shouldn't be speaking on an open system like this."

There was a pause at the other end. Finally, Dominic replied, "You're right. Do what you need to do."

A FEW minutes later, Steve reestablished a connection with Dominic on an encrypted voice link.

"The answer is yes," said Steve, "but it will take me a while. I need your telco, your phone number, your address, and your billing ID. You can type them into this secure link."

"I can't remember my billing ID. How am I going to get that?" asked Dominic. "I'm in Spain at the moment. All my paperwork is back in the apartment in England."

Before Steve could answer, Jonathan's voice interrupted. "Oh, even I know the answer to that, my dear. It'll all be online. Just go and check one of your old emails. I'm sorry, Steve," Jonathan continued. "Dominic can be remarkably old-fashioned sometimes."

Steve heard a few moments of angry whispered conversation. Then Dominic's voice spoke in his ear. "Steve, how long do you think it will take?"

"Not long if it's a recent message," Steve replied. "Give me half an hour."

Steve waited, expecting to hear more.

"Tell me," he said finally. "Are you going to let me know what the fuck's going on? Or am I just playing the part of your handy techno subcontractor again?"

"I'm sorry, Steve." Dominic was abrupt. "I'll get the information for you right now and post it here. Then, when you find the message, call us back. We'll tell you more, I promise."

DOMINIC SANK back into the black leather upholstery of the chrome-framed couch, thinking over what Alfonso had told him twenty minutes before. The news of Bernhardt's death had been a shock. He looked across at Alfonso.

"Will I need to identify his body?"

Alfonso shook his head. "I doubt it. From what I've seen on the police reports, they've confirmed his identity, and a relative is flying in to Barcelona to formally identify him. I think it's his sister, but I can check."

Dominic sat up. "Anna's coming?" he asked. "Oh, poor woman. I should be with her."

Alfonso stood up, walked around to the back of the couch, and laid a hand on Dominic's shoulder.

"She's not coming until Saturday," said Alfonso. "By which time you'll be in San Francisco."

Dominic slumped back into the couch again. "I could really do without that at the moment."

Jonathan leaned across and rested a hand on Dominic's knee.

"Lover, I think it's exactly what you need right now. A Californian wedding. It will be fun. Anyway," Jonathan continued, "we need to meet up with Steve in San Francisco. Then we can find out what's going on with this secret message from Bernhardt."

Dominic pushed Jonathan's hand away. "You can go if you want, Jonathan. It doesn't take two of us. And anyway, it's your friends getting married. I've never met them before."

Alfonso looked across at Gabriel, who picked up the statue from the table. "Why don't you make some coffee for us all, Alfonso?" Gabriel stood up. "Meanwhile, I'll have a look at Adam here and see what I can find."

Gabriel carried the statue over to the balcony and began to examine it closely in the daylight. Alfonso walked to the kitchen.

Jonathan leaned across to Dominic. "I'm sorry, my love. You've had a really bad shock, and I'm being insensitive. On top of that, I was rude just then. Really, I was simply trying to be funny. Will you forgive me?"

"Forgiveness is easy, Jonathan. Forgetting is harder," Dominic replied. He stood and looked down at his husband for several moments before he spoke.

"Yes, you were rude, Jonathan," he said. "But you know it's not the first time. Whenever you ignore me, or you ignore what's important to me. Whenever you belittle me in front of people or fuck someone else—" Dominic searched for the words he wanted to say next. "We're on our honeymoon, Jonathan. Yes, it's been wonderful. Well, to start with. You were wonderful. You made me feel special, and I hope I made you feel special. But since all this has happened—"

Jonathan stood and faced Dominic. His eyes were wide, and he was breathing deeply.

"And how do you think I felt," he said, "when some little German shit tells me my husband was fucking his partner just two weeks before our wedding? Do you think I felt special then?"

Dominic was lost for words. He paused. He wanted to keep his voice calm and steady when he finally spoke.

"Jonathan," he began. "I've told you several times that Karl Michael is lying. Bernhardt and I had nothing more than a friendship and a business relationship. I've also promised to tell you all about Bernhardt. But it's got to be when the moment's right—"

"And when will the moment be right?" interrupted Jonathan.

Dominic could no longer contain his anger. "He's dead, Jonathan! Don't you understand?" Dominic closed his eyes and looked away. "I don't know what I'm feeling right now." He took a deep breath before he looked back at his husband. "If you continue to push me like this, you're going to push me away." He sat down on the couch.

"Perhaps," said Dominic finally, "I should never have accepted your marriage proposal in the first place."

Before Jonathan could reply, there was a shout from Gabriel.

"I've done it!" said Gabriel. "I've found something hidden in the base of this statue. Come and take a look."

IT TOOK Steve less than twenty minutes to find the message store for Dominic's mobile phone number. He felt proud at breaking yet another personal database hacking record. Steve relished the challenge of breaching the security of corporate systems, and he was always careful to leave no trace of his visit. He was already familiar with Dominic's telco, having hacked into it twice before. He was grateful to note the company had failed to strengthen its security since his last visits.

"Hey, Dominic. I've got the message," said Steve after he reestablished the secure video link on his laptop. "Now. Are you going to tell me what this is all about?"

Dominic's face appeared on the screen. He looked downcast, and his voice was subdued.

"Of course," Dominic replied, holding a small object close to the camera for Steve to see. "But before I do, have you any idea what this is?"

Steve peered at the grainy image on his laptop screen. It was about half an inch square, black, with a series of silver studs around its edge. It was wrapped in a clear plastic film, through which some white printing was visible.

"Looks like a memory chip, or a module for a computer," he replied after a brief examination. "Can you hold it still?"

"Excuse me" came Jonathan's voice. "I know you'll think it stupid, Dominic. You usually do. But I've got an idea."

There was a blur of activity as hands moved backward and forward in front of the laptop camera. Finally the hands cleared, and Steve could clearly see a bronze statue of a male nude, apparently standing close to the laptop's camera lens. In the statue's hand nestled the memory chip. Steve took a snapshot of the image, enlarged it, and then rotated it to read some white characters printed on the surface of the chip.

"That's very strange." Steve began to search through pages of serial numbers on the internet. "Where did you get this from?" he asked as he read through a specification sheet on his screen.

"It's quite a long story," began Dominic. "I think it belonged to a close friend of mine from Germany. He was driving from Berlin to meet me here in Spain. The memory chip was hidden inside a small statue."

Dominic paused for a moment, took a deep breath, and continued, "A friend of ours, a Spanish police officer, found the statue. It was in the wreck of my friend's car. He was killed in an accident not far from Barcelona."

Dominic's voice faltered, and Steve switched his screen back to the camera view of the statue.

"Are you all right, Dominic?"

There was a pause. "Not really," Dominic replied, "But I'm sure I'll get over it." Dominic coughed and cleared his throat before he went on. "You said something about it being strange. What did you mean?"

Steve flicked his screen back to the specification sheet he had been reading. "This chip isn't commercially available, as far as I can see," he said. "It's bespoke. Made by a specialist company in China. They usually make stuff for the military or the world's space agencies."

The Deadly Lies

He sat back and thought for a moment. "Do you know what's on it?" he asked finally.

"No idea," replied Dominic. "The only reason I knew anything about it is because my friend, Bernhardt, had sent me a strange text message on his way here to Spain. That's the message I wanted you to retrieve. What did it say?"

Steve leaned over his laptop and brought up another internet page. "Oh yes, the message," he said. "It's certainly weird. Here it is."

Steve copied and pasted the text into the secure message window:
41 38 36.91 68 88 13 53.09 76
Turn to the feet of Adam
03152621
June 1

"Oh, I get it," said Steve as he studied his screen. "So that's a statue of Adam. But what does the rest of it mean?"

"Well, you're the computer whiz," came Jonathan's voice. "We need you to answer that."

The statue disappeared from the screen, and Jonathan's face loomed into view, wearing a broad smile.

"And in just over a day's time, my dear Steve, it will be May 31, and we'll be joining you in San Francisco. Then you'll have this little chip thingy to play with to your heart's content."

"Jonathan," said Steve with irritation. "Could you butt out the way so I can talk to Dominic?"

Jonathan shuffled out of view, grumbling, and Dominic's face appeared again on Steve's laptop screen.

"Can you help us, Steve?" asked Dominic. "Too much has happened in the last twenty-four hours. I don't know what this is about, but Bernhardt's lover was here in Spain, and he warned me to be careful. Then he disappeared, and our apartment was burgled, and our phones and laptop were stolen. Now I find that Bernhardt's been killed on his way to bring me this memory chip. I really don't…." Dominic looked away from the camera.

"Don't worry, mate," Steve said briskly. "I'll sort things out."

He started typing into the secure message window.

"This is the number of a mobile phone I've got here in the States," Steve said as he typed. "Nobody else knows about it. Get yourselves sorted with mobiles and text me so I've got your number. Keep that memory chip well hidden."

Steve looked up at the screen.

"And take care, mate."

Chapter 19

EARLY MORNING sunlight streamed through the skylight windows of 101 Grain Street. Jeff Woodfield shielded his eyes as he padded across the wooden floor of the loft space and headed for the large, airy kitchen to his beloved espresso machine. It was 6:00 a.m., a few hours after the call with Charter Ninety-Nine. He was usually an early riser, even when he was late to bed the night before. Today there was much to do. It was the first day of the hackfest, and for the first time, he planned to leave it entirely in Nick's hands.

Jeff intended to make only an occasional guest appearance in front of the admiring audience of geeks and programmers. Then he would withdraw to think through more pressing matters. He needed time to revise the plans for the assault, to consider the Ninety-Nine's options now that the Originator had disappeared. And of course, there were the British connections to deal with.

Preparing his first caffeine hit of the day, Jeff pressed the button on the coffee grinder. He needed a strong shot today, so he carefully measured the freshly ground coffee into a chrome filter holder, locked it securely in the head of the espresso machine, placed two espresso cups under the twin nozzle, and released the steam valve. The coffee's rich aroma filled his nostrils, and he inhaled deeply.

"Hey, made enough for two?"

Jeff looked around to see Nick walk naked into the kitchen.

"Do you want coffee or a blow job?" Jeff smiled, admiring the tumescent end of Nick's hardened cock.

"Both would be good," Nick replied, absently scratching his back with one hand and his cock with the other. He yawned, walked over to stand behind Jeff, and wrapped his arms around him. He slid his hands across Jeff's bare chest and gently toyed with his nipple rings.

Jeff turned off the steam valve and reached behind to wrap his hand around Nick's erection. "Well, the coffee's made, so don't let it get cold. Drink up. Then I'll take care of this for you."

He squeezed hard and got an appreciative groan from Nick in response. After one more squeeze, he let go and reached for a tablet computer that lay on the countertop. He picked it up and swiped through several screens until he came to a map.

"And while you're drinking it," said Jeff, holding the computer in one hand and picking up a cup of coffee with the other, "you can tell me where our young British friend ended up last night and prove to me your little tracking device is working."

Nick sighed, took the coffee and tablet computer from Jeff, and walked away from the kitchen. He set his coffee cup down on a low metal table and stretched out full-length on the leather couch. Jeff followed and knelt down on the floor beside him. He reached forward and began working Nick's cock with his hands, cupping the balls and sliding his tongue around their circumference. Nick groaned but continued the task Jeff had assigned him.

"He's on the move," Nick announced after a few moments. Jeff paused as he drew his tongue up the length of Nick's cock.

"Where's he off to?"

Nick scanned through the history log of the tracker.

"He stayed at that place where I dropped him last night, a couple of blocks from here," replied Nick. "About ten minutes ago, he set off, heading toward Route 101. He's not coming here. And I reckon he's in a vehicle. Oh fuck—" He dropped the tablet computer as Jeff took Nick's cock deep inside his mouth.

Nick lay back on the couch and thrust his pelvis upward. As Jeff pumped his mouth rhythmically up and down, Nick's moans of appreciation increased in volume. Suddenly Jeff pulled back and looked at Nick with a grin.

"I'll finish that in a moment," he said and reached across for the discarded computer. "You've got some work to do first."

Nick groaned with disappointment, took the tablet from Jeff's outstretched hand, and slumped back on the couch.

"You sure know how to edge me," said Nick, staring at the screen. He looked up. "Why are you fucking with me this morning?"

Jeff reached forward and slid one hand tenderly over the curls of hair on Nick's chest. The other he used to gently massage a spot just below Nick's balls.

"I'm not fucking with you," said Jeff, "but I do want to bring you right to the edge. Then when you finally come"—Jeff leaned forward—"you're going to explode." Once again he took Nick's cock in his mouth.

"Wait, wait, wait." Nick sat up, his hand resting on Jeff's head. "I can't handle this." He cupped his hand under Jeff's chin and lifted it up and away from his cock.

"I've gotta tell you, sexy guy. You've always given good head. And I know you're gonna do so this morning. But you also gotta know, our British friend has just arrived at the Saint Francis Memorial Hospital."

THE TRIAGE nurse was a cute young Venezuelan called Alejandro. Tight ringlets of black hair covered his head. His long eyelashes curled up at the tips and looked almost fake. He sat with Steve in one of several small examination cubicles that formed part of the emergency room at Saint Francis Memorial Hospital. Steve described his symptoms to Alejandro and, unbidden, went on to recount what had happened in the front seat of the Tesla the night before.

The Venezuelan's eyelashes flickered as he rapidly scribbled notes.

"And you think that this man may have…." Alejandro paused, seeming to consider the best English expression to use.

"I don't know what he did, mate, but it's throbbing like crazy now," replied Steve. "And not in a good way," he added as the triage nurse's eyes widened.

"Will you permit me to examine you?" Alejandro stood up. "Please, lie down on the bed here, and I will prepare."

Steve needed no second invitation. He stood up and pulled off his loose-fitting sweatpants to reveal he was wearing no underwear. Steve had decided that any layers of clothing were chafing and too uncomfortable. He lay back on the bed and tried to avoid getting an erection during the examination by the young male nurse. He forced himself to think of Margaret Thatcher.

"I'm glad to see you're already shaved," Alejandro said as he carefully inspected Steve's groin. "We'll probably need to take an ultrasound scan, and you've made that real easy for us."

"Happy to oblige, mate," replied Steve, lifting his head off the bed to wink at the nurse.

Alejandro looked back at Steve and smiled. "Does this hurt?" He pressed with two gloved fingers a little below the base of Steve's penis.

"Fuck, yes," responded Steve, recoiling from Alejandro's inspection. "It's like someone's hammered a fuckin' nail in!"

"I apologize." Alejandro sat back and removed his gloves. He stood up and walked across to a small sink, where he washed his hands.

"I believe there is some kind of small, hard object in your perineum," said Alejandro as he dried his hands. "It's about four or five millimeters in size. The doctor will probably want to scan it first. Then we can consider how to remove it."

Steve sat up, rested his hands on his knees, and peered down at his crotch.

"Does that mean you're going to operate?" He stared at Alejandro. "How long am I going to have to stay here?"

"It seems to be just below the surface," replied the nurse. "I'm sure it will be a simple procedure. You'll be discharged in a few hours if everything goes okay. We're not busy this time of the morning."

"Procedure?" Steve groaned. "That means anesthetic and needles and knives and stuff." He looked down at his crotch once more. "Am I ever going to fuck again?"

NICK LAY stretched out on the black leather couch, his hands tucked behind his head, a broad grin on his face. As he peered down the length of his torso, he could see his erect penis slowly beginning to detumesce. He could feel the last waves of orgasm ebb away, and he released a deep sigh as the muscles throughout his body relaxed.

Jeff walked back from the kitchen, a glass of freshly squeezed orange juice in one hand and a towel in the other. He set the glass on the table beside Nick and looked down at his partner's body.

"How was your hackfest wake-up call?" he asked, and he tipped his head and smiled. "Did I hit the spot for you?"

Nick sighed again, a long, contented sigh.

"Fuck yes," he replied. "You sure know how to milk a guy dry. I could lie here all day."

A towel landed on Nick's face, and he slowly reached for it with one hand. "I guess that means you want me up and about now." He dragged the towel down to his cock and began cleaning up.

"Damn right," said Jeff. "Plenty of work to be done today. Fortran and Cobol will be here soon. Then we've got the interns arriving, the caterers, and then the eager delegates will be at the doors, ready for us to start in just a couple of hours."

Jeff squatted down alongside Nick and kissed him long and slow on the lips. "And you, my computer prince," he said, running his hand over the hair on Nick's chest. "You are in charge. I'll be around, but this is your show."

He kissed Nick once more, then stood and walked across to a set of sliding glass doors, where the sunlight was streaming in. He opened the doors and stepped out onto a balcony that gave a view over the bay.

"Get your ass out here!" Jeff called back through the open doors. "I need to brief you, and I don't want to risk some damn bug picking up what we've got to say."

Nick gave his cock one last dab, threw the towel on the floor, picked up the glass of orange juice, and took a long drink. He stood and padded across the floor. Jeff watched as his partner sauntered onto the balcony.

"I can see you've been working those upper arms again," Jeff said admiringly. "You can put them to good use later. I need a massage."

He sat at a round wooden table on the balcony. "Now, to business. Who've we got coming?"

Nick listed the delegates for Jeff. "Ten code writers. Ten system architects. Five data analysts. Five fiction writers. Five creative writers, ten storyboard artists, and five assorted composers and lyricists. Fifty in total."

"What the fuck's a 'creative writer'?" asked Jeff. "I thought all writers were supposed to be creative."

"It's what they call them in the industry these days." Nick pulled out a chair and sat opposite Jeff. "Dunno why. Perhaps it makes them feel special."

Jeff rolled his eyes. "Well, as long as they're not constrained by some corporate straitjacket mentality. We want them to think big. Think broad. In a few months, when the assault happens, we need people who can dream the impossible."

Nick leaned back in his chair and absently scratched the hollow of his chest, between his well-defined pectoral muscles. "If it's only a few months away," he said. "We can't recruit too many from this lot. The clearance will take too long."

Jeff leaned forward and rested his arms on the table.

"How many d'you think we can take? Six? Seven?"

Nick shook his head. "I'd say four or five tops. The risk is too great otherwise. Now that the DG chip is missing, we've got to be on our guard against infiltration."

"Okay," said Jeff. "I'll go with that. Now. You're running the hackfest this year. Tell me what you're going to do."

Nick stopped scratching and lifted his hand to show four fingers. "So, there are four sections to each day. Briefing, pitching, building, and presenting. The main theme is storytelling."

He stood and began pacing the balcony as he outlined the plan for the hackfest. "We start by telling them their brief is to tell and retell stories in new and different ways. We tell them we're looking for the next big internet storytelling platform. We want audiences to engage, to share, to be part of a global narrative—"

"Good, good," interrupted Jeff. "Meanwhile, you'll monitor the coders and data analysts. The bored ones are usually the best. They go off on their own little cyber adventures—"

"And that way," concluded Nick, "we'll find the star hackers."

"No." Jeff shook his head and leaned back in his chair. "We've got enough hackers in the Ninety-Nine. When the assault happens, it's far more than a hack. It's a wholesale rewrite. We need fast coders with imagination, with originality, and with flair."

From far below came the sound of a ship's horn, long and mournful.

Jeff looked across at Nick.

"We're going to rewrite the world."

Chapter 20

IT WAS midafternoon by the time Dominic and Jonathan had collected a replacement mobile phone and returned with it to their apartment in Sitges. Jonathan went out to the balcony to text Steve the new phone number. Dominic entered the bedroom and started to pack their suitcases. After several minutes he stopped and called out to Jonathan.

"Have you sent that text to Steve yet? If you have, I could do with a hand here. Alfonso's going to be back in just over an hour."

Jonathan left the balcony and walked over to the bedroom door. "Have you decided if you're coming to San Francisco after all?" he asked.

Dominic was standing by the bed, a half-filled suitcase in front of him.

"Just now, Jonathan," he said, "I really don't want to go to San Francisco. But I think I probably should." He turned away and resumed folding a shirt. "Anyway, you should go to your friends' wedding. It would be rude of you not to. And in between, we've got a lot to talk about." He carefully placed the shirt in the suitcase and looked up at his husband paused in the doorway.

"Don't just stand there," said Dominic. "Can you deal with our carry-on bags? Get everything out of the safe, and sort out some books for the journey."

"Books?" asked Jonathan. "I thought you said we had a lot to talk about?" He walked over to the safe and took out a bundle of passports and travel documents.

"We have," replied Dominic, "but I'd also like to catch up on some reading. Anyway, I don't want to stay here another night. Not after everything that's happened. And it was very kind of Gabriel to invite us to stay with them tonight."

Jonathan began to sort through the documents from the safe. "I suppose so," he grunted. "But maybe we're seeing a bit too much of those two when really we need to be alone." He stopped for a moment and looked up at Dominic. "As you say, we've got a lot to talk about."

"Yes, I know." Dominic walked to the wardrobe, unloaded some clothes from their hangers, and carried them to the bed. "But we've got to be at Barcelona Airport very early tomorrow morning. It will be much easier to get to there from Gabriel and Alfonso's place, rather than from here. Besides"—Dominic began carefully folding up jackets—"Alfonso will be driving us to the airport. He's a policeman. Somehow I feel safer if we've got his protection."

Jonathan snorted. "He's hardly the Spanish SWAT team, Dominic. He's a traffic cop, as far as I can work out." He picked up a leather holdall, set it on the table, and then glanced across at Dominic. "I would have preferred an evening with you, that's all. Talking over things."

Dominic said nothing. Neither of them spoke for a while as they continued with their packing. Finally, Jonathan went over to the bed and sat. He looked up at Dominic and laid a hand on his arm.

"I need to know, Dominic. About you and Bernhardt. You said we could talk on the flight tomorrow. But I can't wait that long. Please, tell me."

Dominic studied his husband. Jonathan's eyes were glistening with tears. Dominic sighed. He set down the clothes he had in his hand and knelt on the floor in front of him. Then he leaned forward, placed his hands on Jonathan's thighs, and gazed up into his face.

"Jonathan, it's not what you think. Yes, long ago I loved Bernhardt. I was infatuated with him. But that's all in the past."

Jonathan leaned forward and rested his hands on Dominic's shoulders. "But you did go to see him before our wedding. Didn't you?"

Dominic nodded.

"If it was just business, or some legal discussion," said Jonathan, "then you wouldn't be so mysterious about it now. Dominic, what aren't you telling me?"

Dominic sighed and gripped Jonathan's thighs more tightly in his hands.

"Two nights ago, Jonathan, we stood on the beach, waiting for Karl Michael. And you said that everybody tells convenient lies. I've not lied to you, Jonathan. But neither have I told you the whole truth."

Jonathan's hands tensed, and he gripped Dominic's shoulders.

"I did go to stay with Bernhardt," continued Dominic. "And it was just before our wedding. Bernhardt was helping me with a personal legal matter. It was sort of business."

"What sort of legal matter?" asked Jonathan.

"He was helping me to get access rights," replied Dominic. "It's quite complicated in Germany."

"Access rights?" Jonathan looked confused. "Access to what?"

"Access to whom, Jonathan. Not to what." Dominic looked down, away from Jonathan's eyes as he spoke.

"Bernhardt was helping me get access to my son."

KARL MICHAEL walked along the rows of expensive yachts moored in Port Sitges. The afternoon was hot. The sun burned the back of his neck, and his feet ached from walking. He regretted not giving himself the luxury of a rental car, but he had made the decision to reduce the likelihood of being traced while he remained in Spain.

At the end of a row of gleaming white yachts, he found what he was looking for. *Teaghlaigh* was a fifty-five-foot Azimut S-type yacht. Standing on the deck was a tall, well-built man with a bald head and a small scar across his forehead. He was wearing a pair of white chinos, a tight-fitting white T-shirt, and trainers.

"Excuse me," Karl Michael called from the walkway. "I'm looking for Janet Downpatrick. She's asked me to meet her here."

A woman emerged from a doorway onto the deck and stood alongside the man.

"Karl Michael," she said. "You're late. Come aboard. Viktor will help you."

Karl Michael walked gingerly up the narrow gangplank that led from the walkway to the yacht. He took hold of the arm Viktor extended to help him and was pulled firmly onto the deck. Viktor maintained his grip on Karl Michael as Janet Downpatrick spoke to him.

"Take him below, Viktor. I'll join you in a moment."

Viktor escorted Karl Michael to the doorway from which Downpatrick had just emerged. He directed him down a flight of steep stairs to the lower level of the yacht. Once there, Viktor pushed Karl Michael forward to a small table next to a shuttered window.

"Sit," said Viktor.

Karl Michael slid onto one of the two bench seats on either side of the table. Viktor stood at the end of the table, his arms folded across his broad chest. His head just brushed the low ceiling of the cabin. There was no natural light; the only illumination came from overhead spotlights. Air-conditioning hummed, and Karl Michael shivered as his body reacted to the sudden drop in temperature after the heat outside.

An uncomfortable five minutes of silence passed before Janet Downpatrick entered the cabin.

"Oh, but Viktor," she said, "you've not got our guest a drink. He must be very thirsty, walking all this way from the town. Get him one of our specials."

Viktor left the cabin, and Janet Downpatrick sat on the bench opposite Karl Michael.

"So tell me," she began, "when will the Americans launch the assault?"

Karl Michael felt light-headed, and his mouth was dry. He had only met Janet Downpatrick a few times. The first had been in Berlin, when she seemed friendly and generous in her concern for him and how much she would pay in return for his help. Now, confined in the cramped cabin of this yacht over a thousand miles from Berlin, he felt very alone.

"They won't start until they've got the DG chip back again," he began. "But there's a new development. They now have secured entry to the banking networks."

Janet Downpatrick leaned forward as Karl Michael continued.

"They're concerned that without the DG chip, the assault cannot be sustained and—"

"Is that true?" interrupted Downpatrick.

Karl Michael nodded.

"Without the DG chip, they have a shorter window of time to modify the global history records for all the targets. There's also a greater risk that the assault could be traced and neutralized."

Janet Downpatrick leaned back on the narrow bench seat and tapped the fingernails of her left hand on the tabletop in a rapid rhythm. She stared hard at Karl Michael while she did. He looked away and ran his finger around the inside of his shirt collar, which felt tight against his neck.

Finally, Downpatrick gracefully slid along the bench seat and stood.

"That's good. So if we can retrieve and destroy the chip, then the threat of the assault is ended? Are you sure they don't have all the access they need now? Couldn't they manually rewrite certain key master history records?"

"Yes, but only on a small scale," replied Karl Michael. "The whole purpose of Bennie's work on the History Writer project is to create a massive assault that's undetectable."

"Ah yes, your boyfriend, Bernhardt Freude," mused Downpatrick. "He had the only copy of a chip that would provide an undetectable link to the core of the financial networks. He steals it from his very own organization and drives all the way here to meet his onetime lover, Dominic Delingpole." She placed her hands on the edge of the narrow tabletop and leaned down to bring her face close to Karl Michael's.

"What was it? A lover's tiff between you two? Did he stop fucking you all of a sudden?"

Karl Michael closed his eyes and breathed heavily. "That happened a long time ago." He opened his eyes and stared at the wall in front of him, avoiding Downpatrick's stare. "I believe he suspected Charter Ninety-Nine had been infiltrated. That's why he was taking it to Dominic. Someone outside the group he could trust."

"He guessed you were the traitor, didn't he?" said Downpatrick. "He must have been furious when he finally found out. But don't worry," she continued, a smile forming on her face. "He won't ever come seeking retribution. He's dead."

Karl Michael felt a chill draft from the ventilation panel above his head and shivered.

"How do you know?" he asked.

"We followed him from the Pyrenees. He turned off the *autopista* just after Girona," replied Downpatrick. "He stopped, and we had to drive past as there's nowhere to turn off. We waited farther down the road, but he never reappeared. After a long wait, we drove back and saw a motorbike cop had discovered the wreckage of his car. It was clear Freude didn't survive. Unfortunately, we were unable to recover the DG chip."

Karl Michael felt his arms tense, and he clenched and unclenched his fists. He turned slowly to glare at the look of amusement on Downpatrick's face.

"You've known all this time, haven't you?" he said. "Yet you didn't tell me. Just what kind of a woman are you?"

Before Downpatrick could answer, Viktor returned to the cabin, holding a tray with three glasses on it. He placed it carefully on the table in front of Karl Michael and stepped back.

"What kind of woman?" asked Janet Downpatrick. "I am your generous host. The woman who supplied you with an enormous sum of cash to get us access to the History Writer project." She picked up the tallest of the glasses from the tray and set it down in front of Karl Michael.

"And now," she continued, "I realize you've had a shock, and you're thirsty from your walk. So here, this will refresh and rejuvenate you."

Karl Michael picked up the glass and took a long drink from it. Janet Downpatrick took the other two glasses from the tray and handed one to Viktor.

"And you've been successful, Herr Meyer," she said, raising her glass in toast. "Well, almost. We know where the DG chip is, and I'm certain we'll recover it and destroy it. Even better, we've got access to Charter Ninety-Nine meetings through your mobile phone codes."

"You can't possibly have that access," protested Karl Michael. He tried to stand, but his legs buckled, and he collapsed back on the seat.

"Oh, but we have," replied Downpatrick. "And thank you. You've helped the cause of the free world enormously. The risk to the stability of the established order presented by those do-gooders in Charter Ninety-Nine will soon be gone."

She watched as Karl Michael swayed, trying to keep his eyes open. Beads of sweat had broken out on his forehead. She turned to Viktor Krasov.

"You can thank Viktor here for your boyfriend's accident," she said. "He implanted a software fix in the computer of Freude's sports car. He did it when Freude stopped at the service area." She looked back at Karl Michael. "There's no end to what you can control remotely these days."

Karl Michael could no longer focus on Downpatrick's smiling face.

Downpatrick set her glass down on the table and leaned in close to Karl Michael.

"Your lover is dead, Karl Michael," she continued. "And before he died, you betrayed him. Which means you can never be trusted. How can I be sure you won't betray me? I suspected you were also becoming too close to Delingpole. So—" She straightened up. "—all good things must come to an end."

Karl Michael felt the glass slip from his hand as he collapsed forward onto the table.

Chapter 21

STEVE HAD tried to translate his humiliation into exhibitionism by imagining he was lying back in a sling in a fetish club in London's East End. His imagination failed him; there were far too many women present. Alejandro, the Venezuelan male nurse with the long eyelashes, had disappeared to minister to another admission. His replacement was a stern-faced female nurse, who kept commenting that she had never seen a man with his legs up in birthing stirrups before. The anesthetist was a jolly fair-haired woman from Minnesota. And the doctor who performed the procedure between his legs had announced herself as "Sandra, the slickest scalpel south of Sacramento."

"There you are, young man," announced Sandra the scalpel after less than five minutes. "You either got hit by a piece of stray buckshot, or you were playing a very strange sex game last night."

The stern-faced nurse tutted loudly and held out a small plastic dish to the doctor. "Here you are, Doctor. I'll dispose of it for you."

"No, no, let me see it first," said Steve, trying to sit up.

"You lie back, young man," said the doctor. "I haven't finished down here yet. If you move again, you'll be walking like John Wayne for a long time to come."

She turned to the nurse. "Put it in a sample tube, and give it to him." She looked up at Steve. "It sure is the weirdest souvenir of San Francisco I've ever seen." Then she winked and turned back to finish closing the small incision she had made. There followed a few minutes of silence, during which Steve tried to blank the mental picture of what was happening down there from his mind.

"You Britishers," the doctor continued. "You're not like *Downton Abbey* in real life, are you?"

Steve lay back and closed his eyes. He imagined what he would do to Nick the next time he met him. He was furious the American had beaten him, not once, but twice. He wondered if he was being tested in some way. Steve was still not entirely sure what the hackfest was all about. When he received the invitation four months previously, he spent time researching it as thoroughly as he could. But in all the references he found, it seemed little more than an interesting ego trip for the multimillionaire dot-com success Jeff Woodfield. Steve was flattered to be invited, and he had looked forward to meeting several internet coders whose work he admired.

"Here, take it," said the stern-faced nurse. Steve felt something being shoved into his hand, and his fingers closed around a small plastic tube. He opened his eyes, to see the nurse bending down to whisper in his ear.

"Watch yourself in this God-fearing country of ours called America," she said. "Especially beware the coastal cities. They are the Sodom and—"

"Nurse!" the doctor called out. "Keep your preaching outta the emergency room, will you?"

The nurse turned her head to glare at the doctor, looked back at Steve, and whispered the word "Beware" once more. With a final scowl at the doctor, she straightened up and left the room.

Steve brought the tube close to his face to examine the object inside more closely. It was about a quarter of an inch long, muddy brown in color, and had a tiny piece of wire sticking from one end. He recognized it immediately from the work he had done monitoring the flight patterns of rare British birds. It was a micro tracking device. For the first time, Steve had found himself being the hunted instead of the hunter. And he was determined to reverse the roles as quickly as he could.

JEFF LOOKED up as he heard the lift doors open.

"How's it going?" he asked as Nick stepped out of the lift and walked across the wooden floor toward the steel desk where Jeff was seated.

"Well, it's nearly midday, and no one's picked a fight yet," replied Nick, as he perched on the edge of the desk and rested his leather rigger boot on the arm of Jeff's chair.

"But here's some real news for you," Nick continued. "Our young British friend is on the move again." He handed a tablet computer to Jeff. The screen displayed a map of the northeastern area of San Francisco. A small red circle flashed close to Coit Tower.

"Is he coming here?" asked Jeff, looking closely at the screen.

"Nope. He left the hospital about a half hour ago."

"What was he doing at the hospital, I wonder?" Jeff mused. "Do you think it's to do with the tracker?"

Nick looked affronted. "I was damn careful when I installed it. Anyway, it's still working. You can see he's back at the place I dropped him last night."

As he spoke, the red circle started to move slowly across the map.

"Not anymore," said Jeff. "Looks like he's heading south."

The two men tracked the small red circle as it moved along the streets of San Francisco. After a few minutes, it headed north onto Highway 80.

"Shit. He's going across to Oakland," said Nick. "What the fuck's he up to?"

Jeff handed the tablet computer back to Nick. "You'd better go after him. Take the Dodge. He'll recognize the Tesla after you picked him up last night. He's less likely to spot you in the Dodge. I'll take over the hackfest for now. Follow him, and let me know where the hell he's going. We want to recruit him, but we need to know we can trust him."

NICK WAITED impatiently for the automatic garage doors of 101 Grain Street to open. As soon as they slid far enough apart, he stamped his foot down on the gas pedal. Tires squealed as the large Dodge van shot backward out of the garage. A horn sounded, and a man's voice shouted angrily as a UPS delivery driver swerved to avoid the truck. Nick slammed the Dodge into drive, accelerated to the corner of Battery Street, and hung a right, hardly lifting his foot off the gas pedal.

The traffic got heavier as he neared the busy intersection with Market Street. Nick saw the approaching traffic lights turn amber, and he stepped hard on the accelerator and swerved around a dawdling powder-blue Ford Fiesta in front of him. He ignored a chorus of car horns and swerved in and out of the slow-moving traffic. Nick glanced at the dashboard map display, which showed a flashing red circle. Steve's tracker had reached the naval training station, midway along the Oakland Bay Bridge.

As Nick looked up, he slammed his foot down on the brake pedal and narrowly avoided crashing into a garbage truck stopped in front of him. He pulled the Dodge out from behind the truck and accelerated down First Street to the intersection with Route 80. As the Dodge accelerated up the entry ramp to the Bay Bridge, Nick looked again at the dashboard display. It showed Steve was approaching the end of the bridge and entering Oakland. Nick reckoned he would catch up with him in just a few minutes. In his head, he thanked the city planners for putting the bridge tollbooths on the approach to San Francisco and not on the lanes he was taking that led out of the city.

The midday sunlight was bright, and the waters of the bay glowed an intense azure, matching the clear blue of the sky. Nick took one hand off the steering wheel to reach up and take a pair of mirrored sunglasses from the compartment above his head. Not only did they shield his eyes from the glare of the reflected sunlight, but the glasses would help disguise him, hopefully buying him time when he finally caught up with Steve.

The traffic was light on the bridge, and Nick weaved the Dodge van in and out of it with ease as he closed in on his target. All the while, he went over in his mind what he was going to do when he got close to the runaway British skinhead. His aim was to keep a low profile and find out who Steve was contacting.

By the time Nick reached the end of the Bay Bridge, the map on the dashboard display showed Steve's tracker was heading along the Aquatic Park toward the Berkeley Marina. Nick was now less than half a mile behind him. He reached forward to the glove box, pulled out a Giants baseball cap, and placed it on his head with the peak forward and low over his eyes. He scanned the road ahead of him, trying to work out which vehicle Steve might be traveling in.

Nick looked back at the map on the display screen and could see the red marker turning off the freeway, headed down to Berkeley and University Avenue. He looked up at the road again and moved the Dodge into the right-hand lane. There were only a handful of vehicles directly ahead of him. The fourth car in front was a yellow San Francisco taxi. Nick was certain Steve had to be in it.

Once the road straightened out into University Avenue, it continued on to the heart of the city of Berkeley. Nick eased past the few remaining vehicles that separated him from the taxi and settled the Dodge close behind it. A glance across at the red circle flashing on the map confirmed he was now trailing Steve and the tracker.

After ten blocks, the yellow cab slowed and indicated right. It pulled to the curb outside a boarded-up restaurant called the Santa Fe. Nick pulled the Dodge van over into a parking space two cars behind the taxi. He watched as the man in the back of the cab leaned forward and spoke to the driver. The curbside door opened, and the passenger stepped out onto the sidewalk.

Nick took off his sunglasses and stared. The passenger was not Steve. He was a big bear of a man with long white hair tied in a ponytail and a white beard. The man turned and looked straight at the Dodge van. Nick hurriedly put his sunglasses back on as the man walked toward him and stood alongside the vehicle. He tapped on Nick's window.

"Hey, are you Nick Poole?"

Nick lowered his window. "Who are you?"

"My name's Anders," said the man, speaking with a Scandinavian accent. He leaned on the doorframe and reached in to place his large bearlike hand on Nick's shoulder.

"If you're Nick Poole," Anders continued, "then I have a message for you. It's from Steve. He asked me to give you this."

Anders reached into his pocket, pulled out a folded sheet of paper, and handed it to Nick. It was a hospital leaflet, inviting him to give blood. Scrawled across the middle were two words.

Fuck you.

STEVE TURNED to Sinon with a triumphant smile on his face.

"Looks pretty pissed, doesn't he?" he said. They were in the back seat of a taxi parked across the street from the boarded-up Santa Fe restaurant. They watched as Anders strode away from the Dodge van and back to his taxi. The taxi headed off down University Avenue and turned right at the intersection with Sacramento Street. Steve looked down at the screen of his mobile phone. A red dot flashed on a map of Berkeley.

"It's not moving," said Steve. "Looks like Anders delivered the tracker. The hunter has become the hunted. We'll know for sure if the tracker starts moving when nob-head over there drives off."

There was a screech of tires, followed by the sound of car horns, as the Dodge van lurched into the traffic on University Avenue. The red dot began moving across the map on Steve's phone.

"Perfect," he said. "Anders probably only managed to drop the tracker into the car, but at least I've got one over on that bastard now." He turned to Sinon. "How come you know Anders, anyway?"

Sinon smiled. "Oh, you know. First trip to San Francisco, when I came to Folsom Street Fair, ten years ago. Anders liked twinks in leather. I obliged. We sort of keep in touch. Didn't know he was doing GayBnB now. Otherwise I'd have stayed at his place."

Steve slipped his phone back into the pocket of his MA-1 jacket and turned to Sinon. "You okay about me staying at yours temporarily? I mean, I can't go back to Anders's place for the moment." Steve looked out the window. "That shithead Nick knows I stayed there, and he's going to be gunning for me now."

"Yeah, no problem," said Sinon. "After our session onboard the plane, we can carry on where we left off." He reached his hand down between Steve's thighs. Steve gave a yell of pain.

"Shit, sorry, mate." Sinon withdrew his hand hastily. "I forgot about your injury."

Steve looked around at Sinon and smiled wanly. "Yeah, mate. It's going to be strictly above the waist for the next couple of days. Anyway, I've got stuff to do. I need to work out what the fuck's going on."

"Well, I can help there." Sinon pulled an earpiece out of his pocket and plugged it into his phone. "My name's Sinon, remember? The Greek left behind with the wooden horse of Troy? I'll go back to the hackfest like nothing's happened and report back to you what they're up to. Plus, you can listen to this." He took a few moments to adjust an app on the phone, then handed the earpiece to Steve, who shoved it into his ear. He heard Nick talking on the phone in his van.

"Shit, mate," said Steve, looking wide-eyed at Sinon. "How the fuck did you manage that?"

"You weren't watching closely enough just now." Sinon grinned. "Anders not only dropped the tracker into your friend's van, but he also slapped a bit of chewing gum I'd given him onto the back of Nick's shirt. There's a small transmitter inside it. It'll take Nick a while to find it. And until then, you've got something interesting to listen to."

Chapter 22

Gabriel looked up at the kitchen clock as he sliced baby squid into small pieces for the tapas. It was nearly eight o'clock in the evening. Alfonso had returned home over two hours ago with Dominic and Jonathan. As soon as they arrived, Gabriel had sensed there was a chill in the relationship between the two Englishmen. Their body language betrayed it immediately. Alfonso showed them to the guest room, while Gabriel went to the kitchen to begin the supper. He was preparing eight different types of tapas, including his signature dish, baby squid in white beans and garlic.

In the two hours since Dominic and Jonathan arrived, Gabriel had hardly seen his husband, apart from the regular occasions when he came into the kitchen to make more coffee for their guests. The rest of the time, Alfonso was locked in discussion with the two men. The three of them sat on the balcony, talking and watching the sun set over Barcelona.

Cups rattled behind Gabriel as Alfonso entered the kitchen.

"How is my husband," asked Gabriel, "the newly appointed marriage guidance counselor of Barcelona?"

Alfonso set the tray he was holding on the worktop. He stood behind Gabriel, wrapped his arms around his waist, and rested his head on Gabriel's shoulder.

"I am desperately in need of *un aperitivo*." He sighed and kissed his husband on the neck. "Are all Englishmen as complicated as this? I'm so glad I'm a Latin. We're so much more straightforward."

Gabriel laughed. "Alfonso, do you know how racist that just sounded? Surely you must know by now, all *men* are complicated. It doesn't matter where they come from."

Alfonso released his arms from around Gabriel's waist and began to massage his husband's neck. "My dear Gabriel, do you know how *sexist* that just sounded? Surely you must know that all *people* are complicated." He stopped his massage for a moment and kissed Gabriel on the neck again. "That's what makes the world so interesting."

Gabriel finished slicing the baby squid, picked up the chopping board, and tipped the squid into a frying pan of white beans and garlic. He set down the chopping board and turned to face Alfonso.

"And just at the moment, do you think our two newlyweds in there believe complication is interesting?" asked Gabriel. "They seem to be very unhappy." He turned back to the stove and began stirring the squid into the white beans. "I don't understand how Jonathan can be so upset with Dominic. Especially after Dominic received the news about the death of his friend. Surely Jonathan should be more sensitive than that? And anyway," he continued, turning up the heat under the frying pan, "why isn't he delighted at the news of a son? Isn't that what marriage is about?"

Alfonso walked over to the large glass-fronted wine cooler by the entrance to the kitchen. He opened the door, took out a bottle of cava, and set it down on the counter next to his laptop.

"Marriage means different things to different people," said Alfonso. "Surely you know that, Gabriel? I'm not sure that Dominic and Jonathan have given much thought to children, so far."

Gabriel stopped stirring and lifted the spoon from the frying pan to taste the juice. "Ah, I always love this dish. We were lucky to get these squid today. They were almost the last ones."

Gabriel resumed stirring the pan and looked at Alfonso. "Well, I'm certain that at least Dominic had thought about children. After what you've told me, he's known about his son for over two years. That's as long as he's known Jonathan. I suppose that's why Jonathan is angry. Dominic never told him about the boy, not even when they were preparing to get married. Then he tells him on their honeymoon. I'd be upset if you were to withhold a piece of information like that from me, Alfonso."

His husband failed to respond, and Gabriel stopped stirring again. "I presume you're not?" he asked teasingly.

Alfonso was skimming through police updates on his laptop screen. He seemed to ignore the question, or was oblivious to it. "Jonathan's certainly not happy" was all he said.

Gabriel resumed stirring the pan of squid.

"I wonder why Dominic didn't tell him," Gabriel continued. "I would be so proud if I was a father. I would want everyone to know. And if I were Jonathan, I would be proud of him. Why do you think Dominic hid the information from him?"

Alfonso looked up. "The three of us have been talking for nearly two hours in there, and Dominic still hasn't given a proper answer to that. But I think I can guess why."

He picked up a pen and began writing notes on a piece of paper.

Gabriel dropped the spoon into the frying pan, turned to face Alfonso, and folded his arms. "So are you going to tell me?" he asked. "Or is your Latin Cinderella here to be kept out of the grown-up's conversation?"

Alfonso stopped writing and put down his pen. He picked up the bottle of cava, walked over to his husband, and kissed him slowly, using his tongue to explore the fullness of Gabriel's lips and mouth.

"There," he said after nearly a minute. "Prince Charming will invite you to the ball. Only please don't call those two boys in there grown-ups." Alfonso set the bottle down on the worktop and reached for long-stemmed glasses from the cupboard above their heads.

"I have a theory," he said. He put the glasses on the worktop and started to open the bottle of cava. "I think Dominic is like your cousin Pedro."

Gabriel raised an eyebrow, and Alfonso continued.

"Apparently, back in England, Dominic was only 'out' in certain circles. He and Jonathan lived separately. They only met at weekends, usually at Jonathan's place. That was when Dominic was out as a gay man. The weekends and when he and Jonathan went away on holiday together. Dominic learned to break his life into little compartments. You know as well as I do that lots of gay men do that."

Alfonso expertly lifted the cork from the bottle of cava and began filling the four glasses.

Gabriel nodded. "It's true. Gay men never stop 'coming out.' People assume you're straight. Each time you meet someone new, you have to choose whether to go through the whole coming-out conversation all over again. It gets boring."

Alfonso finished pouring the cava and set the bottle on the kitchen worktop. He took a glass in either hand and gave one to Gabriel.

"Dominic put the news about his son in the compartment that included Bernhardt," said Alfonso. "The man who was his brief German love affair when Dominic was twenty years old. It fitted in that compartment, because it was around the time, when he knew Bernhardt, that his son was conceived." He touched his glass against Gabriel's. "*Salud*, my love."

"It must have been a very confusing summer for Dominic all those years ago," said Gabriel. "A love affair with a woman and a love affair with a man. Does he think he's bisexual?"

Alfonso laughed. "Why don't you come and ask him yourself? I could really do with your support. I've never considered myself the best diplomat in the world, and I'm beginning to run out of patience with those two."

Gabriel turned back to the stove.

"I'm nearly finished here," he said. "Then I promise I'll come and join you. What was so interesting on your laptop, by the way?"

Alfonso picked up the two glasses he had poured for Dominic and Jonathan and headed toward the doorway.

"Oh, it's a report from Sitges. They've found a body in the water at the port."

JANET DOWNPATRICK held the phone away from her ear for a few seconds as a woman's voice shouted from the earpiece. After the tirade had subsided, she put the phone back to her ear.

"I'm sorry, ma'am," Downpatrick said, "but be confident that we will find them again. We know they're flying to London first thing tomorrow, connecting with a flight to San Francisco in the afternoon. We're booked on the same flights. It will be useful to have Viktor with me. He just has to finish some housecleaning here first."

There was a dull thud above her head, as Viktor continued to box up the contents of the yacht, ready for their departure.

Downpatrick listened patiently as the verbal tirade exploded in her ear again. Holding the phone in one hand, she walked over to one of the cabin windows, opened the blinds, and revealed the lights of Port Sitges. It was nearly ten o'clock in the evening, and the sun had finally set. In the distance, she could see the flashing blue lights of police cars. Downpatrick allowed the voice to continue its rant in her ear for several minutes before she seized her chance to speak again.

"The German was no longer needed, ma'am," said Downpatrick. "He had become untrustworthy. In my opinion, he was always unreliable. I dislike traitors. Especially when we pay them well." She paused and took a sip from a glass of unsweetened hot lemon Viktor had prepared for her. She listened patiently for a moment.

"That's not a problem," Downpatrick responded. "I have the codes for the Charter Ninety-Nine calls. I'll be notified when they happen, and I can listen in."

She turned as Viktor Krasov entered the cabin and signaled he wanted to speak to her.

"Please be assured, we will recover and destroy the DG chip by the end of tomorrow." Downpatrick nodded to Krasov. "Yes, ma'am. I understand. Please excuse me now, but I have to go."

Janet Downpatrick ended the call and threw the mobile phone down on the tabletop.

"I dislike working with politicians, particularly those in the church. They panic too easily." She turned to Krasov. "Yes, what is it?"

"There are police everywhere in the port, ma'am," he replied. "We should delay the evacuation until they've gone. It will avoid attracting their attention."

She looked at him coldly for a moment.

"Then how am I expected to travel to London tomorrow?"

Krasov returned her look, unblinking.

"They won't be concerned by a single woman such as yourself on an evening's walk in the port," he replied. "I have arranged for a taxi driver friend of mine to collect you outside the secure entrance. If you walk down there on your own, the police will simply take you for another spectator at the scene of their investigation. Santos will drive you to the airport hotel for the night."

"And what am I supposed to do for clothes?" asked Downpatrick.

Krasov shrugged. "I do not need any." He walked to the doorway, stopped, and turned to look at Downpatrick.

"I will try to bring something for you later," Krasov relented. "But only if I see the police have gone. If you take a suitcase now, they may want to question you. It's your choice."

ALFONSO SIDESTEPPED to avoid bumping into Dominic, who appeared at the kitchen doorway.

"Can I help with anything?" asked Dominic. "I'm feeling very guilty. You're doing all the work, while Jonathan and I just sit in there being waited on hand and foot."

Alfonso handed Dominic one of the glasses of cava. "You can start by drinking this," he said. "I think you'll find it medicinal."

Dominic smiled and took the glass from Alfonso's outstretched hand. "You're being both doctor and therapist this evening, Alfonso. I'm very sorry. Jonathan and I aren't behaving like very good guests. I'd like to apologize for ruining your evening."

Alfonso put his free hand on Dominic's shoulder, pulled him forward, and gave him a hug.

"Don't worry, my friend," said Alfonso into Dominic's ear. "Life has not been fair to you in the last few days. Be gentle on yourself." He released his arm and pulled back to look at Dominic's face. "Be gentle on your new husband as well, my friend. You mustn't allow these extraordinary events to sour the start of your married life. You have so much to look forward to."

Dominic leaned forward and kissed Alfonso on the forehead. "You're an extraordinarily kind man," he said. Then he looked across at Gabriel and added, "Both of you are. It's inspiring to see such a successful marriage."

Gabriel laughed. "It's not always perfect harmony. Alfonso can be impossible at times." He gestured around him. "He ties me to this kitchen most of the time."

"Huh!" said Alfonso in mock anger. "The things I have to put up with from the queen of the cuisine. Anyway," he continued, looking at Gabriel, "you always said you enjoyed being tied up."

Alfonso ducked as a bread roll flew across the kitchen. It hit the notepad Alfonso had been writing on a few minutes before and knocked it to the floor. Alfonso turned to Dominic and shrugged. "See what I mean?"

Dominic laughed and bent down to pick up the notepad. He glanced at the handwritten notes for a moment.

"I'm sorry to be inquisitive," said Dominic, "but what is this?"

"There's been an incident at Port Sitges," Alfonso replied guardedly. "I was making some notes on it."

"What are these numbers?" Dominic pointed at the notepad.

Alfonso glanced down. "Oh, those are the GPS coordinates for where they found the body." He looked up at Dominic. "They've found a body in the water at the port," he added by way of explanation.

"That's it!" cried Dominic. "The first set of numbers in the message that Bernhardt sent me. They're almost in the same format. But they had the sign for degrees and the north and west symbols missing. But now I see this"—Dominic indicated the notepad—"they're clearly GPS coordinates. I'll go and tell Jonathan."

Dominic turned and left the kitchen.

Alfonso stared at Gabriel, who shrugged.

"Well," he said, smiling at Alfonso. "Let's hope their adventure helps to bring them back together again. Why don't you take Jonathan his drink? I think he's going to need it."

Chapter 23

STEVE REACHED over to the small table next to his chair and picked up the glass of India pale ale Sinon had brought for him earlier. He took a mouthful of beer and reveled in its hoppy taste. Steve was a big fan of West Coast America's IPA. He preferred it to the taste of the British original. In San Francisco alone, there were over thirty microbrewed India pale ales to choose from, for which Steve was immensely grateful. He stretched out languidly on the steamer deck chair and looked around him.

Sinon had rented an elegant one-room apartment attached to an old Edwardian inn at the heart of San Francisco's Castro district. The apartment was on the ground floor of the building. A set of timber-and-glass floor-to-ceiling doors opened out onto a small garden. The garden was filled with mature trees and shrubs. Late afternoon sunlight filtered through the leaves, and Steve enjoyed its warmth on his body. The pain from his recent surgery had subsided to a dull ache, and he hoped he could soon stop walking like an extra from *Brokeback Mountain.*

He took a mobile phone from his pocket and switched it on. It was one he rarely used in the UK, and he was confident it would not be linked to him if it was tracked. To reduce the risk further, he kept it turned off, and only turned it on periodically to check for messages. He took another mouthful of beer while he waited for the phone to start up.

Two text messages appeared on the screen, both from Dominic. The first told him of Dominic's idea about the GPS codes, and the second had details of their flight information for the following day. Steve reached for his laptop. After a few moments, he found the message he had retrieved from Dominic's mobile message store:

38 35 25.603 121 48 11.249
Turn to the feet of Adam
03 15 26 21
June 1

He pulled up a mapping website on his screen that converted GPS coordinates to addresses, typed in the coordinates, and waited for the results to appear. A red dot flashed over a California town, no bigger than a crossroads, called Plainfield. It was a couple of miles to the west of Sacramento. Steve switched to the website's street view and explored the town virtually. There was very little to see. Plainfield was predominantly open fields, a few barns, and some houses. He wondered if the street view was out of date. Maybe a new building had been put up in the intervening time. He checked the dates on the photographs. They had been taken in the summer of the previous year. Steve switched the map to satellite view and zoomed it in as far as he could. Of what he could see, there was nothing that looked significant or important.

"Hey, what you up to?" Sinon appeared in the open doorway of the apartment. He was wearing a pair of board shorts and a loose-fitting sleeveless white T-shirt. "How's the beer?"

"The glass is empty, if you're offering," replied Steve.

Sinon stepped out into the garden and walked over to an empty steamer deck chair next to Steve. He stripped off his shirt and sat down.

"I've got to go back to the hackfest soon," Sinon replied, stretching out his legs. "Before they miss me and maybe connect me with you. But I want to catch a few rays before the sun goes for the day."

"Thanks for letting me crash here, mate," said Steve, admiring the curves of Sinon's thighs. "Great spot. How did you find it?"

"A mate of mine introduced me to Johann, who owns it, a couple of years ago," replied Sinon. "Johann's been running this place for nearly twenty years. He came from Holland originally. The year before last, I stayed here for Folsom. Johann's really laid-back." Sinon reached across to Steve and placed his hand at the top of his thigh. "There's nothing that will faze him."

Keeping his hand on Steve's thigh, Sinon leaned over to try to see the laptop screen. "What are you looking at?"

Steve swiveled the laptop around so Sinon could see the screen clearly. "Remember I told you about my friends on their honeymoon in Sitges?"

Sinon started to massage Steve's thigh. "The uptight lawyer and the loopy opera singer?" he asked.

Steve nodded. "Well, Dominic's the lawyer. He had an old lover in Berlin who's involved in some weird internet shit."

Sinon sat up, his hand still resting on Steve's thigh.

"A few days ago," continued Steve, "Dominic got a strange text from this guy. It's a set of GPS coordinates, some code, and the date June 1. Then Dominic found his ex-lover had been trying to give him some bespoke computer chip that's linked to the message."

Sinon took the laptop from Steve and looked at the screen. "So you checked out the coordinates, and they land you at WRI's DarkStone data center?"

"What's DarkStone?" asked Steve. "I've heard of WRI, World Resources Inc. The guys who do all the banking data." He pointed at the screen. "But where's the data center? All I can see is fields and a few barns."

"Don't tell me you haven't heard of DarkStone," said Sinon, typing into the browser on Steve's laptop. "A security expert like you?"

"Well, I know the computer game," replied Steve. "Sure. It was okay, but I reckon the mediocre metacritic score for it was about right."

Sinon stopped typing. "You're kidding me," he said and gave Steve a withering look. He turned back to the laptop and resumed typing. "WRI set up DarkStone back in the late '80s. It's an asset management company, and it's the world's biggest investor. Here we are." Sinon began to read from the screen.

DarkStone was founded in 1988 and manages over four trillion dollars of assets for its clients. It is the biggest shareholder in half of the world's thirty largest companies. It single-handedly manages almost as much money as all of the world's private equity and hedge funds put together. That makes it bigger than any bank, insurance company, or government fund.

Sinon stopped reading and grinned at Steve. "One of my clients," Sinon boasted. "I've had the best, me."

"Oh yeah," said Steve. "I remember now. There was that shithead fund manager who lost everything in the late '80s. He swore it would never happen again. So he built a giant computer to forecast how world events would affect the markets. Shit, I'd forgotten about that." He took the laptop back from Sinon and flicked through the information about DarkStone. "It's the single most powerful computer in the world, monitoring global changes from climate to wars. Investors flock to DarkStone because it can forecast the future."

Steve eyed Sinon. "Did you work on this up at Plainfield, then?"

Sinon stood up and pulled his shirt back on. "I need to get back to the hackfest before they send out a search party and find you lying there." He squatted down beside Steve's chair and placed his hand on Steve's thigh.

"Looks like your friend's computer chip needs to get up to DarkStone in Plainfield by June 1," said Sinon. "The question you need to answer is… why?"

THE CREATIVE Cavern, on the ground floor of 101 Grain Street, was buzzing with activity when Nick arrived. Just under fifty people, from a range of creative backgrounds, were at the hackfest. There were computer coders, designers, artists, sociologists, and writers. Some were seated at the dozen or so large round tables scattered throughout the carpeted space, talking to each other or typing on their laptop computers. Others gathered around whiteboards and flipcharts, slices of pizza in their hands, deep in animated conversation.

Nick made his way to the suspended mobile home. He paused to chat to some of the programmers he recognized from previous hackfests and was introduced to a few new faces. As he reached the first step of the iron spiral staircase that led up to the control room, Fortran appeared at the top and headed down.

"Hey, how's it going, Nick?" said Fortran. He stopped at the foot of the staircase. "Great crowd this year. Some really cool stuff happening." He gestured to a table at the far end of the Creative Cavern. "You should check out those guys at table alpha. They've, like, totally got the whole digital storytelling thing, you know? They've only been going a couple of hours, but, like, they've already built this fictional character. And he's got, like, a Social Security number, a credit rating, and a college record. He's, like, totally fake, yet he exists."

"They should call him Donald," replied Nick with a wry grin. "Nothing much new in what they're doing. I was faking credit ratings in seventh grade to order stuff from Amazon."

"Sure," said Fortran earnestly. "But it's, like, got a whole artificial intelligence attached to it and shit. So they can, like, write a whole life history for some dude. Then, like, his history just appears on all the computer systems across the world. The system creates a consistent history, like when he bought stuff, when he traveled, doctor's visits. And all they do is write in the key events and shit for his life. The system fills in the rest. They've, like, even worked out how to create entries on CCTV trackers. Everything's linked. Everything's consistent."

Nick was impressed. "Yeah, that sounds cool. I'll take a look." He gestured to the control room. "Is Jeff up there?"

Fortran nodded. "Jeff's real excited about table alpha," he added. "There's, like, some science fiction writer from Washington State and a sixteen-year-old superfast coder, who seems to be from Russia. And they've, like, totally hijacked everything. It's awesome."

Nick climbed the stairs two at a time and stepped into the darkness of the mobile home. Inside, Jeff sat alone at the control console. He listened to the conversations at table alpha, his face lit by the bank of video screens. He turned as Nick entered.

"You calmed down yet?" Jeff asked. "One thing's for sure, that British guy is smart. We need to recruit him."

Nick sat down in a black leather swivel chair and put his feet up on the control console. "You want that piece of shit in Charter Ninety-Nine?" he asked, throwing the keys for the Dodge van over to Jeff.

"He's really got to you, kid, hasn't he?" said Jeff, standing up and walking over to Nick. He rested his hands on Nick's shoulders and started to massage his neck. "Which one of your buttons did he push? Was it because he figured out how to send you on a wild goose chase? Or are you pissed because you didn't get to fuck him?"

Nick leaned back into Jeff's hands. He flexed his shoulders as the massage began to ease the tension accumulated during his abortive drive to Oakland.

"Yeah, maybe both." Nick sighed. "Sure, he's smart. And he's done all that neat work on remote device control, which I guess is why we're recruiting him. The question is, can we trust him? I mean, the Originator suspected one traitor in the organization. What if we bring this guy in and he turns against us?"

Jeff stopped kneading and inspected the back of Nick's T-shirt. "It's a risk we're always going to face," he replied. "There are powerful forces who'd like us to stop what we're doing. Even though we can create a better world."

He straightened up and turned the chair around so Nick faced him. "Looks like you've been leaning against some shit today. Take your shirt off."

Nick smirked and obediently pulled the T-shirt over his head to reveal his taut torso. He turned the shirt over and inspected the wad of chewing gum stuck on its back.

"Shit, that's disgusting," he said, pulling at the gum. "I'll never get it off." He was about to throw the T-shirt on the floor when he stopped.

"Hey, check this out, Jeff." He pulled at a black lump in the middle of the gum.

"What is it?" asked Jeff.

"I thought it was a stone or something," said Nick, peeling the black lump clear of the gum. He held it up to one of the spotlights set into the ceiling of the control room and peered at it.

"I've been bugged," Nick snapped. He glared at Jeff. "You still think the Brit's worth recruiting? When he does shit like this?"

"But did he do this?" asked Jeff. "You didn't see him, did you? What if someone else wants to listen in to Charter Ninety-Nine? What if there's another infiltrator?"

Nick picked up a pair of pliers from the control desk and crushed the black lump between the jaws. Then he threw the T-shirt to the floor and sat back in the swivel chair heavily.

"We need the DG chip," said Nick. "And we're running out of time to get it. It's close to the deadline for the opportunity at Plainfield. If we miss that, the assault could be set back months." He frowned. "Maybe it will all be pointless by then."

Chapter 24

It was a quarter to five in the morning. Gabriel helped Dominic and Jonathan load their suitcases into his black Range Rover. As Dominic carried the last of the bags from the elevator to the car, he looked around the underground parking garage. He counted at least three Ferraris and four Aston Martins, as well as several Range Rovers and a beautiful red Bugatti. The sight of so many expensive cars made him think his own Mercedes SLK back in England was far too ordinary.

Dominic placed his bag into the back of the Range Rover and walked around to open the passenger door. He looked up as a fire door clanged open on the other side of the garage. Alfonso emerged, dressed in full police uniform. He came over to the car, his tall boots squeaking on the smooth, polished floor.

"Goodness, Alfonso," said Dominic. "You look very—" He searched for a word. "—very authoritative this morning. It's good to know you're driving us to the airport dressed like that."

"I'm not driving you," said Alfonso, nodding to Gabriel, who climbed into the driver's seat. "Gabriel will drive us and drop us outside the terminal. I'll come in with you to make sure nothing happens." He patted a holster strapped to his thigh. "I'm licensed to carry a gun around the airport." He smiled at Dominic. "Just in case."

Dominic looked apprehensively at the weapon resting on Alfonso's leg. He did not feel reassured. Dominic climbed into the back seat alongside Jonathan and closed the door.

"All set for our next big adventure?" asked Jonathan with a broad grin. He leaned over and kissed Dominic on the lips. Jonathan had cheered up significantly from the night before. Dominic hoped his mood would continue for the rest of the long day ahead of them. After a short stop in London to change planes, they were due to arrive in San Francisco just before three in the afternoon, US time.

"I'm ready," replied Dominic, fastening his seat belt. He peered at his husband and rested a hand on his thigh. "Are you okay this morning?"

Jonathan placed his hand on top of Dominic's and intertwined their fingers. "Not much sleep last night, I must admit, lover. But I was doing a lot of thinking." He squeezed Dominic's hand.

"I trust you completely about your friend, the late Bernhardt Freude," Jonathan continued. "And I'm sorry for acting so jealously. The whole matter's made me think about how you must have felt after I blundered about in XXL and knocked myself out."

Alfonso had climbed into the passenger seat in front of Jonathan and fastened his seat belt. He turned to gaze at Jonathan.

"¡Gracias a Dios!" he said and winked at Dominic. "The boy is becoming a man."

"That's not to say I want a marriage of perpetual monogamy," continued Jonathan, not meeting Alfonso's eyes. "But from now on, we must discuss everything first."

Dominic smiled and kissed Jonathan on the cheek.

"Well, it's progress, of a sort," said Dominic. "Let's hope our love remains strong enough to cope with your need for 'open monogamy,' as you call it."

Gabriel started the engine and drove toward the exit.

"I believe that the love you have for each other is strong," said Gabriel as he negotiated the exit ramp and drove the car out into the still darkness of the morning. "Despite what Alfonso and I have witnessed in the last twenty-four hours." He looked at his husband. "What do you think, Alfonso?"

Alfonso turned to his husband and rested his hand on Gabriel's knee.

"Yes, I think it's strong," he replied. "But for your love to continue, you must be completely honest with each other, do lots of talking, lots of understanding, and lots of sex."

Gabriel laughed. "Is that the secret of our eleven-year marriage, *mi amor*?"

"Oh, but you know it is," replied Alfonso. "Now, pay attention to the road. We have a precious cargo on board this morning."

KRASOV LOOKED through the windshield of the car. Four or five policemen, armed with assault weapons, were positioned by the entrance designated Departures at Barcelona Airport's Terminal One.

"Now do you see why we must wait until San Francisco?" he asked. "It will be impossible to remove the DG chip from Delingpole with so many police here." He turned to look at Janet Downpatrick in the back of the car. "The security is at full alert. And if we fail, there's no second chance."

Downpatrick looked through the side window of the car at the police activity. She hated to admit it, but Krasov was right.

"It's true," she said at length. "If we fail here, we not only risk being caught, but I'd have no choice but to trust our agent in San Francisco to recover and destroy the DG chip." She pulled a lipstick and compact from her bag and studied her face in the small mirror.

"What agent in San Francisco?" asked Krasov.

"You remember," replied Downpatrick, continuing to examine her face. "That queer programmer we hired last winter. He's done well to infiltrate the networks. I'm suspicious of him, of course." She looked up to see Krasov watching her in his rearview mirror. "After all, he's a queer. But we pay him handsomely." She studied Krasov's bicep, flexing beneath his T-shirt. "Although I can't believe he'll have the same persuasive powers as you, Viktor."

She took time to touch up the edges of her lips, then snapped shut the compact and put it back in her bag.

"I don't want Delingpole to see us," she said. "Although in the confines of the terminal, it will be difficult to avoid the possibility."

She opened her door, stepped out, and then leaned back in through the open doorway to continue talking to Krasov. "Go and get rid of the car, and bring the luggage round to the check-in." She stood up and looked around. "I doubt Delingpole's here yet. If we check in now, we can watch for him and keep out of his way. It should be possible, given that we're booked on the slightly later plane to London."

After a moment's thought, she turned her attention back to Krasov. "And put a hat on or something. That scar on your head is far too recognizable."

She slammed the car door, and Krasov drove off.

THE BLACK Range Rover pulled up to the curb outside Departures at the Barcelona airport. Alfonso opened his door and jumped out of the car. He looked around, standing guard as Gabriel stepped out of the car and opened Dominic's door for him.

"A su servicio, señor," he said, bowing low.

Dominic laughed as he stepped out and stretched his legs. "You are never my servant, Gabriel," he said. "Stand up and hug me."

Gabriel smiled broadly, wrapped his arms around Dominic, and hugged him tight.

"You take great care, my handsome Englishman," he whispered. Then he released an arm and extended it to Jonathan, who had slid out of the car behind Dominic.

"Come here, Jonathan," said Gabriel, "so that the three of us can embrace together." The three men hugged.

"Now, you two," said Gabriel, his arms still around Dominic's and Jonathan's waists. "Welcome to the marvelous world of marriage. And you"—he turned to Dominic—"take care of this man of yours. Try not to let him out of your sight again. As for the wonderful news of your son," he added, "I am very envious."

"So am I, now," said Jonathan, smiling at Dominic. "And that is for me to deal with, I know."

Dominic leaned forward and kissed Jonathan. "You will, my husband." Then Dominic addressed Gabriel. "And good luck with your surrogacy visit to California. Jonathan and I are certain you'll make wonderful parents. You have a very strong marriage that can only benefit your children."

Alfonso nudged the back of Gabriel's legs with an airport trolley he had piled with Dominic and Jonathan's luggage.

"Are you becoming sentimental, Gabriel?" he asked. "Because we don't have time. I want to get our friends into the safety of the building." He glanced around. "If someone is out to get them, they are very vulnerable out here. *Venga.*"

Gabriel hugged Dominic and Jonathan one last time and got back into the Range Rover.

DESPITE BEING early morning, the departures hall was crowded with passengers. The three men took a moment to scan the indicator board to find the number of the check-in desk they needed.

"It's down the other end," said Dominic, pointing to the left. "Past the queue for security."

Dominic and Jonathan walked on either side of Alfonso as he negotiated the trolley through the lines of people. After less than a minute, Jonathan pulled hard on the trolley to stop it. He slid behind Alfonso to Dominic's side and gripped his shoulder.

"Get down!" he half whispered.

Dominic crouched alongside Jonathan, hidden behind the trolley.

"What is it?" Dominic asked.

"Over in that queue for the other London flight," Jonathan replied. "I can't believe it, but it's that bloody woman who nearly killed you in London. And her thug sidekick."

Alfonso stared down at Dominic and Jonathan. "What are you doing?" he asked. "What have you seen?"

Jonathan looked up at Alfonso imploringly. "Hide us. There are two really very bad people over there. They nearly killed Dominic in London last year, and the big ugly one took a shot at me. We thought they'd been arrested, but obviously not."

Dominic's hands shook as he held on to the trolley loaded with their suitcases.

"What are we going to do?" he asked. "We can't stay down here like this. But if either of them sees us…."

Alfonso took out his radio. "I can try my friends in airport security," he said. "But without reasonable grounds, there's probably little we can do. And we risk drawing attention to you."

"Alfonso," said Jonathan, "their names are Janet Downpatrick and Viktor Krasov. I'm sure they're on a hundred wanted lists around the world. If you just tell your chums now, they can arrest them straightaway."

"If they're on a hundred wanted lists," replied Alfonso, "then they're hardly likely to come through an airport. They'd be picked up immediately, even if they used fake names."

Again, Jonathan looked up at Alfonso imploringly.

"All right," said Alfonso. "I'll try."

Dominic took his mobile phone out of his pocket and tapped out a text message.

"What are you doing, my love?" asked Jonathan.

Dominic finished the message and pressed Send.

"If those two are flying to London," he said, "who's to say they're not following us out to San Francisco? It's a strong coincidence, them being here, isn't it? What if it was Krasov or Downpatrick who got into our apartment? They broke open the safe, so they'd know our flights."

Jonathan nodded. "You just texted Steve, didn't you?"

"Yes," said Dominic. "It's a long shot, but he rescued me last time. Perhaps he can do the same again."

THE PEOPLE standing in the queue behind Janet Downpatrick and Viktor Krasov were beginning to get restless.

"It's impossible," said Downpatrick. "Your computer must be wrong. We both have ESTA visa waivers for the United States. Dammit, woman." She stared hard at the perfectly made-up attendant behind the desk. "We were only there last month."

"Then perhaps," said the woman patiently, "your ESTAs have expired. I'm sorry. You may travel to London now if you wish. But you will not be allowed to continue your journey on to the United States. The airline is not permitted to carry you. We would be fined heavily if we let you on the plane."

Janet Downpatrick took out her mobile phone.

"Oh very well," she said as she typed a number. "Check us in to London. We'll talk to somebody sensible there."

She turned to Krasov. "We've got no choice," she said. "We may have to use that queer coder we hired. He's in San Francisco, getting himself further into Charter Ninety-Nine."

"Do you really think he'll do anything?" Krasov asked. "He's paid to be a coder, not a heavy."

"I'll pay him another hundred thousand," replied Downpatrick. "He'll do anything for money." She held the phone to her ear. "I'll let him know what's happened. If we fail to get to San Francisco, he'll have to recover the DG chip from Delingpole when he lands."

Chapter 25

"THIS IS much more my style," said Jonathan. He stretched out his long legs in front of him and relished his second glass of cava of the morning.

He and Dominic were in the business class lounge at Barcelona Airport. It was quiet, with only a handful of other passengers scattered throughout the long, richly furnished room. Voices murmured softly, and somewhere in the distance, a large-screen television played the breakfast news—to the interest of no one.

Jonathan turned to Dominic, reached out his hand, and massaged his husband's arm.

"You know, my love," he said, "hobnobbing with the rich operagoers at Glyndebourne has rather robbed me of my innocence to sustain the second-rate." He took a mouthful of cava.

Dominic set down his coffee cup on the arm of the black leather armchair. He leaned forward to pick up a glass of orange juice. "It's just after six in the morning, Jonathan. How can you possibly drink cava at this time?"

"When it's free, my love," replied Jonathan, "I can drink it anytime."

Dominic took a sip from his glass of orange juice. The breakfast menu had described it as "freshly squeezed Seville orange juice." "I must admit," he said, "I'm actually really looking forward to the long flight to San Francisco."

He set down his glass, gathered up their empty plates from the low table in front of them, and stood.

"Steve was very quick to work his magic with the computer," Dominic continued. "Not only did he stop Downpatrick in her tracks, but he managed to upgrade us to first class all the way to America."

Jonathan nodded. "He's a genius. But I do feel rather vulnerable, knowing that foul woman and her poisonous sidekick are still on the loose." He looked at the plates in Dominic's hand and grinned. "That's very kind of you to offer. More of those wonderful pastries, please. And hurry back," he added as Dominic turned and headed for the self-service food counter. "I've got things I want to talk about."

The Deadly Lies

While Dominic replenished their plates, Jonathan looked around. There were a dozen other passengers in the lounge. They were all men, dressed in business suits, earnestly tapping away at laptop computers or looking at their mobile phones. Jonathan wondered why they felt the need to look busy and important, even at 6:30 a.m. As a landscape gardener—and occasional member of the chorus for the prestigious Glyndebourne opera—Jonathan never wore a suit, except if he was performing in a modern-dress production.

He reached forward and picked up one of the complimentary notepads and a pen from the coffee table in front of him. He drew a line down the middle of the paper, wrote his name on the left of the line and Dominic's on the right. He placed the notepad back on the table as Dominic returned with the food.

"So tell me," said Dominic, setting down the plates. "What are these things you want to talk to me about?" He sat and turned his gaze on Jonathan. "Or can I guess?"

"Alfonso's right," said Jonathan, reaching for one of the plates piled with pastries. "This boy you see before you is finally becoming a man." He picked up a pastry and bit into it. "Mm, *buñuelos*," he said, his mouth full. "Stuffed with egg custard. I love 'em."

"I hope," replied Dominic, "that now the boy is becoming a man, he isn't going to become boring."

Jonathan gave Dominic a look.

"Did you just roll your eyes out loud at me?" asked Dominic with a smile.

"I'm trying to be serious for a minute." Jonathan put his plate in his lap and leaned forward. "Look. We've just got married. I love you—"

Dominic opened his mouth to speak.

"No, don't say anything yet," said Jonathan. "Hear me out. I love you madly. And you love me. And I want that to last forever. I was serious when I proposed to you in that hospital bed last year. 'Till death us do part' and all that." Jonathan took another bite from his buñuelo. "But here's the thing. I don't think being married means we now own each other—"

"Jonathan," interrupted Dominic. "I know what you're going to say. And before you go any further, I must tell you that I've been doing a lot of thinking too."

Jonathan paused, the final slice of pastry frozen in midair.

"Don't look so worried," said Dominic, placing his hand on Jonathan's thigh. "I had a long talk with Gabriel last night. He gave me a lot to think about." He leaned forward and took a bite from the pastry in Jonathan's hand. "They are good, aren't they?" He rolled the buñuelo around in his mouth.

"I think that Alfonso and Gabriel have a very successful marriage," Dominic continued after he swallowed. "They've known each other for thirteen years. They've been married for eleven. They have a wonderful sex life—"

Jonathan raised an eyebrow.

"Don't pull that face," Dominic said with a mock frown. "Gabriel told me. They're about to start the process to have a baby together. And yet they aren't monogamous. From time to time, they both like to have sex with other men. And it works. And finally, I think I can see how."

Dominic paused and noticed the notepad on the coffee table with Jonathan's scribble on the top sheet of paper.

"What were you going to do with that?" he asked.

Jonathan picked up the notepad. "I thought it would be a good idea for us to make a list of what each of us wanted," he said. "Then we could discuss where we had—differences of opinion. And then we could talk about them."

Dominic took the notepad from Jonathan and retrieved the pen from the table. He ripped off the top sheet of paper and drew a large circle on the sheet below. Inside the circle, he wrote their names.

"I see us more like this," said Dominic. "We're not on either side of a line. We're together, linked through marriage." He set down the pen and reached for his glass of orange juice. "But, as you say, that doesn't mean we own each other."

Jonathan had reached for a second pastry. He stopped, looked up, and his eyes met Dominic's.

"Now you're agreeing with me," said Jonathan. "You're very intriguing, lover."

"Gabriel told me they have two simple rules in their marriage," Dominic went on. "The first is always be honest with each other. And the second is never hurt the other person. You know, I think Gabriel is like me in many ways. Alfonso's more like you."

"You mean he needs lots of sex," said Jonathan with a grin.

"Yes," said Dominic, "and so does Gabriel, much of the time. But not all the time. So when Alfonso feels the need to go and play elsewhere, he talks to Gabriel first. He makes sure Gabriel's never hurt. Sometimes they'll invite a guy round and have a threesome. The thing is, they talk about it. Gabriel knows Alfonso loves him deeply. And he loves Alfonso just as deeply. But he feels strongly that marriage doesn't mean ownership. It doesn't mean control."

Jonathan leaned over to Dominic and embraced him. He rested his head on Dominic's shoulder and planted tender kisses on his cheek.

"I knew you were special, Dominic Delingpole," he said at last. "But you've just reaffirmed that I made the best decision of my life."

Jonathan sat up and held Dominic's hands tightly in his. He looked intently at his husband.

"You are the most precious person in the world to me," Jonathan began. "And I will never hurt you, my love. I will always tell you the truth. What you've just described, the rules in Gabriel and Alfonso's marriage, that's all I want. I want someone I can always trust. Someone who I know will never hurt me." Jonathan looked down and sighed. "I've never had that in my life, ever since I was a boy."

Dominic leaned forward and kissed the top of Jonathan's head. "I know, Jonathan. And I've spent most of my life not being truthful. Or at least," Dominic corrected himself, "I've been sparing with the truth. Convenient lies, I think you called them."

Jonathan pulled back and gazed at Dominic. "Please disregard I ever used those words. A relationship based on convenient lies can never last."

Then he leaned forward and kissed Dominic on the lips.

"But open relationships, with the right ground rules," Jonathan said even as he reached for another pastry, "can last for years. Did you know that San Francisco State University's done lots of studies on gay relationships?" He took a mouthful of the pastry, then held it out for Dominic to take a bite.

"They've been doing it for the last decade," Jonathan continued. "They've found that half of gay relationships are open. And quite a lot of them have lasted for twenty, thirty years or more."

"Yes," replied Dominic. "Gabriel told me about that last night. He even told me that the pioneer of gay porn in California, a man who has a very open relationship, has been with his husband for over forty years."

"There you are, then." Jonathan sat back in his armchair and finished the pastry. "It's true. We gays are leading the way to healthier, more honest, and above all, sexier marriages."

A grunt sounded from behind them, and Jonathan turned to see a man in a business suit shaking his head.

"Have you been listening to our private conversation?" asked Jonathan.

The man ignored the question. "The trouble is," he said, "you gays want to have your cake and eat it too." He grunted again and went on, "But then, so do we straight people."

He sighed.

"I just wish I could talk to my wife the way you guys talk."

Jonathan laughed. "I'll tell you another thing we can do. We can leave the toilet seat up without anyone nagging us about it."

SINON CROSSED the floor of the Creative Cavern at 101 Grain Street and joined the five people at table alpha. It was about eight in the evening, and no one was giving any signs of wanting to stop for the day. The Creative Cavern was buzzing with activity.

The floor around table alpha was littered with large pages of flipchart paper—pages covered with diagrams of database structures and scribbles of half-written computer code. The table itself was strewn with discarded pizza boxes and crumpled soda cans. Some of the boxes still contained curled, stale-looking slices of pizza.

A disheveled teenager wearing jeans and a T-shirt bearing the logo Truth is Relative drew on a sheet of paper on the floor. At the same time, he addressed the group. He spoke with a strong Russian accent and a rapid, staccato delivery. An older man in the group interrupted the teenager.

"Alex," said the man, "are you telling me there are multiple backdoors like this already in the US banking networks?"

Alex laughed and ran his fingers through the ringlets of his curly mop of brown hair.

"Not just US networks," he replied. Alex slammed the tip of his black marker pen against the flipchart paper and drew a broad circle. "All. All networks in world." He looked up with an expression of conceit on his face.

The older man shook his head, appearing skeptical. "It's not possible. Not on the scale you're talking about. When it comes to software, the banks are the most cautious of all organizations. Especially in the US. Shit, we're still using old-fashioned checks here. The rest of the world has long since switched over to contactless and wireless."

Alex pointed his marker pen at the man and shook his head. "You are naïve, my friend. American banks are not cautious. Just cheap. They make money but spend nothing on their systems. Or their programmers."

With his arms folded across his chest and a look of defiance on his face, Alex stood and addressed the table. "They pay peanuts, and they get"—he smiled—"us. We work for little money. We maintain their ancient computer code. And we insert little backdoors from time to time. Is easy."

Sinon's mobile vibrated in his pocket as a message arrived. He took it out and checked the screen.

Plan changed. I am unable to travel to US. Nor can Viktor. You must intercept Delingpole and destroy the DG chip. Use force if necessary. Additional fee arrangements to follow.

Chapter 26

THE THREE-TONE chirrup of Grindr erupted on Steve's phone at regular intervals. He was perched at a table in QBAR, about five minutes' walk from Sinon's apartment. Steve had arrived there just under two hours ago. The place was finally filling up with some cute-looking guys.

After Sinon had left him sitting in the garden of the apartment, Steve quickly got bored. He decided to go for a cruise around the local area. Despite the obvious tourists, the Castro district of San Francisco remained true to its gay liberation origins of the '60s. Whenever Steve returned to the West Coast, he tried to spend at least one evening there, checking out the changes since his last visit.

He usually ended up in QBAR at some point. In his hometown of Brighton, back in England, Steve's regular haunt was a club called Legends. QBAR was similar. It attracted a young twink crowd, and there was a good dance floor.

When Steve arrived, it was still early in the evening, and there was little talent of interest in the bar. He perched on a stool at a small table with his beer. In between checking Grindr, he thought about the impending arrival of Dominic and Jonathan. It was less than a day before they would be here, and Steve had no idea how he could protect them.

It was obvious that Dominic was carrying a valuable—and dangerous—cargo. Recent events made it clear that people on both sides of the Atlantic wanted the little computer chip. It seemed to have been the reason Dominic and Jonathan's holiday apartment was burgled. And the appearance of Janet Downpatrick at the Barcelona airport was no coincidence. She and her sidekick had been booked on the same flight out of London as Dominic and Jonathan. Steve congratulated himself on how quickly he had hacked into their ESTA visa records and deleted them.

The thought of the visa records reminded him of Nick Poole from the hackfest and the close attention he had shown Steve ever since he landed in San Francisco. Was Nick also involved with Downpatrick? Were they both after the computer chip?

Steve rubbed his crotch at the memory of Nick's attack in the front seat of the Tesla. Why was Nick so interested in tracking Steve? Perhaps there was something more sinister behind the hackfest. Steve had planned to question Sinon in more detail about the event, but when he left the apartment earlier, Sinon said he was not returning until after midnight.

Steve took another drink of beer and stared out the window of QBAR. Once Dominic and Jonathan landed at San Francisco Airport, they were going to be very vulnerable. Steve tried to think of a way he could get them some kind of protection. He picked up his phone and switched to another app. It was one he preferred to use when he wanted to hook up with guys into leather or uniform. After several minutes thumbing through his list of bookmarked profiles, LeatherCop appeared on the screen.

Steve had met Mike from the San Francisco Police Department two years ago. It was at the Folsom Street Leather Fair. Mike was wearing a leather police shirt, leather chaps, tall boots, a Muir cap, and mirror sunglasses. It had been a good night at Mike's apartment. It was only the next morning Steve discovered Mike was a real police officer, based at the airport. That was two years ago, and now was the time to call in the firm hands, not to mention thighs, of LeatherCop.

JEFF PACED up and down, his boots clattering on the wooden floor of the loft space of 101 Grain Street. Nick was in the kitchen area, brewing coffee. They had left Fortran and Cobol to supervise the evening stragglers at the hackfest. The eager ones who wanted to work long into the night. Nick had given strict instructions for the doors to close by midnight.

The late-night call of Charter Ninety-Nine had just started, and there was a gloomy mood among the participants.

"Can you repeat that, Britannia?" said Jeff. "I just want to make sure I heard you right."

"Um, yes," said an English voice from the speakers. "So, we decided to check through the European police reports for the last couple of days. And it seems that the Spanish police discovered the body of Bernhardt Freude in a car accident just south of Girona in eastern Spain, two days ago."

"Hey," said a new voice on the speakers. "East Coast here. Why did no one in Europe check this earlier? Once you knew Bernhardt had taken off, surely—"

"East Coast," interrupted Jeff. He stopped pacing. "Don't waste time trying to point the finger of blame at people. It's not helpful. Britannia, do you think it was an accident?"

There was a pause. Nick carried two cups of coffee across from the kitchen and handed one to Jeff.

Britannia spoke again.

"That stretch of road is a notorious accident black spot in Spain. He was driving a sports car. The police are still examining the vehicle, but—"

"Yeah, yeah," cut in East Coast. "So we'll probably never know. My question is, where the hell is Karl Michael?"

Britannia attempted to interrupt.

"Okay, I should have said 'Germany' and not used names," responded East Coast. "Sorry. But it looks mighty suspicious, don't you think?"

"I was going to tell you," said the English voice. "We had a text earlier. Germany can only join by messaging. Apparently they've had a problem with voice communications."

Jeff looked at Nick. "What the fuck's going on?" he asked. "We could launch the assault in a few months. Less if we finish the History Writer files sooner. But with Bernhardt dead, and now it looks like Karl Michael's gone—" He took a sip of coffee. "—I think we're under attack."

The voice of East Coast came from the speaker. "Did you say we're under attack, Jeff? 'Cos that's what I've been thinking for a while. Ever since Bernhardt disappeared. You know what? I say we shut down the project. At least until we know what the fuck's going on."

"Um, excuse me again," said Britannia. "If you switch to the message service on your screens, you'll see Germany has joined us."

Jeff looked up at the display on the wall and read a series of messages as they slowly appeared on the screen.

Dominic Delingpole has the DG chip. He arrives in San Francisco from London at 14:25 tomorrow. An agent will intercept him and recover the chip. It is in hand. We agree with East Coast. The project should be shut down.

Jeff looked at Nick, who shook his head.

"It stinks," whispered Nick. "Who the fuck's this agent in San Francisco? If there is one, we'd know it."

Jeff nodded. He turned back to the screen.

"There's no reason to shut down the project. Once we get the DG chip tomorrow, the assault can still go ahead. With or without the Originator."

He leaned in to Nick and whispered close to his ear. "Tomorrow, we'll go to the airport. I'll use my contact there to intercept Delingpole. He'll never get to the arrivals hall."

STEVE'S EVENING had been frustrating. Mike, or LeatherCop, had moved to Washington State nearly a year ago. Despite Steve's best efforts of persuasion, LeatherCop would not, or maybe could not, pull any strings for him in the San Francisco Police Department. Annoyed, Steve left the twinks of QBAR and went for a walk down the street.

It was a clear evening, and the Castro was busy. He was tempted to go back to the apartment, find some reasonable talent on Grindr, and hook up for the evening. If Sinon came back early, they could make a threesome of it.

Steve paused when he reached the Castro Theater. It was screening *Trainspotting*, one of his all-time top-ten movies. As he weighed up the options open to him for his evening's entertainment, the nagging ache from his groin confirmed his decision. For the moment, an evening of sex would probably end with a lot of unwelcome pain.

Steve sighed and chose *Trainspotting*.

IT WAS just on midnight when Steve emerged from the Castro Theater. He shook his head to clear the ringing in his ears. It was a long time since he had been to a gay movie sing-along of *The Adventures of Priscilla, Queen of the Desert*. Here in San Francisco, the audiences clearly sang more enthusiastically, and far louder, than the sedate British audiences of Brighton. Steve had failed to notice that *Trainspotting* was on every night that week, except tonight. He tried to persuade himself it was an easy mistake to make. Maybe it was the painkillers the hospital had given him. Perhaps he should have avoided drinking beer while taking them.

Only when Hugo Weaving began to mime his way through the opening musical number of "I've Never Been to Me" did Steve realize his error. By then he was trapped in the middle of a row. Steve decided to sit it out. Maybe the film would be better than he remembered.

Two hours later, Steve stood outside the Castro Theater and swore he would never go to another gay movie sing-along again, not even if they did one for *Trainspotting*. He looked at the time on his mobile. It was after midnight. Dominic and Jonathan would have landed at Heathrow Airport by now. He needed somewhere to talk to them, and he needed a drink.

He walked to the Twin Peaks Tavern on the corner, pushed open the door, and went inside. It was busy but not packed, as he had expected it to be. While he waited to buy a beer at the bar, a text message from Dominic announced that he and Jonathan were settled in the first-class lounge at Heathrow, ready to talk.

Steve picked up his beer and headed for a spare seat at a table near the back. There were two other people sitting there, a middle-aged man and a woman. They were clearly Castro tourists, probably from out of town, on the gay tour of San Francisco. They eyed the shaven-headed Steve suspiciously as he walked up to the table. Steve had chosen not to wear his skintight jeans because of the continued soreness after his operation. Instead, he wore a pair of long sweatshorts. But he still wore his 14 hole Grinders boots and navy blue Fred Perry shirt.

"Seat's not taken, is it?" asked Steve, sitting at the table.

"It sure ain't now," growled the man. He looked at his wife. "You ready to go, Dolores?" He scowled at Steve and added, "It's suddenly got real crowded in here."

Steve smirked and saluted as Dolores and her husband squeezed past him and made their way over to the far end of the bar. He opened his laptop and plugged in the headphones. After a few moments, Dominic's face appeared on the screen.

"You guys okay?" asked Steve.

Dominic smiled and held up a cocktail glass to the camera. "We're here in the first-class lounge, thanks to you."

Jonathan's face appeared alongside his husband's.

"Can you believe it?" asked Jonathan. "Dominic drinking alcohol at half past eight in the morning. I'm afraid I'm a very bad influence."

Steve laughed. "About time, mate," he said. "Any sign of the Downpatrick woman?" As Steve spoke, he brought up another screen on his computer.

"No sighting so far," replied Jonathan. "But it was a terrifying few minutes back in Barcelona. Even with hunky Alfonso parading his weapon—"

"She's getting to Heathrow in about thirty minutes," interrupted Steve. He switched the screen back to Dominic and Jonathan and saw the looks on their faces.

"Sorry, mate," Steve continued. "I just checked on the flight records. She took the one that left just after yours. But don't worry. She can't leave London for the States. I made sure of that. No airline's going to take her when she hasn't got an ESTA visa waiver."

"Is that gorilla with a shaved head flying with her?" asked Jonathan. "Although I must say, they're each as bad as the other. He just has better tattoos."

Steve nodded. "Yes. They both got the flight." He could see Dominic had slumped back in his seat. "Look, don't worry. You're in the first-class area. There's no way they can get to you. You'll be on your way here in a couple of hours. I'll be at the airport to meet you."

Dominic leaned forward again. "Yes, but what do we do then? Bernhardt didn't really give me any instructions for the computer chip apart from the location and a date. What are we supposed to do with it?"

Steve waved his hand again. "I'm shacked up with this really cool guy called Sinon. He's pretty well worked it out. He reckons the chip gives access to a bunch of financial computer servers near Sacramento. Once we've got the chip here, we can analyze it."

Steve took a drink of his beer before continuing, "Sinon's a great guy. From England. He'll help us sort this one out."

Chapter 27

THE BUS lurched again. Pete put his foot down in the gangway and held on to the seat in front to steady himself. Alongside him in the window seat, Captain Roberts laid her hands on a brown cardboard folder resting on her laptop to stop the contents falling to the floor.

Pete looked forward to see what the holdup was. The bus was in a slow line of traffic, crawling toward construction work. The highway narrowed to a single line past the works. It looked like they were close to Union Street, not long before they arrived at their stop to get off.

He shifted his gaze to Captain Roberts as she tidied the collection of documents in the cardboard folder. It contained about fifteen battered pieces of paper belonging to Pete, including mortgage payment receipts, utility bills, his old driver's license, and a letter from the Department of Veterans Affairs. In the last year, since Pete had become homeless, he had kept them safe and dry, whatever the situation he found himself in.

"I can't see it's going to be any different this time, Captain Roberts," said Pete. "I've been to the Social Security a million times. They just kick me out."

The Salvation Army captain looked over her reading glasses at him. "Pete, it will be different now. You've got someone who'll explain your case for you." She paused before she added, "Calmly." Captain Roberts patted his knee. In the confines of the cramped bus seat, Pete felt uncomfortable.

"These documents are very conclusive," she continued. "If you'd gathered them together like this in the first place, you could have maybe sorted this mistake out three years ago."

"Mistake?" Pete's voice got louder. "It's a helluva lot more than a mistake, Captain Roberts." He grasped the back of the seat in front of him and breathed hard.

"I've been destroyed these last three years," he continued, staring straight ahead of him. "I lost the house, the car, my pension. And no one believed me." He looked at Captain Roberts. "So you've gotta understand if I get a little skeptical about all this shit."

Captain Roberts sighed.

"The woman we're meeting is a very experienced lawyer in matters like these. She's going to represent you at the Social Security hearing this morning. The person from Washington Law Help said she's dealt with a lot of similar cases before. She's highly recommended and is doing it for you pro bono."

Captain Roberts took off her reading glasses and looked kindly at Pete. "That means it's free. Just keep calm, once we get in there. Let her do the talking, and I'm sure it'll be just fine."

"Mr. Brown, delighted to meet you."

The woman's voice was strong and authoritative. It was a deep voice, coming from someone who appeared to be little more than five feet tall. Pete reckoned she was no older than thirty. She wore a tailored pinstripe suit, a white blouse, and he noticed her shoes were ankle-high, stiletto-heeled boots, with some kind of intricate pattern embossed on the leather. The woman extended her hand toward Pete as he stepped into the small, windowless waiting room. Her fingernails were long and painted a vivid red. The bracelet on her wrist was laden with small metal charms, and it jangled as they shook hands.

"My name's Sandra Levy," she continued briskly. "I'm a lawyer with Braithewaite's here in Seattle. I specialize in identity theft." She turned to Captain Roberts. "Captain, thank you so much for contacting me. This is a most intriguing case. I've discovered that Pete's not the only person who's been affected in this way."

Sandra Levy indicated two molded-plastic chairs at the small round table in the middle of the room. "Please, take a seat." The young lawyer sat down opposite them and opened a large ring binder of papers.

Captain Roberts pushed the brown cardboard folder she had been clutching across the table. "Pete's brought all the paperwork you asked for," she said. "I hope it's going to be useful."

Sandra pulled the folder toward her and smiled. "Oh yes. This is the start of reclaiming your place in the world, Mr. Brown."

Pete looked up at the mention of his name. Sandra was staring straight at him, her head slightly tilted, a broad smile on her face. He was struck by how bright and sparkling her eyes were, even in the flat fluorescent light of the room.

"Mr. Brown," she continued. "I'm afraid you are what we call a cyber ghost. You no longer exist in the computer systems of the United States. That means you can't function as a person in real life."

She picked out a document from her ring binder and passed it across the table to Captain Roberts and Pete. "What's surprising in your case, Mr. Brown, is that you have completely disappeared. What usually happens in the case of cyber ghosts like you is that the Social Security Administration makes an error and puts you on their Death Master File."

"Oh my goodness," said Captain Roberts, putting her hand up to her mouth.

"Yes," continued the young lawyer. "Sounds pretty gruesome, doesn't it? The SSA started the Death Master File in 1980. It's supposed to stop identity fraud. The problem is, people who are alive, like Mr. Brown, get stuck on it by accident."

She pointed to the document on the table in front of Captain Roberts and Pete. "Those are the statistics. Each year, over twelve thousand people in the US are declared dead when they're very much alive. It screws up their lives. Banks won't touch them. Their homes can get repossessed. They lose their pensions." She looked directly at Pete. "Very similar to what happened to you."

She searched through the ring binder and pulled out a spiral-bound report. "Except in your case, things are different. We ran this report on your presence in cyberspace." She opened its cover and began to flick through the pages. "You don't even come up on the Death Master File. You don't appear anywhere, on any database on the internet. It's as though you've been wiped off the earth."

STEVE LEANED back in the leather passenger seat and rested his Grinder boots against the glove compartment of the electric-blue Range Rover Sport. He looked out his window at the blue waters of San Francisco Bay as the car sped south along the Bayshore Freeway. A sign flashed past showing Airport—2 Miles.

"Go on, then," said Steve, turning to Sinon next to him. "Where do you get your cash for swanky motors like this, then?"

Sinon's window was down, and his left arm rested on the sill, his hand holding the roof of the car.

"Same way as you," he replied. "I work for whoever pays me. And just at the moment"—he looked across the front seat at Steve and winked—"I've got a bloody good client paying me bloody well. So I thought I'd get a decent wagon to go get your friends from the airport." He laughed. "Sit back and enjoy the ride. It's a long drive up to Plainfield. You wanna do it in comfort, don't you?"

Steve took out his laptop and rested it on his thighs. He pulled up a map of Plainfield on the screen and switched to a street image view.

"What the fuck are we going to do once we get there?" he asked. "Do you know where this data center is? And what are we supposed to do with this DG chip? It's hardly going to have a sign saying Plug Me in Here, is it?"

"I know how to get to the data center," replied Sinon. "I told you, I did some stuff with WRI a couple of years ago. The entrance is in a barn. There's an elevator that takes you down to the server rooms."

Steve had reopened the text message Bernhardt sent to Dominic. "Presumably these other numbers are the access code. But what's with the date?"

"That'll be the expiry for the access code," replied Sinon. "That's why we've got to get them up there today, before the code expires."

Steve closed the text message and turned to some of the files he had downloaded to track down his father.

"What's that you're looking at?" asked Sinon.

"My dad lives up in Seattle," replied Steve. "Or rather, he did. He seems to have disappeared off the map. I've been into all the main indexes. But his records have vanished."

Sinon waved his hand in the air and made spooky noises. "Another cyber ghost," he said with a grin. "There's a lot of that in the States. The electronic records are crap here. I guess you tried his employment records. Where did he work?"

Steve was trying to get an internet connection, without success.

"Funnily enough, it was WRI," he replied, looking up at last. "He worked in security."

Sinon's hands twitched for a moment on the steering wheel.

"Really?" he said. He signaled and pulled over to the right-hand lane to turn off at the airport exit. "How long ago was that?"

DOMINIC LOOKED at his watch and turned to Jonathan.

"Quarter to three, bang on time." He looked out the window at the clear blue California sky. The plane stopped taxiing, and the captain shut down the engines.

Dominic and Jonathan were not used to flying first class. None of the passengers around them seemed to be making the usual frantic scramble for jackets and hand luggage that happened in economy. Instead, the cabin crew calmly brought coats and bags to people's seats.

"This has been rather wonderful," said Dominic. He kissed Jonathan on the lips. "But I do feel something of a fraud. What if they were to find out now we'd only paid for an economy ticket?"

"Sh," said Jonathan, kissing Dominic back. "Steve is a very clever man and has only done what other people would give their eyeteeth to do. After all, it's just another of those convenient lies." He took hold of Dominic's hand and squeezed it tight. "You worry far too much, my dear. How often do you tick the box on the internet saying 'I have read the terms and conditions'? It's just another of modern life's little fibs."

Jonathan took in the expression on Dominic's face. "Oh my God, I shouldn't have asked a lawyer that, should I? Don't tell me you do read the terms and conditions?"

Dominic laughed and leaned in toward Jonathan. "No, I don't. But I hardly think it compares with the fraud we've just committed on this airline."

A handsome young flight attendant with short, curly black hair and dark brown eyes arrived with their jackets and carry-on cases.

"Mr. Delingpole? Mr. McFadden?" he asked. "Can you get ready to deplane, please?"

Jonathan rolled his eyes at Dominic and turned to the young flight attendant.

"Dear boy," said Jonathan, "I thought this was a British airline. And for that reason, I thought I would never hear such a ghastly expression as 'deplane.'" He eyed the flight attendant up and down. "You only get away with it because you are young and remarkably cute."

The flight attendant blushed. "I'm sorry, sir," he said with a bow of his head. "It won't happen again. Would you get ready to leave the aircraft, please? You're booked through VIP immigration, and we'd like you to leave first, if you don't mind."

Jonathan winked at Dominic. "I imagine young Steve has worked his magic once more."

The two men stood and stepped out into the aisle. Jonathan stretched his arms up and sighed contentedly. He dropped them and rested his hands on Dominic's shoulders.

"Do you have that chip thingy for him?" asked Jonathan.

Dominic nodded. "I've got it in my jacket pocket. Maybe we can finally find out what Bernhardt was up to. I just wish he hadn't involved me. Especially on our honeymoon."

Jonathan leaned forward and kissed Dominic. "Lover, life is never dull with you."

"Are you ready, gentlemen?" asked the cabin attendant. "If so, would you follow me? We'll have you and your luggage out of the airport in fifteen minutes. VIP immigration is very efficient here."

Chapter 28

STEVE LOOKED around at the other people waiting by the greetings barrier in the crowded San Francisco arrivals hall. Several carried boards or pieces of card bearing the name of the person they were waiting for. In different circumstances, Steve would have done the same for Dominic and Jonathan. Except the board would have featured a photograph of two cute naked guys, with Dominic and Jonathan's names in large letters emblazoned across the image.

But the last thing Steve wanted today was to draw attention to his friends. He had to get them out of the airport and into Sinon's Range Rover as quickly and as safely as possible.

He turned as Sinon walked over from the newsstand, a bag of cashew nuts in his hand. Sinon looked from side to side as he walked, scanning the crowd.

"Any sign of them yet?" asked Sinon.

"It's a bit soon, mate," replied Steve. "They only landed about twenty minutes ago. You know how long us Brits have to wait in the American immigration line to enter this lousy country."

"Yeah," replied Sinon. "Well, you know better than most about that. Have you texted them?"

"Yeah. I sent Dominic a text as soon as we got here. No reply yet."

Sinon looked around again, scanning the faces in the crowd.

Steve watched him with curiosity. "What are you hoping to see, somebody in a black suit wearing sunglasses, a piece bulging on his hip?"

Sinon laughed and nonchalantly leaned against the arrivals barrier. "Nah, mate," he replied. "Just wondered how we're going to get them out safely. That's all."

Steve pointed in the distance behind them. "Through the exit doors, like everyone else. We've got no choice."

Steve put his boot on the lower rail of the arrivals barrier alongside Sinon. "By the way, mate," he continued. "Tell me more about the time you were working at WRI. What were you doing there?"

Sinon took a handful of cashews and shoved them in his mouth.

"Oh, nothing much," he replied, looking away from Steve to scan the arrivals hall. "It was some database project. I was running the trials for them."

"But you went to Plainfield," said Steve. "So it was something to do with DarkStone. Financial stuff, yeah?"

"Oh yeah. But like I said, nothing special."

Steve was about to ask more, but his phone vibrated as a new text message arrived.

"This'll be Dominic, I guess," he said. He pulled out his phone and read the message.

Thanks for VIP immigration! We're about to get picked up now. See you at the Marriott? Dominic x

"Shit!" exclaimed Steve. "I didn't do any fucking VIP immigration. Someone's got them."

DOMINIC AND Jonathan pushed their trolley, laden with bags, toward the small exit door. There had only been a dozen other passengers at San Francisco's VIP immigration, and they waited barely fifteen minutes. By the time they completed the formalities and the chatty immigration official stamped their passports, the airline had brought them their luggage. They were waved through customs and on to a long narrow corridor leading to the exit.

"I wish I could do it this way every time I come to America," said Dominic. "How the other half lives, eh, Jonathan?" he continued. "Maybe when you're a rich and famous opera singer—"

"Don't hold your breath, lover." Jonathan laughed. "It's been a while since I trod the boards. Now, when I'm a rich and famous landscape gardener—"

"Hey, Dominic."

A tall shaven-headed man stepped forward. He wore a maroon polo shirt, straight-leg jeans, and leather rigger boots. The man extended his hand in greeting.

"My name's Jeff," he said. "I hope you enjoyed the VIP treatment. We thought you'd want to get away from here as quickly as possible."

Dominic shook Jeff's hand. He glanced at Jonathan and then back at Jeff.

"Hello, yes, I'm Dominic," he replied. "This is my husband, Jonathan. Thanks for the VIP treatment. Are you going to take us to the Marriott now? I've told Steve we'll meet him there."

Jeff took hold of the handle of the trolley. "Let me take that. You've had a long journey. The Dodge is just outside."

Jeff pushed the trolley through the automatic doors and out into the afternoon sunshine. Dominic and Jonathan looked at each other, then followed him. The noise of the airport hit them immediately. Jet engines screamed overhead, and the rumble of traffic was constant.

Jeff stopped by a large black American van. A man jumped down from the driver's seat and walked around to the back.

"This is Nick," said Jeff. "He's been talking to Steve more than I have. He'll be able to fill you in on the details once we get on the road to Sacramento."

Nick nodded at Dominic and Jonathan and began loading their luggage into the back of the van.

"Sacramento?" shouted Dominic above the noise of the airport. "I don't understand."

"We're going to meet Steve there," replied Jeff as he opened the side door of the van. "You've got the chip with you, haven't you?"

Dominic held on to the handle of a brown holdall Nick was about to load into the car and looked back at Jeff.

"Just a minute," he said. "Who exactly are you two? We were supposed to meet Steve here. He didn't mention anything about VIP treatment. Or you."

Jeff smiled. "I'm sorry. I should have explained. I run the hackfest here in San Francisco. Steve told you about it, I guess?"

Dominic nodded.

"Well, he told us you guys were in a bit of trouble. We just wanted to help. I pulled some strings at the airport to get you through immigration quickly."

Nick gently tugged the brown holdall away from Dominic's hand and put the bag in the back of the van.

"Steve's gone on to Plainfield," Jeff continued. "He mentioned that too?"

Dominic nodded again. "We spoke to Steve while we were waiting at Heathrow. He said we had to go to Plainfield, near Sacramento, because that's where the coordinates in the message were for. What do you know about all this?"

Jeff indicated the open door of the van. "It's too noisy out here," he said. "Get in the Dodge. I'll explain everything on the way."

Nick put the last of the bags into the van and closed the back. He walked round to the driver's door, opened it, and jumped in.

Dominic pulled out his mobile phone and leaned toward Jonathan to talk in his ear. "I'll call Steve."

"They've got our bags, lover," replied Jonathan. "I don't think we've got much choice."

"FUCK, FUCK, fuck, fuck, fuck," said Steve, frantically typing on his laptop keyboard. Beside him, Sinon drummed his fingers on the steering wheel of the Range Rover as they lined up to leave the car park.

"How could I have been so fucking stupid?" Steve said. "I'm an amateur."

Sinon pulled up to the exit barrier, wound down his window, and shoved the parking ticket into the slot. After a few moments, the barrier lifted, and the Range Rover shot forward.

"Is the tracker doing anything?" asked Sinon as he swerved in front of a taxi. He began to weave through the traffic, headed for Route 101.

"It's moving," Steve replied, gripping his laptop as the car swayed violently from side to side. "If it's still in the Dodge, where Anders dropped it, then they're headed south on 101." He looked up. "That doesn't make sense. Sacramento is north."

"I guess they're going to avoid the city and cross the bay past San Mateo," replied Sinon. "How far ahead are they?"

Steve looked at the map on the screen. "Only a couple of miles. But they're moving fucking fast."

"Don't worry," said Sinon, slamming on the brakes to avoid crashing into a line of traffic ahead of them. "Once we get past this shit, so will we."

THE DODGE van screeched across to the exit lane and headed for Route 92 to cross the bay. Dominic was terrified. He looked at Jeff, who sat opposite him.

"Does he have to drive so fast?" he asked. "What's the hurry?"

Jeff ignored his question. "I presume that was Steve Brown you just called?"

Dominic said nothing.

"It's okay," continued Jeff. "Presumably he told you that Nick and I were dangerous, and he's going to come rescue you?"

It was true. Steve had told him to pick a moment when he and Jonathan could escape from the van. Dominic looked out the window at the scenery flashing past. If they continued at this speed, he could see no possibility of getting away.

Jeff smiled. "We're not dangerous," he said. "Just determined. We could have removed the DG chip from you at the airport. But we need the access codes, and I thought you might be more amenable to handing them over, once we're a little more isolated from the city."

Dominic looked at him coldly. "So you kidnapped us instead. I can't believe you ever had anything to do with Bernhardt. He was a very gentle man."

Jeff nodded. "Bernhardt was also brilliant," he said. "And he's created a marvelous plan for us to set the world right once more. I don't want it sabotaged at this late stage."

"Bernhardt? What plan has he created?"

Jeff smiled again. "I thought it would be useful to bring you along for the ride, and perhaps by the end of it, you'll understand why it's so important." He leaned toward Dominic. "What do you know of Bernhardt's Charter Ninety-Nine?"

Dominic shook his head. "He never mentioned it to me."

Jeff looked surprised. "Bernhardt never said anything? I thought you were close friends and business colleagues?"

Dominic glanced at Jonathan, who was sitting beside him. But Jonathan had his eyes shut and was clinging tightly to the armrests on either side as the car rocketed down the freeway.

"Bernhardt and I collaborated on matters of European law," replied Dominic. "Plus, I have specialized knowledge in Anglo-American trade law, which I advised him on. But that was it."

"Then what do you know of the concept of the 99 percent?" asked Jeff.

"Is that something to do with Stiglitz's famous article in *Vanity Fair*?" asked Dominic. "I remember Bernhardt getting very excited when it came out back in 2011."

Jeff nodded. "Yup. So you know about our American economist, Joseph Stiglitz. Basically, he said that one percent of America's population takes a quarter of the country's income. One percent controls 40 percent of the nation's wealth—"

"And one day, the other 99 percent will rise up," added Dominic. "I remember the article. So what's Charter Ninety-Nine? Some kind of revolution in the planning?"

"Bernhardt set up Charter Ninety-Nine in 2010," Jeff began. "The year before Stiglitz published his article. Bernhardt was called the Originator. Sure, Charter Ninety-Nine is a revolution. A revolution to overthrow the one percent. The one percent now control politics, commerce, and the media. Bernhardt's project is based on a series of brilliant computer programs written by Karl Michael and young Nick, our driver up front. Bernhardt called it the History Writer project."

Jeff turned and looked forward. They had crossed the bay, and the highway began to veer north as it merged into interstate 580. He leaned toward Nick.

"What time will we be there?" he asked.

Nick glanced down at the satnav on the dashboard. "If I can keep up this speed, we'll be there in ninety minutes."

"See if you can get us there faster," said Jeff. He turned back to Dominic.

"Charter Ninety-Nine has coders in five countries," he continued. "They're working to rewrite our society's history. Ever since the 1970s, our world has become a virtual society. It exists on computers, somewhere in the cloud. We've now got to the point where that virtual representation of our society is more trusted than reality itself."

"You mean," said Dominic, "in the way that you know you've got money in your bank account, but the person at the bank tells you, 'computer says no'?"

"Exactly," replied Jeff. "It's true for every aspect of our lives, not just financial matters. Our health, our identity, our employment, all our communications, our social interactions. They're all virtual. The History Writer project has the power to rewrite that virtual world completely. We have the power to rebalance the world. Make it fair once again."

Jonathan opened his eyes and stared at Dominic. "Sounds like what young Steve did," he said, "when he upgraded us to first class. Except on a bigger scale."

"But surely," said Dominic, "even if you could hack into the computers, someone would find the changes? They'd be inconsistent with the information somewhere else. Eventually they'd get fixed."

Jeff shook his head. "Not if you tied up all the loose ends. It's like telling a story. In a novel, the author makes sure everything is consistent. I'll give you an example."

Jeff took a notepad out of the seat pocket in front of him and sketched a stick figure of a man.

"One of our coders ran some tests about two years ago," said Jeff. He wrote the name *Peter Brown* above the stick figure.

"Using computer programs written for the History Writer project, he hacked the online records of a couple of employees at WRI here in Northern California. He used the programs from the History Writer project and eliminated those people from the virtual world. Any reference to them, whether financial, personal, medical, email, war record—anything. Then he rewrote their virtual life histories to storyboards we'd devised."

Dominic was momentarily lost for words.

"That's simply cruel," he said finally. "What gave you the right to manipulate the lives of those poor people?"

Jeff put the sketchpad on the seat beside him. "We had to use nonentities for the tests," he said. "We didn't want the trial to use high-profile people, in case it didn't work out and the hacks got discovered."

Dominic closed his eyes for a moment and tried to imagine what it would be like if his world was similarly turned upside down.

He opened his eyes again. "And did it work out?" he asked. "Did you wreck their real lives, the way you destroyed their virtual ones?"

Jeff looked shocked. "Oh, we didn't wreck their lives. Well, maybe in the case of an early test," he conceded. "The rest are living very comfortably, with guaranteed incomes." He looked triumphant. "We proved the virtual world is more credible than the real one. With the History Writer project, we're now ready to launch our assault on the one percent."

Chapter 29

STEVE LOOKED out at the farmland stretching to the horizon on either side of Interstate Highway 80. They had been driving for nearly an hour and a half. For the first part of the journey, Sinon had expertly steered the electric-blue Range Rover through the busy afternoon traffic, catching up with the black Dodge van. After twenty minutes of high-speed chase, they left the suburbs of Oakland far behind, and the traffic eased. For the last fifty minutes of the journey, they had maintained a steady ninety miles an hour along the interstate. Steve wished their speed would attract the attention of the police patrols. It was the only way he imagined they could rescue Dominic and Jonathan.

His earlier phone conversation with Dominic, when they were leaving the airport, had been abruptly cut short after little more than a minute. When he called back, the phone went to voicemail. Steve sent texts, but there was no response. He had no more contact with them, and no idea what to do once the Dodge van finally stopped.

Steve considered the options. Both he and Sinon were well built and physically fit. The chances were high they could overpower both Jeff and Nick, especially if Jonathan threw himself into the fight. But what if Jeff and Nick had weapons? As far as he knew, every person in America carried a gun.

He looked at Sinon. "Any good at martial arts, mate?"

Sinon nodded. "I can handle myself. Why? Have you got a plan?"

"No," replied Steve. "But we're going to need one soon. We're nearly at the junction for Plainfield. What do we do then?"

Sinon thought for a moment. "I don't reckon Jeff or Nick are going to do anything to harm your friends," he said at last. "They were great guys when I came to the last hackfest. It was a big party, and we built some cool stuff."

"If they're great guys," said Steve, "why have they kidnapped Dominic and Jonathan?"

"Maybe they haven't. Look, the message Bernhardt Freude sent to Dominic said there was a time limit. It's today. We don't know what time today. I guess Jeff and Nick reasoned they had to get to DarkStone as soon as possible."

Steve shook his head. "But then why can't I get through to Dominic on the phone? It would be a bloody sight easier if I could. Then we'd know what the fuck was going on up front."

DOMINIC WAS trying to piece together all the new information he was learning from Jeff. The more he heard, the more it made sense. The legal frameworks Bernhardt had asked him to work on over the years were all concerned with the theoretical defusing of corporate power. Bernhardt had only ever shown him elements of the legal structures. But they seemed to restore rights to individuals and establish greater responsibility and accountability for large organizations. Bernhardt had once casually mentioned he was involved with a worldwide movement, but he never referred to Charter Ninety-Nine. Dominic felt his friend and former lover had never trusted him. Now that Bernhardt was dead, Dominic would never find out why he had been excluded.

Jonathan opened his eyes and looked at the speedometer. "He hasn't slowed down," he said and closed his eyes again. "Why do we have to be in such a hurry?"

Jeff leaned forward. "It's because of the date in that message Dominic received. We've got until midnight to get inside the DarkStone data center and plant that chip you have. From tomorrow, the access codes that were in Bernhardt's message will no longer be valid. Now he's dead, it could take us a long time to find a way inside."

"So tell us, Jeff," said Dominic. "What's so special about this chip you want?"

Jeff picked up the notepad again and drew a circle below the stickman he had previously drawn.

"Most computer networks have strong barriers against hackers," he began. "They're called firewalls. Every little home computer has one. The big networks have big firewalls, like this." He drew his pen around the perimeter of the circle he had just drawn.

"We can usually penetrate a firewall for a short period of time," Jeff continued. "But for an assault on the scale we've planned, we need to get inside the world's data systems for much longer. We need something inside the firewall that's trusted." He drew a small square inside the circle on the notepad.

"That's the Dormant Gateway chip. The DG chip. Karl Michael and Nick designed something that's really neat. It can sit inside DarkStone's data center at Plainfield until we're ready. It can wait for months, maybe years. Then, when we're set, we briefly penetrate the firewall and activate it. The chip's in a data center that's trusted worldwide. WRI have made sure of that. The DG chip draws in all the rewritten histories we've prepared, through the firewall, and sends them back out into the world's networks. The virtual world is transformed."

He ripped the page from the notepad and handed it to Dominic.

"Here you are," he said. "A little keepsake. This is a key moment for Charter Ninety-Nine. We're close to rewriting the world."

Dominic looked down at the crude sketch. He crumpled it in his hand and thrust it into the outer pocket of his jacket.

The van pulled into the right-hand lane of the highway and began to slow. Dominic looked through the window and saw the turnoff sign for Plainfield. He turned back to Jeff.

"What if I don't have the chip?" he asked.

The van lurched as Nick's hands twitched on the steering wheel.

"Shit, Jeff," called Nick from the front. "You didn't frisk him at the airport?"

Jeff stared at Dominic. "You're kidding me, of course."

Dominic said nothing. Jonathan opened his eyes and glanced from Jeff to Dominic.

"Please, lover," Jonathan said to Dominic. "Don't play games with this man. Just give him the bloody chip. I don't want you murdered in the middle of a field."

SINON FOLLOWED the black van off the interstate and onto the Lincoln Highway, which headed for Plainfield. They passed a gas station and diner before the road led into open countryside, with no sign of human habitation around them. After less than a mile, the Dodge van pulled off the road onto a dirt track that headed into the fields.

"Okay, Steve," said Sinon. "What's the plan? We're about to need it."

"Why aren't they going on to Plainfield?" asked Steve. "It's still a few miles ahead."

"I guess they need to deal with us first. They know damn well we've been following for the last hour."

The Range Rover bumped its way along the dirt track behind the Dodge van for another hundred yards before the van pulled into a clearing by some trees and stopped. Sinon brought the Range Rover to a halt in the middle of the track, with the engine ticking over.

"What are they doing now?" he asked.

His question was soon answered when the side door of the van slid open and Dominic and Jonathan stepped out, followed by Jeff.

Steve slammed his door open. "I'm not waiting here," he said. "You stay with the car and get ready to ram them if they try anything." He jumped out and strode toward the three men who stood beside the Dodge van ahead of them.

Sinon watched the departing figure of Steve for a moment. Then he switched off the engine, reached beneath his seat, and pulled out the gun he had hidden there earlier. He opened his door, jumped down, and followed Steve up the narrow track.

DOMINIC AND Jonathan stood back as Nick jumped down from the driver's seat of the van and pushed past them to get to the rear door. He opened the door and started to unload their luggage.

Dominic looked at Jeff. "Shoot me if you like. I'm not giving you something that will ruin the lives of millions of people in the way you describe."

Jonathan looked imploringly at him. "Dominic," he pleaded, "don't say that. What about us?" He took hold of Dominic's arm. "It's not worth it. Just give the man his chip, and they can take us back to that petrol station, and we can go back to San Francisco."

Dominic brushed Jonathan away and glared at Jeff.

"You seriously plan to turn people's lives upside down?" he asked. "Hoping you might create a fairer world? What's the guarantee? You could cause devastation like we've never seen." He shook his head. "No wonder Bernhardt didn't tell me the reality behind what he was doing. I would never have agreed to help him."

Behind them, there was the thud of bags hitting the dirt as Nick threw their luggage out of the van. When the back of the van was empty, Nick started to open each bag in turn, tipping the contents onto the rough ground.

"Dominic," said Jeff, "we're not in the habit of using guns. We don't want to shoot you." He stepped forward and stood directly in front of Dominic. He was several inches taller than Dominic, and his frame was broad and intimidating.

"Bernhardt always said you were stubborn," said Jeff. "Brilliant but stubborn. We know you've got the chip. All you have to do is hand it over. We'll finish what we have to do at the data center, then take you back to the city."

"Hey, Delingpole," a man's voice came from behind them.

Dominic turned to see Steve facing them, standing stock-still. Behind him stood a man pointing a gun at Steve's head.

"Delingpole," said the man. "You and Jonathan walk over here. Slowly. Don't do anything stupid, or Steve's dead."

"Sinon, what the fuck are you doing?" asked Jeff.

Sinon briefly motioned with the gun toward Jeff. "Shut up, Jeff. Or you'll be dead too. Raise your hands." He glanced over at Nick. "And you too, Nick. Both of you. Get down on the ground."

Nobody moved. The only sound was that of distant traffic on the interstate.

"Hey, Sinon," said Nick. "You don't have to do it this way—"

"I said shut up!" shouted Sinon. "Do as I say. Now." Sinon shifted his legs apart slightly and steadied the gun on Steve.

After a long pause, Jeff raised his hands above his head and knelt down. Nick watched for a moment. Then he too put his hands above his head and knelt on the bare earth.

Dominic stood where he was.

"Who are you?" he asked.

"That doesn't matter," replied Sinon. "Just give me the DG chip and I'll leave you all in peace."

"If you so much as touch Steve," said Jonathan, "I'm going to rip your fucking arms off."

Dominic turned to Jonathan. "Come on," he said. "I'm not going to sacrifice Steve. I can't make that choice."

Dominic started to walk forward, and Jonathan followed him. When they were within a few yards of Steve, they stopped. Dominic started to reach into the inside pocket of his jacket for the small package containing the chip.

"Oh no you don't," shouted Sinon. He swung the gun to point at Dominic. Steve seized the opportunity to turn and lunge at Sinon. At the same time, Jonathan threw himself forward.

There was a single shot.

Sinon fell to the ground. Steve landed on top of him and slammed his head into Sinon's nose. Sinon's fingers loosened from around the gun, and Steve grabbed it from him. Steve scrambled to his feet and stood back from Sinon, who still lay on the ground, holding his nose.

"So, you say you can handle yourself?" said Steve triumphantly. "Thank fuck I wasn't on your side."

Dominic looked round. Jonathan was lying motionless on the ground. He could see blood oozing through Jonathan's shirt.

"Steve," Dominic called out. "It's Jonathan. He's been hit!"

Steve looked up in horror. "Check his pulse," he said.

Dominic bent down and desperately felt Jonathan's neck for a pulse. He heard the sound of feet running behind him and turned to see Jeff coming toward them. He was carrying a first aid kit.

Dominic turned back to Jonathan and saw the bloodstain spreading rapidly across his shirt. He ripped the shirt open, revealing a large wound in Jonathan's chest.

Jeff appeared at his side. "Okay, Dominic," he said, "I'm trained as a first response paramedic." He knelt on the ground and checked Jonathan's pulse. He leaned close to Jonathan's mouth and checked for breathing.

Finally, he shouted back to Nick. "He looks bad, Nick. Call emergency. Maybe they can send a chopper. Go bring that Range Rover down here. We'll see if we can get him on the road fast."

He turned back to Dominic. "Okay, Dominic. You want to keep your buddy alive? Hand over the DG chip."

Chapter 30

STEVE PUT the Range Rover into reverse, looked over his shoulder, and cautiously inched the car back up the potholed road. Jonathan lay unconscious on the back seat, his head cradled in Dominic's lap. Jonathan's chest was strapped with a large dressing, which temporarily stopped the flow of blood from the gunshot wound.

Steve glanced down at Jonathan's unconscious form before he looked back out the rear window of the Range Rover.

"I wish I'd shot those fucking guys," he said. "I had the gun in my hand."

"Steve," said Dominic quietly. "Not now. They let us go at least. And they've called the air ambulance. Just get us away from here."

As the dirt track widened out, Steve found a place to turn the Range Rover around. Once they were moving forward again, he accelerated down the road. The car lurched as it bounced from one pothole to another.

"Careful, Steve," said Dominic from the back seat. "Let's get him there with all the pieces he's still got."

As they approached the end of the road, Steve could see the parking lot next to the diner. He looked up to the sky as he heard a helicopter approaching.

"They're here already," he announced excitedly to Dominic. "He's gonna be okay. I'm sure of it."

Steve swung the Range Rover into the parking lot, and the car slid gently to a halt. Behind them, the roar of the helicopter became deafening as it hovered in a field next to the parking lot for a moment before finally landing.

After a few minutes, two paramedics ran across with a gurney. Steve held the rear door of the Range Rover open while they assessed Jonathan's condition. One of the paramedics turned to Dominic.

"He's hanging in there, buddy," said the paramedic. "But I'd say he's lost a lot of blood. We'll get him over to the emergency center right away. Do you wanna ride with?"

Dominic nodded. He turned to Steve. "When the police arrive, can you go back and get our bags?" he shouted above the roar of the helicopter. "That's if they're still there."

"Oh, yes," replied Steve. "If I run into those two shits—"

"No." Dominic held up his hand and pointed a finger at Steve. "If you run into them, let the police take over. Don't go looking for revenge. Don't put yourself in danger."

"Okay," shouted Steve. "I'll take it easy. I guess Jeff and Nick will be running around the data center anyway. Getting ready to change the world."

Dominic smiled. "Maybe," he said. He reached into his jacket pocket and pulled out a crumpled piece of paper. "But if you see Jeff again, give him this." He handed the ball of paper to Steve. "Tell him I won't be needing it anymore."

Steve leaned forward and hugged Dominic awkwardly. They separated, and Dominic followed the paramedics as they pushed the gurney, with Jonathan strapped to it, across the parking lot toward the helicopter.

Steve looked down and unfolded the crumpled piece of paper. At the top of the sheet he read the name Peter Brown.

DOMINIC DOZED, sitting upright in his chair, sedated by the rhythmic sound of the respirator and an aria from Puccini's *Madame Butterfly*. Late afternoon sunshine streamed through the window of the fifth-floor hospital room.

It was ten days since Jonathan had been shot. The hospital said he had lost nearly four pints of blood. Despite that, his brain function appeared to be normal, but he remained in a coma. Dominic spent most of his time at the hospital in Sacramento, sitting at Jonathan's bedside. The room was large and airy. The window looked out over a busy main street that ran by the hospital. Dominic played opera tracks he knew Jonathan loved on a music system he had bought and read him the poetry of Maya Angelou and Walt Whitman, two writers Jonathan often read for pleasure. Dominic had checked into a small motel down the street from the hospital but spent little time there. He would get a change of clothes and a few hours' sleep and then return to the hospital.

The door creaked open. Dominic stirred from his doze and opened his eyes. He turned to see who the visitor was.

"Alfonso!" he said as the tall Spaniard cautiously stepped into the room.

Dominic stood up, and the two men hugged each other. Alfonso held on to Dominic for several minutes before he slowly loosened his arms and placed his hands on Dominic's shoulders. For a moment, he looked across at Jonathan, lying in the bed, before he turned back to Dominic.

"Gabriel brought me straight here from the airport," said Alfonso. "He's gone to the hotel, but he'll be back in a while. What's the news?"

Dominic shook his head. "No change since we last spoke two days ago. It's going to be a while, they say."

Alfonso dropped his hands from Dominic's shoulders and walked over to the bedside. He reached out and laid a hand on Jonathan's arm. Then he bent down and gently kissed Jonathan on the forehead.

Dominic brought a second chair across to the bedside. "Sit with me, Alfonso," he said. "It's been lonely these last few days."

The two men sat silently as "The Humming Chorus" from *Madame Butterfly* started on the music system. Dominic's shoulders began to shake, and Alfonso placed his bearlike arm around them.

"You're not alone anymore, Dominic," he said. "We're here for you now."

After several minutes, Dominic looked at Alfonso. His eyes were red, and he wiped them with his hand.

"I don't know what I'm going to do, Alfonso," he said. "Jonathan could be here for months. They say they can't transfer him back to England. But there's going to come a point when I need to go back. I'll have to work." He looked at Jonathan's motionless form. "But I can't leave him."

Alfonso squeezed Dominic's shoulder.

"Don't think about it just yet," he said. "One day at a time, my friend."

"After everything that's happened between us in the last few weeks," Dominic said, "I really thought our marriage was over before it had begun." He looked back at the still, calm form of Jonathan lying in the bed. "Now, I can't imagine a life without him."

Alfonso squeezed Dominic's shoulder tighter.

The door behind them opened. Dominic turned to see Steve enter the room.

"Hi, Steve," said Dominic. He released himself gently from Alfonso's arm and stood. "This is Alfonso, from Barcelona. You'll have seen him on the video call we had a few weeks back."

Steve nodded. "Hi, Alfonso." Steve looked past the two men at Jonathan. "Any change?"

Dominic shook his head. "When are you going back to England, Steve?" he asked.

Steve shrugged. "I'll be around for a while. I've had some good news, I guess."

He pulled out the crumpled sheet of paper Dominic had handed him ten days before.

"I was right," Steve began. "This Peter Brown that bastard Jeff so casually experimented on is my father. Not only that, it was Sinon who did the work at WRI, rewriting the employees' records. Charter Ninety-Nine got Sinon to change the records of six people." He crumpled up the piece of paper and shoved it back into his pocket. "He nearly destroyed my father's life."

Dominic stood and walked across to Steve. "And the good news is, you've found him, I hope?"

Steve nodded. "Yeah. I spoke to him an hour ago."

"And how is he?" asked Dominic.

"Oh, you know," said Steve. "Same old dad. Grumpy as shit. I'm driving up to Seattle tomorrow. I'll help him get everything straight again."

Dominic laid a hand on Steve's shoulder. "I'm glad it's worked out," he said. "Any sign of Jeff or Nick?"

Steve pulled away from Dominic and walked to the window. "I've not been back to Grain Street," he replied. "If I did, I'm pretty sure I'd end up trying to kill them."

He looked back at Dominic.

"I know you did it for Jonathan," he said. "I can understand that. But I wish you hadn't given those bastards the Dormant Gateway chip." He looked out the window. "You know the world's fucked now?"

Dominic smiled. "Well, the chip wasn't going to be much use to them."

Steve turned. "What do you mean?"

Dominic resumed his seat next to Alfonso at the bedside. "The chip was wrapped in some protective packaging in my pocket. When I reached in to hand it to Jeff, it didn't take much strength to snap it in half before I gave it to him."

Steve punched his fist in the air. "Fucking legend," he crowed. "And Jeff didn't bother to unwrap it in the heat of the moment." He leaned his back against the window. "You took a helluva fucking risk. What if Jeff had decided to check it out before leaving us there?"

"Jeff didn't think I was a risk-taker. I had a hunch he trusted me," said Dominic. "He's the kind of person to see me as a simple, run-of-the-mill lawyer." He reached forward, took Jonathan's hand, and slowly massaged his fingers.

"I suppose I was a run-of-the-mill lawyer once," Dominic continued. "Before I met this man."

"Well, I think you're a fucking legend," said Steve. "And you worked out Bernhardt's message had GPS codes in it. As soon as we had that, we were rocking."

"What I don't understand," said Dominic, "is how Sinon got mixed up with the Downpatrick woman."

"Money," said Steve. "He told me he had a client paying him a shitload of cash. That must have been her. He won't be working for a few years, once they put him away in jail."

Dominic nodded. "And Downpatrick wanted to stop the History Writer project, which is why she got Sinon to intercept the DG chip. She must have some very influential friends in high places, the one percent, who don't want the world order changed."

He sighed and continued. "I suppose I gave them a helping hand. By destroying the chip, I've let the one percent continue to get richer. But I couldn't let thousands of people have their lives ruined, like your dad. Even if it could be for some greater good."

"There's something I must tell you," Alfonso spoke up. "You remember that police report of the body in the water at Port Sitges? I was reading it the night you and Jonathan stayed."

Dominic nodded.

"I'm afraid they identified it as the body of Karl Michael Meyer. He was the man you met on Balmins beach, wasn't he?"

Dominic stopped massaging Jonathan's hand. He sighed and leaned back in his chair.

"Yes," he said. "And he was Bernhardt's partner. And he designed the DG chip." He glanced at Steve. "I think Charter Ninety-Nine's History Writer project is going to be out of action for a long time."

"There's more," said Alfonso. "The police investigation shows he was onboard a yacht moored in the port shortly before he died. Our investigators also discovered that Janet Downpatrick and Viktor Krasov had been on the same yacht."

"So they're wanted for murder?"

Alfonso nodded. "For the moment, they've disappeared. But don't worry. There's a coordinated hunt for them across Europe. We'll catch them this time."

Dominic's phone began to ring. He took it out of his pocket and answered the call. After a brief conversation, he turned to Steve and Alfonso.

"I'm sorry," said Dominic. "I'm just going outside to take this call. It's…." He hesitated for a moment. "It's rather private."

Steve went to the door. "Don't worry about me, mate," he said. "I need to go pack. I've got to get ready for the drive to Seattle. I'll leave you in peace."

He embraced Dominic and whispered in his ear, "He's fucking tough, is Jonathan. He'll pull through."

Steve shook hands with Alfonso, blew a kiss to Jonathan, and was gone.

Alfonso began to head for the door. "Why don't I leave you to take your call, Dominic?" he said. "I can come back later with Gabriel."

"No," said Dominic. "Actually, I think I'd like you to stay. It's my lawyer from Germany on the phone."

Alfonso walked across to the window and looked down at the traffic below.

Dominic sat next to the bed. He held the phone to his ear with one hand. With the other, he reached out and gently stroked Jonathan's arm.

The call lasted no more than three or four minutes. When it ended, Dominic put the phone back in his pocket and leaned forward to rest his head on Jonathan's shoulder. The recording of *Madame Butterfly* had ended. The only sound in the room was the rhythmic noise of Jonathan's respirator.

Alfonso crossed the room and placed his hand on Dominic's shoulder. "Is everything all right, my friend?"

Dominic sat back in his chair and turned to Alfonso. "I'm not sure how I feel," he began, "because really, it's marvelous news." He looked back at Jonathan and sighed.

"My lawyer's been talking to my son in Germany," he continued. "He's told him all about Jonathan, and everything that's happened to us."

Dominic stood up and turned to Alfonso. "My son finally wants to meet me, Alfonso," he said. "And he wants to meet Jonathan." He looked back at Jonathan, lying in the bed.

"So Jonathan has to get better. Because we both have to go back home. Together."

DAVID C. DAWSON is an author, award-winning journalist, and documentary maker living near Oxford in the UK. He has traveled extensively, filming in nearly every continent of the world. He has lived in London, Geneva, and San Francisco, but now prefers the tranquility of the Oxfordshire countryside.

David is a Mathematics graduate from Southampton University in England. After graduating, he joined the BBC in London as a trainee journalist. He worked in radio newsrooms for several years before moving to television as a documentary director. During the growing AIDS crisis in the late '80s, he is proud to say that he directed the first demonstration of putting on a condom on British television. After more than twenty years with the BBC, he left to go freelance. He has produced videos for several charities, including Ethiopiaid, which works to end poverty in Ethiopia, and Hestia, a London-based mental health charity.

David has one son, who is also a successful filmmaker.

In his spare time, David tours Europe on his aging Triumph motorbike and sings with the London Gay Men's Chorus. He has sung with the Chorus at St Paul's Cathedral, The Roundhouse, and the Royal Festival Hall, but David is most proud of the time they sang at the House of Lords, campaigning for equal marriage to be legalized in the UK.

David is an Award winner in the 2017 FAPA President's Awards for Adult Suspense and Thrillers

Website: www.davidcdawson.co.uk
Blog: blog.davidcdawson.co.uk/#home
Twitter: @david_c_dawson
Facebook: www.facebook.com/david.c.dawson.5
LinkedIn: uk.linkedin.com/in/davidcdawson
Email: contact@davidcdawson.co.uk

The Delingpole Mysteries: Book One

A young journalism student lies unconscious in a hospital bed in Brighton, England. His life hangs in the balance after a drug overdose. But was it attempted suicide or attempted murder? The student's mother persuades British lawyer Dominic Delingpole to investigate, and Dominic enlists the aid of his outspoken opera singer partner, Jonathan McFadden.

The student's boyfriend discovers compromising photographs hidden in his lover's room. The photographs not only feature senior politicians and business chiefs, but the young journalist himself. Is he being blackmailed, or is he the blackmailer?

As Dominic and Jonathan investigate further, their lives are threatened and three people are murdered. They uncover a conspiracy that reaches into the highest levels of government and powerful corporations. The people behind it are ruthless, and no one can be trusted. The bond between Dominic and Jonathan deepens as they struggle not only for answers, but for their very survival.

*Award winner in the 2017 FAPA President's Awards
for Adult Suspense and Thrillers*

www.dsppublications.com

Also from DSP Publications

THE BISTI BUSINESS

A BJ VINSON MYSTERY

DON TRAVIS

A BJ Vinson Mystery

Although repulsed by his client, an overbearing, homophobic California wine mogul, confidential investigator B. J. Vinson agrees to search for Anthony Alfano's missing son, Lando, and his traveling companion—strictly for the benefit of the young men. As BJ chases an orange Porsche Boxster all over New Mexico, he soon becomes aware he is not the only one looking for the distinctive car. Every time BJ finds a clue, someone has been there before him. He arrives in Taos just in time to see the car plunge into the 650-foot-deep Rio Grande Gorge. Has he failed in his mission?

Lando's brother, Aggie, arrives to help with BJ's investigation, but BJ isn't sure he trusts Aggie's motives. He seems to hold power in his father's business and has a personal stake in his brother's fate that goes beyond familial bonds. Together they follow the clues scattered across the Bisti/De-Na-Zin Wilderness area and learn the bloodshed didn't end with the car crash. As they get closer to solving the mystery, BJ must decide whether finding Lando will rescue the young man or place him directly in the path of those who want to harm him.

www.dsppublications.com

THE CITY OF ROCKS

A BJ VINSON MYSTERY

DON TRAVIS

A BJ Vinson Mystery

Confidential investigator B. J. Vinson thinks it's a bad joke when Del Dahlman asks him to look into the theft of a duck… a duck named Quacky Quack the Second and insured for $250,000. It ceases to be funny when the young thief dies in a suspicious truck wreck. The search leads BJ and his lover, Paul Barton, to the sprawling Lazy M Ranch in the Bootheel country of southwestern New Mexico bordering the Mexican state of Chihuahua.

A deadly game unfolds when BJ and Paul are trapped in a weird rock formation known as the City of Rocks, an eerie array of frozen magma that is somehow at the center of the entire scheme. But does the theft of Quacky involve a quarter-million-dollar duck-racing bet between the ranch's owner and a Miami real estate developer, or someone attempting to force the sale of the Lazy M because of its proximity to an unfenced portion of the Mexican border? BJ and Paul go from the City of Rocks to the neon lights of Miami and back again in pursuit of the answer… death and danger tracking their every step.

www.dsppublications.com

A Reno PD Case File

A serial killer known as the Confessor is kidnapping and torturing gay men, and Reno Police Department Evidence Technician Leif Carson is determined to catch him.

His personal life isn't any less stressful. Despite being a virgin and having zero experience with men, he can't stop thinking about his best friend's ex, Rafe Castillo. Rafe is suffering from PTSD, but that doesn't stop Leif from wanting to be with him.

Complete opposites, they're an amazing fit once they do get together—until Rafe's PTSD gets in the way and he walks away from the relationship before it has a chance to truly blossom. Even though he has intense feelings for the man, Leif has no choice but to let him go.

When the Confessor kidnaps Rafe, Leif does everything possible to locate him before he's murdered. Rafe's near-death experience changes him profoundly, but the danger isn't over yet. Leif and Rafe will have to face pure evil together if they're going to last.

www.dsppublications.com

Vice City: Book One

After twenty years as an enforcer for the Vice family mob, Nicholas Pierce shouldn't bat an eye at seeing a guy get worked over and tossed in the river. But there's something about the suspected police mole, Miles, that has Pierce second-guessing himself. The kid is just trying to look out for his brother any way he knows how, and the altruistic motive sparks an uncharacteristic act of mercy that involves Pierce taking Miles under his wing.

Miles wants to repay Pierce for saving his life. Pierce shouldn't see him as anything but a convenient hookup… and he sure as hell shouldn't get involved in Miles's doomed quest to get his brother out of a rival street gang. He shouldn't do a lot of things, but life on the streets isn't about following the rules. Besides, he's sick of being abused by the Vice family, especially Mr. Vice and his power-hungry goon of a son, who treats his underlings like playthings.

So Pierce does the absolute last thing he should do if he wants to keep breathing—he leaves the Vice family in the middle of a turf war.

For more great fiction from

DSP PUBLICATIONS

visit us online.
WWW.DSPPUBLICATIONS.COM